T0023387

# MY BIG FAT ITALIAN
# BREAK-UP

ALSO BY NANCY BARONE

THE HUSBAND DIET TRILOGY
*The Husband Diet*
*My Big Fat Italian Break-up*
*Storm in a D Cup*

OTHERS
*Snow Falls Over Starry Cove*
*Starting Over at the Little Cornish Beach House*
*Dreams of a Little Cornish Cottage*
*No Room at the Little Cornish Inn*
*New Hope for the Little Cornish Farmhouse*

# MY BIG FAT ITALIAN BREAK-UP

Book Two of
The Husband Diet series

Nancy Barone

An Aria Book

First published in the UK in 2022 by Head of Zeus Ltd,
part of Bloomsbury Publishing Plc.

Copyright © Nancy Barone, 2022

The moral right of Nancy Barone to be identified
as the author of this work has been asserted in accordance with the
Copyright, Designs and Patents Act of 1988.

All rights reserved. No part of this publication may be reproduced,
stored in a retrieval system, or transmitted in any form or by any
means, electronic, mechanical, photocopying, recording, or otherwise,
without the prior permission of both the copyright owner and the above
publisher of this book.

This is a work of fiction. All characters, organizations, and events
portrayed in this novel are either products of the author's
imagination or are used fictitiously.

9 7 5 3 1 2 4 6 8

A catalogue record for this book is available from the British Library.

ISBN (PB) 9781803287683
ISBN (E): 9781803287669

Cover design: Nina Elstad

Typeset by Siliconchips Services Ltd UK

Printed and bound in Great Britain by
CPI Group (UK) Ltd, Croydon CR0 4YY

Head of Zeus Ltd
First Floor East
5–8 Hardwick Street
London EC1R 4RG

WWW.HEADOFZEUS.COM

To Mamma.

# I

My Big Fat Tuscan Dream, Two Years In…

'Surprise!'

I jumped, my day planner and multicolored Post-its exploding all over the floor like a mini piñata.

'Jesus, Julian, do you *want* to give me a heart attack? It's not June 1ˢᵗ yet, you're not due until tomorrow, did something happen?'

My fiancé grinned and bent to pick up the pieces of my life as he always did. Even the black-and-white ones.

'Sorry, love. I couldn't wait until tomorrow, so I took an earlier flight back. I *missed* you.'

I'd missed him, too, but I'd grown used to it by now, as every week or so he was off on some book tour and hobnobbing with his agent in the States, leaving me to run this Italian madhouse of a farm and B & B rolled into one. And to think I'd practically bullied him into resuming his writing career even before we'd moved here to Tuscany.

'Welcome home,' I said, giving him a quick hug as I grabbed my notes back, fretting over the shopping list in my head. Yellow Post-its for the cleaning products I needed to get, brown for the bread and focaccia goods I didn't have time to bake today. Green for the produce I'd send the kids out into the orchard for later and pink for desserts. Guests always loved desserts. It was my special touch as the owner of A Taste of Tuscany.

We were only hours from receiving the first guests of the season. In other words, The Matera Brainstormers – an international group of female writers who had met here last year and enjoyed it so much they'd decided to make it a tradition and branch out to Tuscany.

So far, they were the only ones who had booked this year. After a successful first year (beginner's luck?), things now were not going as well and I was beginning to feel a twinge of panic. We'd left a secure, albeit suffocating life in Boston to start a new and relaxed life in a new country, but so far I hadn't got to the relaxed part yet.

I blew my hair out of my face as my bag slid off my shoulder and when I yanked it back, I took the thin strap of my sundress with it, the rip sounding loud in the quiet kitchen. *Damn.* I didn't have time to go upstairs and change, not now.

'Slow down, honey,' Julian said. 'Come and sit.'

'I can't. I have to go back into town.'

'Have a break. Come, I'll pour you a glass of iced mint tea.'

Iced tea. That would be the closest I'd come to relaxing in weeks. Which reminded me.

'I need to go down to the cellar and get some wine… And fresh flowers – I need to pick some fresh flowers…'

He put a hand on my shoulder.

'Relax. I already did all that. And I also went down to the orchard and picked some strawberries and peaches.'

Aww, bless his soul...!

'And the pears? Did you pick the pears?'

'I picked the pears. Erica, honey, come and relax.'

'I can't,' I insisted. 'They'll be here in a few hours.'

He poured some homemade tea into a tall glass. 'Sit down. Drink this. I'll go. You can go for a swim and chill out.'

Swim. Chill out? Those were foreign words to me. I hadn't been anywhere near our pool yet, living my summer vicariously through the happy sounds of my kids splashing around. But this afternoon they were at a birthday party. I'd have the whole pool to myself. Even half an hour would restore me. I knew I should make time to relax if I didn't want to end up in a loony bin by the end of the summer. But it just never happened.

Delegate. Could I do that? The idea was certainly tempting. Even twenty minutes floating on my back with an empty mind would do me good. But what if he forgot something? Well, I could always send him back. I eyed my lists, then Julian.

'You're sure?'

'I'm sure. And when I get back, I'll come and join you in the pool.' He bent over and kissed my mouth, his lips lingering over mine. 'And just for us, I'll get a chocolate mousse for *bedtime*...'

Ooh. Saturday was definitely looking up now.

He ran a finger down my cheek and chuckled at the look on my face.

'Erica, honey, I was thinking... now that things have slowed down a bit, don't you think it's time we set the date?'

That was the problem. Business hadn't slowed down a bit, but definitely ground to a terrifying halt. There was nothing I wanted more than to be Mrs. Foxham. He'd proposed inside a hot-air balloon two years ago and we'd set a date at least three times since. But there had always been something: the mumps (my now ten-year-old daughter Maddy), the measles (my fourteen-year-old son Warren), a sprained ankle (me) or Julian's busy book tour schedule. Our wedding plans were now beginning to sound like a running joke between us. Only neither of us was laughing anymore.

But first I wanted to make sure I'd be OK before he committed to me. Financially OK. This was the one fly in my Tuscan champagne. Julian had invested a lot of his own money in our new life and business and the first year we'd been beating bookings away with a stick. But now? *One* booking all season. Why? Had my kick-ass manager skills gone downhill since I'd left my Boston job at The Farthington Hotel? If so, it was time to get back on track and pronto.

'I know we've been putting it off for some time now,' I apologized as Julian's eyebrow shot up. 'But can't we wait just a little longer?' I tried to negotiate without hurting his feelings. God knew how I'd fought tooth and nail to believe in myself after all that my ex-husband Ira had put me and the kids through. I needed to feel I could still do it on my own and not depend on the 'rich husband'. Nothing bothered me more than that. 'I want to sort the business out first...'

He groaned. 'It's been two years, Erica. No more waiting. Let's go away, anywhere you want, and do it.'

'I—I can't just take off like that, Julian. What about our guests?'

'They'll be OK. Rosina can take care of them. It's not like we've got an army coming in,' he insisted.

'Exactly, you see? I need to figure out what's going *on*.'

He shrugged. 'We can always do that when we get back. One week isn't going to change anything.'

Now, I know that money gave him the confidence not to worry about much these days, but it was starting to feel like he didn't understand my worries. Didn't he care as much as me anymore? Or was I the official family worrywart?

'What about our responsibilities?' I insisted. 'The kids need us.'

But he was shaking his head. 'Erica, it's always something with you. I'm getting a little tired.'

'Tired… of me?' I asked, instantly meek.

The prospect of losing him hadn't occurred to me, I'll be honest. But seeing the look in his eyes, I was beginning to worry.

He'd taken a leap of faith to follow me out here, abandoning his cushy job as a principal, and precisely my children's principal in Boston. Those who don't know me yet may think I'm the smooth seductress mom, but they'd be sooo wrong. I'm anything but smooth.

In fact, despite the gazillion diets I've tried, I still have my share of lumps and bumps, although some are still in the right places. And over all those skinny-assed women courting him shamelessly, he'd gone and chosen the one frazzled, stressed-out workaholic freak– *moi*.

At that time, a mother of two and married (albeit in name only), my life had been suffocating me like a size four dress.

I had too much stuff to fit into it, trying to juggle all the balls in the air on my own. Because my better half (ha!) had spent all his time and money, most of it mine, on sneaking around with a woman half his age. To do so, he'd dispensed himself from all fatherly duties, leaving me to graduate to the all-in-one position of mommy and daddy.

Truth be told, Ira and I had been slowly and very painfully dying as a couple. Until the day he tried to badger me into a stomach bypass because I was 'too big for him to handle'. I know, right? In any case, just a few minutes before they were to take me into the operating theatre, I found out that he was cheating on me. Which had given me the push I needed to face him. And believe that even if he and I were done, my life was far from over. I still deserved to be loved.

And then one fine day, Julian had come along and torn my pants off. Literally speaking. And, between a parents' night and a school sports event, it had soon become apparent that Principal Foxham had wanted to spend more and more time with yours truly. And when Ira finally did the unmentionable and went baseball batshit crazy on us, who was there to protect us? You got it – Principal Julian Foxham, former baseball star (it turned out) and lover extraordinaire.

And when he'd agreed to move to Tuscany with us, the rest was history. I ran the B & B and he continued his writing career, globetrotting from one book tour to another. And dealing with my lingering insecurities.

I repeated my question. 'Are you growing tired of me?'

He exhaled, but it wasn't quite a sigh, bless his soul.

'No, honey, not tired of you, but tired of waiting. When are you finally going to let go and give up to the good life?'

*The good life.* He was right. With this need to stay financially independent through my business, I'd carved myself something that was more a trench than a happy routine. Then again, if I didn't succeed, everything the kids and I had been through before Julian would have been for nothing.

And yet, deep in my heart I knew he was right. What the hell *was* I waiting for? We loved each other. Maddy and Warren adored him – the one loving father they'd ever had. Even now that he dashed around the world, he still found time for them, when Ira couldn't even be bothered to praise them for anything, be it their artwork or their marks. Here in Italy, Julian had even learned Italian so he could speak to their teachers and get to grips with their curriculum. Need I say more as to why I adore this handsome, sexy, caring man who believed in me enough to follow me halfway across the world?

So why couldn't I let go and try to relax? If things went belly-up, we'd face it as a family. It wouldn't be my fault, right? Plus, wasn't I in my dreamland now, where only good things could happen to us? So what if this season was a disaster? I'd make it up the next. Julian was right. We had a safety net. It wasn't like we were poor.

'Well?' he prompted softly.

I looked up, conscious I was being ridiculously recalcitrant. Julian was everything I'd ever wanted. I took his hand. 'Uhm...'

He studied me through eyes that were knowing but never sure.

'I'm kidding!' I cried. 'Let's do it! Let's set the date once and for all!'

Julian beamed and wrapped his arms around me. 'Erica…'

Truth was, I was the one beaming, so grateful he'd actually stuck around all this time because, let me tell you, a lesser man would have sent me packing. So yeah, we were going to do it. We were finally going to get hitched.

There was only one thing. (Are you at all surprised?)

'Can we just not run away and do it overnight, though?' I pleaded. 'I want our families to be there in case they don't believe it.'

Actually, my stepmother, Marcy, would have an absolute fit. She never seemed to accept that Julian and I were an item. She didn't not like him – in truth, she thought the world of him. She simply didn't like him with me, because in her opinion, I hadn't put up with my first husband, Ira, long enough.

'So we're finally doing it,' Julian said as if he still couldn't believe it.

I laughed and threw myself into his arms. 'Yes,' I gushed, taking his face between my hands and giving him a whopper of a kiss. 'But with your tight schedule?' I asked. 'When did you have in mind?'

'September 24th?'

My mouth fell open. 'But that's in less than four months…'

He shrugged. 'We'll get everything done on time.'

Which was my cue to worry all over again. Because at this point I feel bound to tell you that Julian is the biggest procrastinator in the world. And not only that – his plans always seemed to change on a dime.

For instance, the original idea when we moved to Tuscany was for me to run the B & B while he bred horses and ran a farm and wrote in his spare time. But now, when he returned from his book tours, he secreted himself in his study to write his next novel. So we'd had to hire more workers for the fields and the stables.

But to look at him, you wouldn't think he lived out of his suitcase, always stylishly casual and freshly pressed (by yours truly, of course). Always cool, calm and collected, while I was the one always charging around like a headless chicken in my cheap sundresses and my flip-flops, baking, cooking and running errands and keeping the farmhouse in top shape. Not impossible for someone who ran the Boston Farthington like clockwork.

Of course, with our farmhands doing all the work, what worries did he have, at the end of the day? As soon as his book about his former life as a baseball champion had hit the shelves, he'd sky-rocketed back to fame, appearing on TV shows and in the papers. He was a celebrity reborn.

And to think that when I met him I'd thought he was just my children's new school principal (I kid you not) who had simply been very kind to me during my divorce, stopping by with apple pies to cheer me up. And it had got to the point I'd literally had to will myself to stop thinking about him all the time, let alone believe he could be interested in me. Doesn't ring any bells? Boy, where have you *been* to miss out on the most exciting part of my life? The worst of times, but also the best.

So you can imagine my surprise when I found out my kids' principal was a celebrity. Even if everybody else did, how was I supposed to know? I don't follow sports. I simply don't have the time. Nor do I know anyone in the jet set, contrary to Julian. So I can't exactly say I'd seen any of this coming.

Truth be told, I was the one who'd badgered him into finishing the novel that had been lodged in the drawer of his nightstand for years, the rest being history. And now we were getting *married*? Surreal. Even I didn't believe it. And now, in retrospect, maybe I shouldn't have believed it.

'Right. Sorted!' he chimed. 'Finally. Now all we have to do is make you write your vows in your own blood.'

I giggled and checked my watch. 'Silly. Now go and run those errands like you promised. You'll find me in the pool.'

*If I don't suddenly remember any last-minute chores.* But it was looking pretty good. The place was spotless, the rooms ready. Bring on the Matera Brainstormer Ladies…

He grinned. 'Wait for me before you have a swim. The last time you stayed in too long your back packed up and I had to carry you upstairs.'

Which was no mean feat for any guy. Because I was anything but pocket-size.

I grinned. 'Worried about me? When did you turn into an Italian mamma?'

But he had a point. Whenever I didn't dry my hair or I stayed in the water too long, I'd get a stiff neck for days, screaming if even the slightest breeze so much as blew my hair the wrong way. Man, I hated it when he was right. Still, I rolled my eyes.

'I'm not eighty, honey.'

'All the same, I'll be right back and I want you nimble.' And then, humming the 'Wedding March', he turned to go, not without me sneaking a peek at his gorgeous Levi's butt.

When I heard his jeep roar into life, I sauntered down the staircase leading to the patio and took off my broken sundress. Without bothering to change out of my bra and underwear, I sank deep into the water and closed my eyes.

*Ah…* This was it. Things could finally fall into place now that I'd committed to the rest of my life. Marrying Julian. In sickness and in health. In poverty or in wealth. I sighed, pushing the demons away.

Because on the flip side, the children were prospering. With Maddy now ten and Warren fourteen, they'd both passed all their subjects at school and were doing very well. Well, Warren wasn't the quickest learner when it came to languages, but he was trying. Maddy was entering her last year of primary school, and Warren was on his first year of *liceo*, junior high.

And I, too, had come a long way. I'd once been the massively overweight and enormously under-loved Mrs. Ira Miserable Lowenstein. An endless dietary regime I'd dubbed 'The Husband Diet' (involving a cartload of tears and anxiety) had turned me into a slightly lighter woman. Slightly, meaning I was still a big girl. And I'd probably still be in that rut today if I hadn't found out Ira was cheating on me with his stick-figure (and younger) secretary, Maxine Moore. In a way, I have them to thank for the happy turn my life has taken. My life has completed brightened up without Ira.

We'd probably still be married if it hadn't been for that telltale text message in the exact moment I was in the hospital awaiting a stomach bypass. (She was, she wrote, wearing red stilettos and no panties, waiting for *my* husband. While I was battling with a tissue-like robe with blue flowers that was nowhere near big enough to cover even the tiniest ass, let alone mine. You get the picture).

Scratch that – rather than still being married to him, I'd most likely have killed him, judging by the amazing amount of killer fantasies I'd had towards the end of the marriage. At one point I'd gone as far as to consider throwing a hairdryer into his bath on one of his 'let's bash Erica's person' nights. Oh, yes! In those days I could have written a book titled, *A Gazillion Ways to Kill Your Husband.*

Even now, occasionally, Ira will pop into my mind and I marvel at how little I loved myself to put up with him and his cruel words about my looks and how I'd never be the perfect housewife. Of course I couldn't, not while working round the clock. Things had got so bad that I'd begun to grind my teeth in my sleep.

And then, once Ira was finally out of the picture, I'd slowly started to blossom. Thanks first to the kindness and later the love of Julian who had chosen to be with The One Who Didn't Have It All Together. As opposed to some of the other moms who did, and would have given their right arm for just one night with him. Of course, I know that they're not better than me. But boy, do they manage to pretend they are!

Yeah. This was definitely my second shot at life and I'd be damned if I wasn't going to get it right this time.

While the gently lapping waters of the pool caressed my skin, I had a brainstorming session with myself about how to drum up some business this coming summer. I was just about to make a chronological list of the steps to be taken when the telephone interrupted my strategy-building. Could it possibly be a blessed booking? I jumped out the pool, stubbing my big toe on the stone steps, cursing as I limped in all my rotund glory to the cordless phone on the garden table, ow-ow-ing in agony.

'A T-taste… of Tuscany… good afternoon,' I managed through gritted teeth as I shoved my foot under a towel to dull the pain.

'Is that the way you answer the phone? Did you learn *nothing* all those years as manager of The Farthington, for goodness' sake?'

I groaned. Marcy Bettarini Cantelli. My stepmother and my mother's twin, better known as the bane of my younger years and still today a thorn in my side, despite a few sporadic attempts to get along from both sides.

It figured that when I lived within a ten-minute drive from their place, she'd never bothered. Unless it was to criticize my taste in clothes, or to try to sabotage my relationship with my aunts, the lovely Three Ms: Maria, Monica and Martina, of whom she was killer jealous. But now that I was in Italy – and at peace with the world, for once – she called at least twice a week just to rub me up the wrong way, knowing that she could, with the result that I was agitated for days after. Of course, it's mostly on me. I could easily not give a damn. But I do.

Sure, we'd had that stepmother–stepdaughter atonement thing going on when she confessed how she'd come to marry my dad. Who was still in love with her own dead twin. Marcy had suffered greatly for always being second and all. And it'd had a softening effect on me. Because, let's face it, I'm a forgiver by nature. To a certain extent.

When would she ever get over herself? And why didn't she instead aggravate my siblings, Judy or Vince, who lived only a few blocks away from her? Why didn't she disapprove of their lifestyle, like when Judy had had a cheating spate on her saintly husband, Steve, or when Vince had fallen in love with another woman, who wasn't Sandra? So much for being at peace with myself and the world. I know, I've still got some work to do in that department. I'm a Work In progress. But I can accept that, now.

So why did she not torture them? Because I never spilled the beans on their mistakes, while my slip-ups were always thrown back in my face.

'Hi, Marcy,' I groaned. 'Sorry, I hurt my foot.'

'What? When? Are you alright?'

For a woman who had barely spoken to me in my youth except to tell me to stop stuffing my face and sit up straight, Marcy had morphed into one hell of a pain in the ass ever since I found out she wasn't my real mother. I almost preferred her before.

'I'm fine, Marcy.'

'Well?'

'Well what?'

'Aren't you going to tell me how it's *going*?'

Lately, Marcy was starting to speak in italics. And hyperboles. It was her new way of getting everyone's attention. Nothing was nice, good, OK. On the contrary, it was *absolutely fabulous*, *tremendous* or, in my case, *horrendous*.

'Very well, thanks. We've got guests coming tonight.' Albeit the only ones, but I wasn't telling her that.

'Are you booked the last two weeks of August?'

The last two weeks of August – meaning the two weeks

I was going to book in Sicily for sun, sea, sand and around-the-clock room service. She wasn't about to invite herself over, was she? Oh, dear God in heaven, please, no.

'We have plans to come over,' I heard her say.

You know when you hear something crystal clear but you're hoping, against all logic, that you've only imagined it? Absolute horror thrummed through me like electricity down a power line and I was sure she could hear the zing as it zapped up my spine.

Other than that, I was slipping into a state of panic. Marcy, *here*, lounging around this very pool and making me cater to her every need while she downed Martinis and criticized everything from my placemats to my shower curtains? Nuh-uh. Not happening – if I valued my sanity, my marriage and my children's respect for me. Because Marcy would tear apart all the aforementioned in one week flat.

I could already see it, like a train wreck in slow motion, or one of those nightmares you can't wake up from. Because all Marcy wanted, bless her selfish little soul, was to look *fabulous* while others looked like shit. And Marcy always got what she wanted. But not this time, if I could help it.

Because if she flew out for the last two weeks of August, once she knew the wedding was in September, there was no way I was getting rid of her until then. Which meant that I'd have to put up with her for the best part of six weeks. Not happening.

'Uhm, actually, I think the cottages are pretty much completely booked all summer,' I lied.

'Oh, that's OK.'

Yes! I silently punched the air in triumph, feeling a bolt of pain shoot through my back. Looked like Julian was right to nag me, after all.

'If you're completely booked, no problem. We'll just sleep in your house, then,' she conceded as, slack-jawed, I scuttled for some excuse, but could think of absolutely zilch.

'I can't believe I have to invite *myself* over,' she tsk-tsked.

And I couldn't believe she just had. I remembered living under the same roof with her and let me tell you, it was not good. Granted, I knew I'd have had to call her sooner or later, because I couldn't get married without inviting her, now could I? But I wasn't prepared for this super-deluxe ambush.

At this point you might be asking yourself, Why the hell doesn't she just tell her stepmom she's getting married? Ah, if you only knew Marcy! Because she'd fly over this instant to take over the preparations and take it upon herself to make all the important decisions, my wedding dress included. It would be an absolute disaster-fest like my first wedding. Believe me, the less time she spent here bossing everyone around, the longer I'd stay sane.

'So it's settled,' she concluded. 'I'll call you as soon as we have our flights.'

And then, somewhere between telling me about Judy's new toy (and for a moment, I honestly thought she meant a new lover) and Vince's new teenage delivery boy (and here I couldn't somehow help thinking they were the same person), she blew *kissie-kissie, bye-bye* noises at me and hung up.

I clicked the phone off with a huff. Kissie-kissie, *bye-bye*? What the hell had got into her? Jesus, was there no escaping her? Did I have to move to the North Pole to get some peace and quiet?

I let myself drop onto a lounger, the pain in my throbbing toe and my back nothing compared to the sensation of impending doom. Just what I needed – my stepmom to *step in* and make my life a misery all over again. For six endless weeks.

I had dinner and drinks served on the terrace at sunset for my ten Matera Brainstormers – talented, smart women from every corner of the world.

Despite the relaxed atmosphere, it was clear they were already in work mode, discussing their plots in the making and helping each other out with the tricky bits. In other words, when to kill off the mother-in-law (or stepmother, in my case), how the heroine should find out her husband is cheating and how the alpha male should defuse the bomb in time to save the world.

From a distance I observed them, wishing I'd had that kind of support in life when I'd needed it.

'Erica?' Elizabeth called. 'We were wondering how you manage it all with very little help.'

I grinned. 'Just a good dose of folly.'

At that, Sheila, a successful thriller author and genuine all-American with a sense of humor as sharp as a blade, cackled in delight.

'And a good dose of something else! We've seen your partner on TV. Friggin' compliments are in order!'

'Partners are overrated,' I informed them, and they laughed.

Elizabeth nodded. 'Don't we know it. But, honey, it's OK to have the almost-perfect life. What's the deal?'

I frowned. 'The deal?'

'Yeah,' Kim, a beautiful American married to an equally beautiful Swede, wanted to know. 'Tell us the truth. What's the fly in your champagne?'

I sighed. 'Jesus, how much time have you got?'

They laughed and Ingrid, an amazing chef and one of the sweetest women alive who had recently bought a house in Abruzzo, shook her head. 'We've all been there, you know. The expectations, the disappointment. What's yours?'

Elizabeth smiled at me knowingly, pulling out a chair for me.

I grinned. 'You need writing material? I'm your gal. Where do I start? A dysfunctional stepmother who can't accept that I exist, yet who tries to rule my life as if it were hers?'

'Ouch,' said Dominique, a crazy-smart woman who had worked with the United Nations. 'My mother lived to be a hundred and one and never once nagged me.'

Sheila turned to her. 'That's an insanely long time to go without a fight.'

At that, Cassie, who had a home not far away but lived in the States, giggled. 'Mothers and daughters get along just fine if moms mind their own business.'

We all laughed. What a wonderful group of easygoing, intelligent and independent women this was. We were on the same wavelength. So far from Marcy or Judy or my sister-in-law, Sandra.

'I have my aunts to thank for their big buckets when the family boat started leaking,' I finally said. 'And my best friends Paul and Renata. They keep me sane. Or at least looking sane.'

'I love my mom,' Christine said as she downed her vodka. 'But hell, she tends to rule with two iron fists. A toast to all moms.'

We laughed and I toasted to both of mine, the larger-than-life stepmom and the faded but beloved memory of my real mother, Emanuela. And with that, I left them to it.

I loved seeing people having fun and relaxing. Julian was right. It was time for the good life.

In September, after the wedding, I could start to take it easy. A new shuttle bus service would ferry Maddy and Warren to their schools so I wouldn't need to throw my clothes on and hop out the door to do the school run and get back to work without having a stroke first. Yes. Soon I'd be living the good life. But even as the evening breeze caressed the fields, carrying with it the fragrance and the whispers of swaying, unripe green wheat, I couldn't help but wonder exactly how much had changed in my own personal pace of life. If I was still worried about the B & B and always running around like a headless chicken when instead I should be, as Julian always said, chilling, what exactly had improved in my life in the past two years? Well, for one thing, I was slowly learning to love myself, even. And my body? Well , I was no Angelina Jolie. But I was a work in progress. Weren't we all, in some way? So it seemed to me that I was the only obstacle to our happiness.

# 2

## If It Ain't Broke…

So who, you might ask, did my first wedding call (or cry for help) go to? Why, to my partner in crime, my BFF of a thousand years and costume designer Paul Belhomme, of course. He'd seen me through thick and thin (well, almost thin) and knew everything about me, as I him. He'd know what to do.

'Woo-hoo! About time, sunshine!' he hollered over the phone all the way from Boston while Julian stood behind me, hands on my shoulders, listening in and grinning.

Julian was no fool. He knew that if he had Paul Belhomme's stamp of approval, he was home free. Paul is my alter ego, my friend, my family, my insides.

'I can't believe you finally said yes to the poor guy!' he cried. 'I've only been waiting for this moment like forever!'

'You and me both, mate,' Julian said into the mouthpiece.

I grinned. 'Well, get your ass over here pronto, then. I need you.'

'I'm on the first flight, sunshine!'

My lifeline was on his way. And that was all I needed to know.

When I called Renata, my BIFF (Best Italian Female Friend), she was over in a flash.

'Hello, *bride!* I've brought you some fresh bread from Fernando's, Nutella *cornetti* (croissants), strawberry jam and a couple of bottles of *Fragolino* dessert wine to celebrate!'

As far as gluttony was concerned, I'd met my match. Only she, of course, was half my weight.

Crazy as a nuthouse, Renata hadn't changed since I met her one early morning two years ago. We'd only been in the farmhouse one night, when a tap-tapping had woken us. I'd honestly thought it was a woodpecker knocking away on a nearby tree at the crack of dawn. But no. The tap-tapping had become a pound-pounding and with a groan, Julian had flipped back the coverlet and jumped into his jeans before padding downstairs.

'It had better be the bloody milkman,' had been his first words on his first morning in Italy.

I remember sitting up. Who the hell could it be? Apart from the *notaio*, the notary officer, who had overseen the sale transaction, I'd thought that no one knew about us. We hadn't even been to the supermarket yet. But I was so wrong. The word had gotten out that we, the *Americans* (although Julian is English), had bought the Colle d'Oro farmhouse to open a B & B.

And they'd poured into my kitchen, a gazillion beautiful, friendly kids followed by a couple in their late thirties, as Julian stood in total confusion.

'*Ciao*, Erica. *Come stai?*' she'd said throwing herself at me. How are you?

I'd immediately dubbed them The Sunshine Family – Renata, her husband, Marco, their twins, Chiara and Graziano, and their youngest, Andrea.

She was a pretty, petite woman with huge turquoise eyes. Her husband was tall and good-looking in a wholesome way, and they were both easygoing and genuine. Renata wore a simple flower-print dress that did nothing to hide a generous bosom. Her blondish hair had been swept up in a hasty, harried ponytail, but I caught a glimpse of the tattoo on the back of her neck and the way Marco held her by the waist even as they all piled in. I liked them instantly.

Before we could speak, they introduced themselves as our neighbors and whipped out a large basket containing a pretty tablecloth, cutlery, crockery and the most colorful food I'd ever seen. Julian had rubbed his face and grinned at me, and I'd shrugged my shoulders. That's what I loved most about him – his naturalness.

Now normally, I hated early birds, especially *happy* early birds, chatting away as if they were on speed. But when the early birds bring you fantastic food and even hot coffee in multiple thermoses, how can you hold a grudge?

So I'd gone with the flow and bit into a *cornetto* and almost swooned on the spot as Nutella chocolate enveloped my tongue.

'Do you like?' she'd asked while feeding her youngest a cookie, her pretty eyes lighting up, searching mine.

'Like?' I laughed. 'This is heaven! Where did you get these?'

Renata laughed. 'Get? I make dem. I show you tomorrow!'

Speaking the international language of male, Julian and

Marco, followed by the boys, had gone down to the stables. Was it really this easy to make friends with people here? Could even I, Erica, the eternally wary, make friends with someone so quickly?

'Thank you for all this food – that was very kind of you,' I said as she tore off a generous chunk of homemade bread, slathered it with jam and handed it to me, licking her own fingers.

'Food is love,' she said. 'Friendship. Many oder tings, too.'

*Many other things, too.* Now that, if you'll pardon my pun, was a mouthful. Since I was a kid my relationship with food had been a difficult one.

But it was so lovely to hear such a universal and heart-warming truth in such a charming accent. Because, funny— for me food had only been a prison. Seen this way, though, I could get used to it big time. And I could learn a lot about life from her.

'Your English is very good,' I marveled.

Renata shrugged. 'I st-huddied English at university, bat I never speak.'

'Why? Tuscany is full of Americans and Brits, isn't it?'

Renata smiled and nodded to her children helplessly. 'I never go out. Dey take up all my energy.'

I decided this woman was my kindred spirit. 'Tell you what,' I offered. 'You teach me your recipes and I'll let you practice your English on me. What do you say?'

'Deal!'

She smacked my upturned hand hard and I couldn't help grinning. If Tuscany was only this – improvised breakfast parties, two men talking horses in two different languages and beautiful children munching on fresh food – I was hooked for life.

That had been two years ago.

Now, I yawned, happy just to sit here as Renata chattered away as usual.

'September 24th is the perfect day for a wedding,' Renata said. 'It's not too hot, it's not windy. It's just perfection. Hey, are you listening to me?'

Her English had improved immensely since then. Now, she sounded like a pure American.

'I didn't get much sleep last night,' I confessed, and she laughed as she presented me with a Nutella croissant, just like back then. The two years that I'd been here, Renata had showered me with food of every kind. She was an amazing cook. It was thanks to her that I had understood that yes, food was indeed love. And it wasn't food that was my problem, but my lack of control over my life. Control your life, she always said, and you control your food. And vice-versa. Boy, was she right. When things went well, food and I were good. When things went badly, food and I became iffy. But with her advice, I was doing better.

'Why didn't you sleep?' she asked. 'You and Julian at it all the time, huh?'

She was one to talk. Renata and Marco were the champions of not being able to keep their hands off each other and sometimes, in front of the kids, he'd place a hand on her breast and all was cool. Julian and I were more prudish in front of others.

Marco was a true Tuscan boy – the very 'salt of the earth' kind of guy born from a large family of farmers and pig breeders on his dad's side. He'd met Renata and got her pregnant while still at university, where she'd constantly heckled her history teacher, who was a blatant capitalist while she couldn't have been more Marxist. She'd sported a hammer and sickle tattoo, smoking joints, dying her then short, spiky hair a dark red and wearing around her neck colorful exotic flags of all the Third World countries.

Nothing enraged her teacher more. The fact that Professoressa Baldini was Marco's mother made it all the better for Renata, who loves a challenge. It took the in-laws three years to forgive them for getting together and having twins, but Renata couldn't seem to care less. She was one of those free-spirited girls whom Marco had been lucky even to try to tame. She was wild but conscientious and a great mother at the same time, like a teenager stuck in her mom's body.

'So this time it's for real! I can't believe you're finally getting married!' she whistled.

'Yeah, neither can I.'

She eyed me. That was all it took, because she knew me very well.

'What's worrying you?' she asked as she pulled on the tip of her *cornetto*, catching the Nutella cream with her tongue and missing some as it fell onto her yellow sundress, the one we'd bought together (mine a few sizes bigger) at the town market.

That was another thing that distinguished Renata and me from the rest of the Italian females living here. Well-to-do Tuscan women wouldn't be caught dead out of a label, but Renata and I had found some very pretty stuff – and cheap, too.

'*Cazzo*,' she swore, dabbing at the stain with a paper

napkin, and looked up. 'Come on, tell Auntie Renata what's bothering you.'

I swung one bare leg from the stool, watching as my white flip-flops dangled from my toes, exposing the tan line on my feet, since I hadn't worn stockings since the beginning of April. I met her eyes.

'Nothing. I'm very happy, of course.'

'But…?' she prompted.

'The business isn't doing well.'

'I figured. But that shouldn't worry you too much for the moment. Think about the important things.'

Which meant my family.

'Well, the kids and I are happy here, but Julian seems more interested in his writing career than running a farm – not that I blame him. But I'm starting to struggle. I need him to be here a bit more.'

'Well, then tell him you need his help.'

Solid logic— in anyone else's head. But not in mine. 'I would, but when we decided to move here, we'd agreed on our roles. If I ask him to write less, I'm afraid he'll think I resent his career. Which is crazy, because I was the one who pushed him to start it again. Or worse, he might even think that I'm not capable of doing everything on my own.'

Renata frowned. 'Erica, no one is capable of doing everything on their own. I'm not, and neither is Marco. You should be honest with Julian and tell him that this was not what you'd agreed.'

'Yes, but you see? We've both stopped short of each other's expectations. And I think that by moving here, I've pushed him into making the biggest mistake of his life.

I'm afraid one day he's going to hate me for it.' There. I'd said it.

Renata shook her head. 'Nonsense. This is where you all belong. Julian is happy with you here. And as far as A Taste of Tuscany is concerned, all you need to do is keep faith while you figure out how to right what you're doing wrong.'

I shook my head. 'But that's the thing, don't you see? I don't know what I'm doing wrong. I understand the business might be slightly different here, but I just don't get it. I've done my research and all my due diligence and stuff. I'm on Facebook, Twitter, Instagram and even TikTok for Christ's sake, but… it's like we're not even on the map anymore.'

Renata shook her head in sympathy. 'Have you tried promoting in a different way?'

'I've tried everything, Renata. Flyers, business cards, word of mouth to my friends in the USA. I don't want Julian to lose his investment.' *Or to get tired of me*, I mentally added.

She patted my knee. 'Silly. You and the children are Julian's investment. Now don't worry.'

'Well, there's one more thing worrying me,' I confessed. Might as well go all the way. 'Marcy is coming to visit. She'll be staying from mid-August to the wedding.'

Women of the same ilk who call themselves friends don't need to explain these things to each other. Renata shivered.

'Marcy? Now *that* is scary. Why don't you hold off telling her about the wedding until after she's flown back home?'

'Because a) she'd never forgive me for not letting her know the date as soon as it was set, and b), for the rest of my living days she'd make me pay for making her travel out twice in the space of two months, rather than hosting her here until the wedding.'

Renata tsk-tsked.

I nodded. 'And don't forget that my aunts will be coming, too.'

'The three Ms and your stepmother in the same house? Oh, Jesus. Here,' she said, offering me another croissant. 'I had a feeling you needed me this morning...'

'Why do we have to go to private afternoon lessons in September again?' Warren groaned at my pondered decision to help them achieve better school results. 'We already know the language. And besides, I've got other stuff to do.'

Ooh, it was going to be one of those days, was it? Well, Warren had chosen the wrong one for a tantrum.

You know when you're already fed up with things and you think, maybe I should go off somewhere, move to a different country, but then that depresses you even more, because you already have gone off somewhere and moved to a different country, but it's not quite like you hoped? That was me right now.

So here's a caveat for you if you're anything like me: always remember that moving away from your old life won't remove you from a daily routine. You might create a new life, but you can't hide from your own problems – they have radar and can find you anywhere on the planet, faster and more accurately than GPS.

'Yes, you do have to continue, and you've both done an amazing job so far. But language isn't everything. You need to learn more about the culture just to understand what you'll be studying. Plus, this coming school year will be more demanding.'

Warren looked at me and then groaned. 'All I want is to play sports, Mom.'

Didn't I know it.

'Will we have exams, Mom? I can't wait to have exams!' Maddy chimed, clapping her tiny hands together in a dreamy mood.

I smiled at my adorable princess. Let her dream on for now. She'd have plenty of time to learn gradually that life was one big, endless exam. One that you didn't always pass.

'I hate exams,' my son whined.

'But think, Warren,' Julian interjected as he came in from the fields, toeing his shoes off and washing his hands in the kitchen sink. And reaching for my pristine dish towel – something that drove me bananas, but as long as he played on my team, he could even wipe his muddy boots on my apron.

'You'll know way more than the senior students at our old school will ever know – plus you get to play in an Italian soccer team. How cool is that?'

Warren pretended to huff but then shrugged. Julian could convince him to walk over burning coals, so strong was my son's admiration for him.

Everything here in Italy was still so new to the kids. They loved being here, but it wasn't without its challenges. Sometimes I wondered if I'd been reckless to uproot my children so completely in the name of my lifelong personal dream of a life in Italy. Whisking them away from their friends, their home, their school (although I'd managed to drag their principal along as a bonus). Had I thrown them both in at the deep end? Or was it a good thing, a life-enriching experience that would make them more prepared for their future? Things with them were good at the moment, but would they remain like that in the long run?

Regarding Julian, I was already worried about testing his patience. I didn't need my children to suffer as well. God, would I be crying and promising to take them back to Boston by Christmas if they weren't happy?

'Of course not, honey,' Julian assured me later as we lay in bed, my laptop on my knees. I was updating A Taste of Tuscany's Facebook page. New photos, some fictitious reviews (well, that's business, right or wrong), some shots of Renata's dishes that guests could hope to taste from her tiny catering gigs.

'But are you sure?' I asked him. 'What if we're wrong? What if they can't adjust? What if I've traumatized them?'

He turned back to look at me as he pulled off his T-shirt. 'Of course not. Kids have amazing adjustment power. They're extremely resilient. You'll see. Now stop worrying and get closer...'

He turned off the lamp and reached for me, playing with my spaghetti straps, nuzzling my throat. Through the open window, the fragrance of the early summer night wafted in, singing a lullaby to my brain and finally relaxing my muscles. He was right. Everything would be OK. I just needed to relax. Not worry about the kids too much. Or about A Taste of Tuscany. *As if*.

'But what about you?' I whispered.

'Sweets, I'm more than resilient.'

'No. I mean, are you happy? You threw away your whole life to follow me here.'

'And you're asking me this after two years?'

'I asked you a mega-gazillion times, Julian!'

To which he chuckled, brushing my hair off my shoulder. 'Silly sausage. If I wasn't happy with you, I wouldn't be here, would I?'

Huh. So if he wasn't happy, all he had to do was walk away? It was that simple? So I guess it had to be true that he was still happy with me, with all he'd put up with since the day we met. I was loud and bossy and ran my household and business like a tight ship. But if you knew me at all, you'd know inside I'm absolute mush.

I lay quietly, mulling it over. Still, loving me and being happy with our life here were two different things. If I was certain that we'd made the right decision in the long run, I'd be happier, too. A new woman, in fact, like you see in those makeover shows like *Ten Years Younger*. Only I'd be ten years happier.

'Besides,' he added, 'isn't this what you always dreamed? A life in the country, a stone's throw from a stunning medieval town full of culture? A slower-paced life, your own business and the house of your dreams?'

It was. It was everything I'd dreamed. 'Sorry. I know how lucky we are. I just… worry about things.'

'Then stop worrying, love. We have it all, for once. And I'll be damned if we don't deserve it. And the business will only get better. Just give it time.'

Even if he wasn't always around, I knew his heart was in the right place. I reached up to caress his jaw. 'You, my love, have a way of reminding me of all the good things we have.'

He chuckled. 'Come here and let me remind you of yet another one, then…'

And with that, he kissed me smack on the lips. He was good at finding me in the dark.

So now I was going to stop worrying about us and go with the flow. Sit back and finally enjoy the benefits of all the hard work that it took us to get here as a family. Despite all the obstacles Ira had put in my path all these years, I'd finally made it to Tuscany. Where we belonged. Where we were happy.

But that wouldn't stop me from continuing my quest to find out why business was slow and trying to figure out if I was making any marketing mistakes. I had a whole lot of investigating to do. And some more marketing research. Perhaps Italians had a different outlook on the B&B business? I'd have to look into that. And find a way to let everyone know we existed. I'd have to extend our social media presence. Be ubiquitous. Make everyone aware that we were here, and in business.

And as far as the wedding was concerned, now that we had a date, I knew I'd dupe Paul into taking care of it. And deal with the consequences if it fell through again. But you have to have a little faith. This time it would be for real. And Paul was perfect for the job. He was the elegant one who knew what was in, what was out and what went with what.

We'd make the ceremony nice and simple, in our very own home (all we had to do was throw a bit of money at the Church in the form of a generous donation), surrounded by all our loved ones. You know, just the kids, Paul, Renata's family, Judy and her family. Vince and his mob, Julian's parents and a few friends. And, oh! I almost forgot to tell my three adorable aunts! They'd practically raised me after my nonna had died, while Marcy just lounged. Marcy hated them with a passion and left every room they entered with a haughty huff. But there was no way I wasn't having them on such an important day.

We called them the three Ms: Maria, Martina and Monica. They owned Le Tre Donne, an award-winning Italian restaurant in Boston. Maria was the cook while Martina was the front woman who took care of the patrons and the look of the place. Monica was the techie who took care of the marketing and the financial side. Together, they were invincible and loved us fiercely as if we were their own.

None of them had ever married despite multiple proposals and Marcy was eternally jealous of them, as they doted on Dad, especially, I'm told, after my real mother died. Zia Maria would feed him his favorite dishes, while Zia Martina would tailor him the finest Italian suits and Zia Monica would give him cutting-edge business advice. Together, the three of them had him covered, much to Marcy's annoyance. She never missed out on the chance to belittle them, despite their beauty, grace and success.

And whenever Marcy drank, which was becoming more and more often according to Judy, she went from passive-aggressive to downright in-your-face, criticizing them for anything and everything, like a helpless, dying angry fish flapping at its destiny. Having them here all in the same house this summer promised to be a bloodbath.

I sighed. So much for not worrying about anything. It was a good thing Paul was coming to my aid.

# 3

## Venues and Menus

Paul's flight was right on schedule and he came out of customs looking as fresh as a daisy. No wrinkly shirts, no messy hair and most of all, come to think of it, absolutely no tired lines on his face after a ten-hour flight. How did he *do* that? Whenever I fly somewhere, I land looking like I've just been through a war.

'Paul!' I cried.

Really cried, swiping at a gush of tears. This was ridiculous. Paul and I didn't do tears. We talked and laughed and pondered, but never, ever, did he let me do tears. Of the two of us, I was the one with the wobbly lower lip, for sure, while he always managed to keep his cool.

Apart from the couple of trips he'd made out in the past two years, I'd hardly seen him, so I'd had to make do with video calls. Even if I couldn't hug him, at least I could see his beloved face or his wacky expressions. Which I wasn't seeing now.

When he spotted me, his face lit up, but he didn't smile.

Not even a teensy, barely noticeable curling upwards of the mouth. Something was definitely wrong.

'Sunshine!' he drawled, wrapping his long arms around me and planting a kiss on my lips. 'You look great!'

'And you look… different.' Weird. Definitely. 'Spray tan?' I tried to guess.

'Botox!' he cried.

'Paul, no! You said you were never going to do anything like that.'

'I said I wasn't going to do it as long as I held out. But when I woke one morning and saw I was starting to look like my mother, I told myself I couldn't come to Italy – and your wedding – looking all leather-bag saggy-faced.'

I was touched. 'Oh, Paulie! You went through all that for me?'

'I wanted to look fabulous, so the minute you called with your news, I booked an appointment. But now I can't move my facial muscles for at least another week. I really want to smile but it hurts!'

That was Paul for you. Honest and prissy. Too bad his gorgeous Latino looks were intended for the other team.

'Hello, mate!' Julian appeared, giving him a bear hug.

'Jules, honey, you look absolutely scrumptious! Italy's treating you well.'

'And so is Erica,' Julian added with a grin. 'Never been happier.'

I flashed him a smile. To think that I'd made this hunk of a man happy was uplifting. Exhilarating, even. So it must be true, after all.

'Right, let's get you home!' Julian said. 'Erica is terrified about this wedding.'

'I am not!' I protested.

Well, it was really a token protest. I wasn't scared of the wedding per se, but that something would happen again, and that the day would come and go without the two of us being any more married than Wile E. Coyote and the Road Runner. Because although I thought I'd 'caught' Julian, he kept on running around the world and there was nothing I could do to keep him still long enough to get married, despite the fact that marriage had been – and still mainly was – his idea.

He rested his hand on the back of my neck as he always did.

'She's terrified that a sudden outbreak of the plague is going to stop us from getting married again, although I've assured her a million times it's not happening.'

'What, the wedding, you mean?' Paul giggled through stiff lips, and I turned to give him my famous hairy eyeball.

'It'll be alright, love. Just have faith.'

Faith. And that was a mouthful, seeing what followed after that.

'Good to see you, doll!' Paul exclaimed when he hugged Renata. 'Your boobs look amazing in this dress!'

She knew all about Paul, although Marco still wasn't convinced about his sexual indifference toward his wife. He'd studied my buddy warily, as if ready to attack him if Paul dared lay a finger on her. Thank God Marco had gone back to work. Paul couldn't resist complimenting a pretty woman and Renata was stunning. Small-boned and big-busted, she represented the epitome of Italian beauty.

'And your ass looks sublime in those pants!' she answered.

That was Renata for you. Looks of a princess, mouth of a stevedore. They got on like a Tuscan villa on fire.

Paul's eyebrows rose in sheer delight as his eyes swerved to mine, then to her again. 'Me too, honey! I've got news!'

'Let me guess. You've found a new lover?' I ventured.

Ever since he and Carl had split up centuries ago, Paul had become the ruthless love 'em an' leave 'em type. But one day, I hoped, as the Tuscans say, his hard head would find an even harder rock to break it open and change his attitude completely. I wanted to see Paul in love with some fantastic guy who loved him to the moon and back. I wanted him to feel the same happiness every day that I did with Julian. No one should ever feel lonely.

Maybe I could shop around and shortlist for him, see if there's anyone in Castellino. I mentally went through a list of the men I was sure were gay and a few were worth investigating. But who was I kidding? Relationships were a minefield to me and I'd hardly made it across myself. But it was my duty to see him through an eventual liaison.

God knew how he was all secure and confident when it was about other people, but when he was involved, he became extremely insecure and standoffish. It was as if he was afraid to get hurt again. But this time I'd hold his hand. (I suppressed a thought of the blind leading the blind.)

'No, no new lover at the moment,' he assured me. 'But I've decided to start my own business. Something new.'

I studied him. A new business? Didn't he know how risky that was? Look at me. He was much safer falling in love at this rate.

'Are you sure, Paul? You're a brilliant costume designer.'

'I know. But I'm sick of the States. I want an Italian life like you. Hell, I already have the important friends and the Italian villa I never live in. Now I just want my freedom.'

Freedom to worry twice as much? I wondered. 'What about your tenants?'

He shrugged. 'I'll give them six months' notice. And live here in the meantime, of course, if that's alright with Julian?'

'Of course it is,' I assured. 'He loves you more than I do, if that's even possible.'

Paul had been in my life since forever and was my first lifeline during the break-up of my marriage to Ira. When Julian had come onto the scene, after sniffing him out, Paul had not only given me the thumbs up, but he'd also practically pushed me into the poor guy's arms.

'So what kind of business are you thinking?' Renata wanted to know.

He waved his hand gracefully over the piles of samples of tablecloths we'd been looking at for the wedding dinner. 'Duh?'

We both looked at the fabrics, then back at him, unsure.

He fake huffed. 'I'm going to be a wedding planner, of course! All I need is a name for the company.'

Now that was a good idea. An amazing one, in fact.

'Then I'm thrilled to be your guinea pig.'

'Hey,' he said, eyes bright. 'Maybe A Taste of Tuscany could be rented out as one of my venues.'

'Sure. What the hell. Maybe that's the answer to my financial woes.'

'Still no bookings?' Paul asked.

'Nope. But I'm working on it.'

'But what's the problem?'

I snorted. 'If I knew, I'd be on it. Truth is, I'm in total darkness. Maybe I should give it all up as a bad idea and you and I could expand your catering business, Renata. And cook for Paul's weddings.'

'With five kids between us? I only take on one job a month. But I do know an amazing chef who could suggest some venues and help you with your menus,' Renata offered.

Paul's face lit up. 'That's it!' he cried. 'Honey, you're a genius.'

Renata and I eyed each other. 'What's it?' Renata asked.

'The name for my new business. Menus and Venues!' he gushed, smacking her a kiss right on the lips.

'So, who are your target customers, then?' I asked.

'Filthy rich snobs, of course! The richest there are! Julian knows everyone in the jet set. Maybe he could spread the word.'

'Eva Santos just got engaged,' Julian offered as he came in, toeing his shoes off as usual.

'Eva Santos? I love her!' Paul began to jump up and down. 'Hook me up, hook me up!'

Little did Paul know that, besides being a great tennis star, Eva Santos was also one of Julian's many famous exes.

I whipped my head round to look at Julian. 'How do *you* know she's engaged?'

Was he keeping in touch with her? Not that there would be anything wrong with that. I mean, not really, just as long as I knew, right?

'*The Daily Mail*,' he answered simply. 'Whenever I log on, she's always on the front page for one reason or other.'

OK, that I could handle. Jealous much, *moi*?

'Jules, please be a star and give her a call for me, will

you? If I can start with her as my first client, then I'm home free.'

'*I'm* your first client,' I objected, but Paul shooed me away.

'You don't count. You're my guinea pig, remember?'

'Gee. I'm touched to the bone.'

'Alright,' Julian chuckled. 'I'll ask around and see who her agent is.'

Which meant he didn't have her direct number. I sort of inwardly sagged in relief. That was one thing out the way.

Paul whipped out a notepad.

'OK, down to brass tacks. What kind of wedding do you want? Large? Small? Modern? Traditional? It all rotates around the dress, you know. Choose your dress and you have your tone.'

I looked up in dismay. What the hell did I know about wedding dresses? My first dress was as much a disaster as the ceremony. A Catholic–Jewish mess where all the in-laws did was avoid each other.

'I want it to be the exact opposite of my first one.'

'Well, considering you were knocked up the first time…' Paul tittered as he poked me with his stylish mother-of-pearl pen. 'OK. Here's what we do. We go dress shopping. I know a woman in Siena who's dressed most of the who's who in Italy and abroad.'

'Yay,' a voice murmured. Mine. 'You know my memories of clothes shopping. I'd rather have my teeth pulled.'

In case you didn't know, when I was a kid, Marcy used to drag me to Macy's every change of season in an attempt to get me some clothes that would fit. Which was a feat, to say the least. Actually, it was embarrassing, excruciating torture, where she'd shout out to the salespeople all the details of my size and why it wouldn't fit, or pulled too much around the hips, or simply made me look like a walrus. I shivered at the memory.

'Ah, but you're not twelve anymore,' Paul insisted. 'This isn't Macy's, I'm not Marcy and we're shopping for your wedding dress! The dress of all dresses.'

'Yeah, whatever.'

Even if I dieted until I died, I'd never be a whippet. I'd never be one of those slim, graceful swans that were all about class and elegance. Which I was OK with. Although from time to time, when I saw a picture of one of Julian's exes online, I wondered how he and I even got together in the first place when we came from completely different worlds.

He was classy, fit and naturally elegant, while I was everything but. He really must have seen in me something that no one else did. Which, by the way, I'm still trying to figure out. When would he tire of my wacky ways and not quite classic poise? And I still dressed like Ernie from *Sesame Street* on the odd day. Note to self: horizontal stripes never did anyone any favors, let alone me. Did Humpty Dumpty wear stripes, as well? I can't remember. Which is also why I needed Paul to take care of the styling, to make sure I looked as fabulous as I hoped this wedding was going to be.

So yes, all in all, with my lifesaver wedding planner by my side, and my life partner who put up with me daily, things had to go smoothly. There were going to be no wedding worries whatsoever. I could get to that day serene and relaxed. One can always hope.

\*

The next Saturday morning, with the Matera Brainstormers just gone, Paul cooked the kids flapjacks in the kitchen, while Julian and I sat at the dining room table in front of our laptops. He worked on his sports novel, while I worked on my mystery novel, Where Have All The Guests Gone? I checked the world news to see if there was any new financial crisis I was unaware of, checked my emails, our website and any sign of life from A Taste of Tuscany on Facebook.

'Still nothing,' I muttered to myself. 'Absolutely nothing.'
Julian looked up from his screen. 'What's that, love?'

'No bookings,' I explained, stabbing at the keyboard to bring up any ideas to save us. I had a couple of marketing ideas in the making.

Out of the corner of my eye, I could see him still watching me. Did I have coffee on my upper lip? Or was he finally starting to worry, too? 'Can't get over how gorgeous I am, huh?' I quipped, still surfing away, a woman on a mission.

'Look at us,' he said, pushing back his chair.

'What?'

'Look at us, sitting at the same table, our laptops back to back.'

'I know, we're cute,' I answered, going back to my task.

Actually, we only did this on the weekends. During the week, he had his coffee in his study and didn't come out until lunchtime. Weekends were a treat for me.

'We look like we're playing Battleship,' he continued.

'Yeah...?' I said, scrolling down the names of all the other

B & Bs in the area, a pad beside me while I checked their availability calendars. And their social media presence. You never knew, there may have been something obvious that I hadn't thought of.

If I could figure out why everyone else was booked and we weren't... This *was* a battle, no bones about it, and our ship was definitely going to be sinking unless I performed a miracle. Remember my words.

Julian stood up with a scrape of his chair and pulled my own back. 'This is ridiculous. Let's go.'

I looked up from the screen, blinking. 'What? Where?'

'Paul?' he called into the kitchen, and Paul appeared in his bright red apron, my bright red spatula in his hand.

'Change your mind about the flapjacks?' Paul asked.

'Watch the kids will you, please? We're going for our usual Saturday morning stroll.'

I frowned. 'We don't have a usual Saturday morning stroll.'

He took my hand. 'We do now. Come on.'

'O-K...' I figured something was on his mind and he needed to talk.

'What's up?' I said finally as he parked on the edge of Castellino.

He flicked the jeep alarm on and put his arm around me casually.

'Nothing. I just think we're becoming computer slaves.'

I snorted. Was this a ploy to get me off the computer? He was one to talk.

'So you're handwriting your books from now on?'

'Silly. I just think we spend too much time working. And worrying.'

That was an understatement. Worrying was my second nature.

'And a walk around the town is going to help?' I asked skeptically.

'Remember when we were in Boston, just getting to know each other, and you told me about your Tuscan dreams?'

'Yeah?'

'Do you remember how you always used to say that getting to Italy was more than half the battle?'

I stopped and looked up at him. 'I was wrong, Julian. The battle starts when you finally get what you wanted. You have to fight even harder to keep it.'

He studied me, kindness in his eyes. He knew me so well. He knew my fears, my insecurities. Only sometimes, as much as I love him, I had the feeling he didn't fully understand how invalidating they were for me. Just because he was confident didn't mean everyone else was.

'Erica, honey. You need to let things be. Things will go as they will, no matter what you do. But you can attract good vibes by sending them out in the first place. Be positive and you'll see that everything will be alright. The kids will grow up a dream here, the business will take off and you will be happy.'

To him it was all easy-peasy. The universe was all in his favor and all his pieces fitted. Well, why not, at the end of the day? Who was to say I was right and he was wrong? Maybe there really was method in his madness. Maybe I should have gone with the flow.

'OK, Julian. I promise I'll try.'

'Good girl.'

So we took the morning off and strolled through the

antique markets, browsing all sorts of old, totally useless knick-knacks. But there was some interesting antique furniture.

'Nice, isn't it?' Julian said, his hand smoothing over the dark wood of an ancient oak table. 'It would look great in one of our annexes.'

He smiled down at me and I tried to smile back, but we'd read each other's minds. *Vacant* annexes. His jaw clenched as he took my hand.

'Come on, love, let's get you a *cornetto*...'

Outside Fernando's bakery-cum-café, we grabbed a table in the shade. Despite the obscene heat for early May, the town center was bustling with locals spilling in and out of bars, eateries and even Margherita's tiny supermarket for those who had a faint heart and preferred to shop indoors where there was air con.

Dogs on leashes waited patiently for their owners to let them have a lick of ice cream and, as it was the weekend, kids were allowed to spend the extra euro on some cheap toy that wouldn't survive the short trip home.

'The town is teeming with tourists. Where the hell do they all sleep?' I observed.

'I don't know,' Julian answered as he sipped his cappuccino. 'Last year we were at full capacity. Could it have been beginner's luck?'

'I don't believe in beginner's luck. Either you've got it or you don't. Maybe we should throw something in besides the welcome package,' I suggested. 'Maybe a free dinner.'

Had this been The Farthington, I wouldn't have needed to be strategizing anything because it was an awesome place. But so was A Taste of Tuscany – the best on offer, in fact.

I'd checked all the other B & Bs in the area on the net and even the ones further afield. No contest. Our premises were undoubtedly the best. And so was our website, through and through. Julian's pictures were like fairy tales in themselves. So I didn't understand. Could it be me? Could I be the problem? But how? I was polite but professional, helpful but unobtrusive. And last year our guestbook was packed with all sorts of compliments and thank-yous. So what the hell was going on?

'A free dinner might work,' Julian conceded.

And then an eerie sensation crossed my entire body, making me shiver as the sun disappeared. I looked up as everyone else around us at the other tables raised their heads in curiosity as a tour bus suddenly loomed in the narrow street, also blocking our view of Piazza Cortini. Apart from the fact that this was a pedestrian-only area, a bus that big was a very disturbing sight for such a small, quiet town.

And then a sea of fair-haired people poured out from the front and back doors of the coach, followed by a little dark man in a panama hat and a badge reading Etruscan Tours. Without warning, he started flapping his arms and shouting.

'OK everrree-baddy! Dis is Castellino, a beauuutiful medieval marrrket town, where many rrrich trrrading merchants come to trrrade in de period of de *Comuni – city states who had their own monetary system!*'

Although his history was more or less accurate, his Italian accent was strong and his demeanor was not that of a happy camper. He looked like he'd been yanked out of bed and had a shotgun pointed to his head under the threat: 'Either your signature or your brains are going to be on this job offer.'

He pointed to his watch. 'Is now ten o'clockke! Come back in de buus at twelve o'clockke, OK? Go to de market – is beauuutiful!'

And that was the end of his cultural spiel. The guy had obviously had enough and simply couldn't be bothered.

In the two years we'd been here we'd never seen a tourist coach because, until now, foreigners had usually come in couples, or families, quietly, delicately, weaving through the town almost as if on tiptoe. This was something new in Castellino. What the hell was going on? I'd be damned if I didn't do some snooping.

That evening after dinner I threw the plates into the dishwasher, the kids into bed and myself onto my laptop at the writing table in our bedroom to find out as much as I could about Etruscan Tours.

But every time I punched the name in, it came up with links to different companies, just like one of those secret shell companies belonging to money launderers in the Cayman islands that you see on TV (if you have the patience to keep up with all the scheming, the crimes and the dodging of the law. Me, I preferred a more honest and direct approach to my business).

My first principle was that I didn't undermine other companies. We actually helped one another out by sending our surplus guests to the others. Even if Tuscans were a competitive bunch in general, in the Tuscan B & B association, we were all linked by friendly business relationships.

So who the hell was behind Etruscan Tours trying to blow everyone else out of the water, and why, most importantly, had I never heard of them if they were so big? I could easily send the association an email requesting info on Etruscan Tours, but it would have been seen as snooping, a big No-no in this field. So I searched more travel blogs far and wide. They were all over the place, named on every single major site, even the ones that I had contributed to over the past two years with entertaining stories about my mother's family and their personal connection to Tuscany.

It soon appeared that I'd have to write another blog about our place. And maybe make some more appetizing offers. Free dinners? Free hampers? More gifts? Any more free stuff and they wouldn't be paying a single Euro to stay! I had to find a solution to this.

'Come to bed, Erica,' Julian beckoned. 'It's past midnight...'

'No can do,' I threw over my shoulder. 'I have to find out who these guys are.'

'Why don't you ask them directly?'

'I could, but I can't find a contact for them anywhere. Which pretty much beats the purpose of advertising, doesn't it?'

I sat back a moment to take stock of the situation with a clear head:

*There can only be two explanations: either Etruscan Tours has simply been hired by a bigger company with a different name, or they are operating under the counter by word of mouth. Which means that they are not registered with the B & B association, not adhering to any of the association rules and regulations and most definitely not paying their taxes. Let me look and see if they are listed among any coach associations... nope nothing here either. Am I spelling it wrong? No, that's what the guy's badge said, and even the big yellow words across the side of the bus said so. Maybe they, too, are operating under someone else?*

'Erica...? What... are you still up? What time is it? Come on, Erica, come to bed, it's bloody three in the morning...'

'Ten more minutes, Julian, I promise...'

With a soft groan, I heard him fall back against the mattress and go quiet. Thank goodness. How was I expected to get any work done with him talking to me all night?

# 4

## External Influences

Paul was on his own mission regarding the wedding preparations. It had taken him days, but through Renata he'd managed to book an appointment with the famous chef who was to do the catering for our wedding. In the space of twenty minutes, he'd dragged me into my Fiat 500L and we'd headed out to meet him over country roads I'd never seen before in the two years we'd been here. Thank God for satnav.

'Alberto Veronesi is the best chef in the whole wide world,' he gushed. 'And I'm in love! He is drop dead gorgeous and talented as hell.'

'You don't even know the guy.'

'That's beside the point. I googled him – all night! He's... everything I always wanted. And he's mine, even if he doesn't know it yet.'

If anyone deserved love, it was Paul. He was the most selfless person I knew. He'd spent half his life saving mine whenever I needed him for absolutely anything: babysitting, cooking, image makeovers, salsa lessons, cheering me on and picking me up – you name it, he'd done it for me. After years of unsuccessful dating and only one true unrequited love, I hoped he'd soon find his share of happiness.

'He's thirty-eight but looks twenty-eight. And... get this... he drives a Ferrari. I've always wanted a boyfriend who drives a Ferrari.'

'Red?' I asked.

'Black!'

'Hot.'

'Wait until you meet him. Apparently, he's even better in the flesh.'

'But is he gay?'

'Not yet,' he said with a wink.

'Paul, please don't get ahead of yourself as you always do.'

'What do you mean "as I always do"?'

I sighed. 'Well, first you ignore them while secretly, irreparably falling in love with them and by the time you find out they're straight, it's too late. You're totally besotted.'

He looked at me for a minute as it slowly sank in that I was onto him. That I had been since we first met. He wasn't fooling anyone with his standoffish stance.

'Nah,' he said. 'This time it's different. He is gay. I've heard rumors.'

'OK, it's your life at the end of the day.'

I backed off with a shrug as we pulled up by an old stone building with a colonnade covered in bright red bougainvillea planted in terracotta pots as tall as Julian and as round as me. There were many cars parked outside what I realized was a quaint little restaurant called De gustibus.

'Oh my God, my heart's pounding! Do you realize that if I can get him to cook at my weddings, I'll have made it big time,' Paul hissed as he took my arm and hustled me inside.

At the bar, he stopped and spoke to a woman in a black apron, who nodded and led us down a dark cavern-like corridor to a larger cave, where someone had his head stuck inside a wood-burning oven.

'Chef Veronesi... what an... an *honor*,' Paul babbled to the (rather nice) butt, being much too enthralled even to appraise it as he normally would have.

A grunt and then the man pulled out and grinned at us. 'You're late.'

'I'm sorry. That's my fault,' I apologized.

'Chef Veronesi, I'm Paul Belhomme and this is my friend, Erica Cantelli,' Paul managed, already lost in the guy's gaze.

A shock of red curly hair cut short and keen golden eyes met mine.

'*La sposa* – the bride.'

He seemed to sneer, the wide, sardonic mouth curled, and I didn't know if he was making fun of me or pitying me. Just by glancing at him, I could tell this guy was arrogance personified, with servants scurrying at his every gesture or grunt as if he were a god. Here, in his world, he meant power. To me, he simply meant food. Food I wouldn't be able to eat until my wedding day, if I wanted to fit into any dress, let alone a nice one. The beautiful ones don't come in big sizes, experience had taught me. And if they do, they don't fit as nicely.

'*Piacere*, my pleasure,' Alberto Veronesi murmured as he directed us to a trestle table laden with so many kinds of food that my aunts' Italian restaurant in Boston looked like a kiosk in comparison.

De gustibus? With all the fare available, it was more like Bust-de-guts.

'*Signora*,' the chef murmured as a waiter presented us with something that smelled more than heavenly.

Oh God, oh God. I could already feel said gut busting and my dress bursting at its lacy seams. And if I broke my diet and ate now, the sluice gates would open again and I'd never be able to gain control of my calorific intake, like surrendering once and for all to a long-lost lover.

I turned to Paul in desperation. 'You try it. I trust you completely.'

The chef's face fell and I instantly knew I'd offended him.

'What?' Paul cried. 'You're not even going to *try* your own wedding menu?'

'No. No fattening foods until my wedding day.'

'No one refuses Chef Veronesi's food,' Paul whispered, but Alberto raised his hand.

'Please, please. Perhaps I should assure the *signora* that none of my food is fattening in the least.'

Not fattening in the least? I looked up, suddenly hopeful and intrigued. In my mind, low-calorie food meant tasteless roughage and that was about it. This man was offering me real, gorgeous food without a lot of calories? Absolutely unheard of.

'I beg your pardon, Chef?' I ventured.

He smiled. 'Steamed, boiled, grilled, baked – nothing fried and absolutely no fat. It's all part of my lean movement.' And then he grinned. 'Cakes excluded, of course.'

'Unbelievable, Chef...'

'Believe it!' he commanded, then grinned. 'And please, call me Alberto.'

Absolutely no fat was fantastic news for me, but for my guests? An absolute disaster. I couldn't feed them what sounded like baby food!

The doubt – and panic – must have shown on my face, because he chuckled and turned to a plate behind him to pass me what looked like a dumpling.

'Just try this,' he said simply.

I eyed him, tempted to ask what it was, but I didn't want to offend him any further, so in the end I found myself opening my mouth. I only hoped that this little gesture of goodwill wasn't going to put me back on the path of hogging out for the rest of my life. To think I'd come so far in the past few weeks. OK, days.

If I couldn't even be disciplined months away from my wedding, I'd never again be able to lose weight. Don't get me wrong. It'd taken me years to appreciate my curviness. I had accepted my body, and even learned to love it, most of the time. The extra weight was now mainly a health issue. And if I let go now, eating literally my weight in my favorite foods, I'd be back to square one again. But damn, it sure smelled good. Well, maybe just one bite. After all, he'd said it was low-calorie, right?

As I chewed, a sensation of sheer stupor followed by a familiar sense of happiness linked to the memory of my grandmother filled me as my tongue rolled around in what could only be described as bliss. I moaned, and Alberto grinned.

'What *is* this?' I tried to ask, but my mouth didn't want

to swallow and thus relinquish this culinary miracle nestling in my mouth.

As Paul dug into his own and groaned, his eyes reflected his own happiness, also caused, might I say, by the not unpleasant view of our chef.

Alberto smiled. 'Tiny pasta satchels of Parma ham, eggplant and pistachio sauce with a sprig of mint. Do you like?'

I closed my eyes and waved my hand in a circle in the typical Italian gesture that meant *Ah-mazing*.

'Good,' he said, his eyes crinkling in a grin, and I hoped Paul would never let this genius out of his sight.

All this flavor and not one ounce of fat? He was too precious to ever let go of!

As Paul continued to eat up Chef Veronesi with his eyes, waiters served us the three pasta, polenta and risotto dishes followed by the fish, chicken and veal entrées. Even the salads and vegetables were works of art. And the fruit salad, drizzled with balsamic vinegar from Modena? Untellable joys.

'*Assaggia*, try it, taste,' Chef Alberto coaxed me as I raised my ignorant eyebrows and let him spoon some of it into my mouth, taken by surprise.

The result? Wow. Jesus. The guy could cook. I had to find another way to bind him to us forever. Because, by the way, he didn't look particularly interested in any of Paul's sexual innuendos.

So about an hour later, after he'd shown us pictures of how the food would be presented, we agreed to sign a contract and, not without reluctance, got back into the car.

'So, what do you think?' Paul rubbed his hands once we were on our way back home.

'He's fabulous, of course,' I admitted. 'You have to get him on board with your business.'

'I told you! I love him. And I'm going to marry him by the end of the year! Mark my words...'

I hesitated. 'Paul, I gotta be honest. I'm not getting the gay vibe at all.'

He winked. 'Ye woman of little faith.'

I rolled my eyes. My friend, ever the optimist.

'Don't laugh. You know I always get what I want. It's only a matter of time.'

Was it really only that? Was everything that easy? You want the straight guy and he suddenly surrenders to the other team (it wouldn't be the first time Paul's transformed a man)? You want to get married and suddenly the man of your life has set a date he'll actually be able to keep? You want to lose weight and... Shazam – done? It just didn't happen like that in life.

The next day, while I was baking (the kids still had to eat, even if I was on a diet, right? Plus, licking the bowl didn't officially count), Julian padded into the kitchen.

'I've got great news, Erica. From now on, I won't be traveling to the States so much.'

Which was a huge thing for me, as last year alone he'd made twenty-six trips to promote his new book. I put my cake mix down.

'Hallelujah! How did you manage that?'

He grinned. 'I found a European publicist I'd like to have over for a bit, if that's OK?'

Now *that* was a great idea. 'Fantastic. Bring him. I'll get the guest room next to your study ready.'

'Her. Her name is Sienna. Sienna Thornton-Jones.'

'Like the chocolates?' I offered.

He grinned. 'Like Lord and Lady Thornton-Jones.'

'Ah, a rich kid, then.'

Julian sighed. 'Remember to behave yourself, OK?'

'K,' I promised. 'Is she any good at least?'

'The absolute best. You'll love her. I'll see if I can get her here by Friday.'

'I already love her if it means I get to see you more.'

So on Friday morning I went into town to get my groceries for a special dinner. And to do some hardy grooming (namely some heavy-duty waxing). After all, I didn't want Julian's new publisher to think he'd shacked up with the Italian version of the chupacabra, a legendary and very hairy goat-eating monster.

But when I got back home, laden like a pack-horse, I found my Bialetti espresso maker and my *good* espresso set laid out on the table . Julian made a dash to relieve me of my five different cuts of meat and all kinds of groceries, including ingredients for an array of quiches and desserts, dangling from each squished, purpling finger, and even a bag hanging from my teeth (the lightest, filled with my rice cakes).

'Hi, honey,' he said, giving me a peck on the cheek.

'Hey,' I wheezed. 'I think I got everything.'

And then I saw her as, in slow motion, she turned to look at me. Straight, long red hair that flowed down to a nonexistent waistline and caramel-colored eyes as big as Bambi's. Delicate copper-colored lips turned into a charming smile.

She was at least six hours early. I suddenly remembered my eyebrows and upper lip that were still red and swollen from the waxing session. All the effort, all the pain and I still managed to look like the chupacabra, after all.

'Erica, please meet Sienna Thornton-Jones, my publicist.'

When my mouth opened (the bag of rice cakes falling onto my foot), she stuck out a long, slender, French-manicured hand.

'Hi, Erica. It's so nice to meet you finally,' came a pleasant, balanced voice, not shrill and breathy like I'd expected coming from a chick with long, sexy red hair and a figure to die for (meaning that I'd have to starve myself to death to look anything like her).

'Hi,' I chirped (or rather squeaked), ignoring the rice cakes that had made their way across the terracotta tiles.

Trying to mask a feeling of total horror at the way I must have looked, I stuck out my hand to the gorgeous woman in the ivory-colored silk dress, pumping it up and down like we were two former poker buddies finally reuniting.

This was Sienna Thornton-Jones, his *publicist*? In this diaphanous dress that looked like a very expensive nightgown clinging to every perfect curve of her oh-so-fit body? Whatever happened to professional workwear? You know, like business suits and knee-length skirts that are *made* to cover up and make you look like you were made of steel... Whatever happened to the kick-ass Margaret Thatcher look, so different from the flesh-fest going on in my kitchen?

And it occurred to me, out of the blue, that this was

the kind of wife Julian needed. One that was in his league, that he could show off to his *people*. Because Julian was a drop-dead gorgeous man who should have stayed in his high-flying milieu of sports stars among his models and endorsements. But here he was, instead, with me, with the kids, his writing, our everyday routine, galaxies away from his previous life. Which he was slowly but surely shaping out according to his desires.

And this woman hit me as extremely sharp and intelligent. The kind of woman who knew what she wanted and didn't waste any time getting it. This woman was me two years ago, if you didn't consider that she was single, slim, classy and beautiful. (No need to laugh. I can see the difference, thank you very much.) But the stamina was the same and the attitude, as well.

Standing before her in all her stunning, sleek beauty, I felt myself instantly levitate and grow back to a size twenty under her very eyes. My white cotton dress looked cheap (another market-trove) and inappropriate for a business encounter. I was also painfully aware of my bingo wings and wished I'd brought a cardi with me, but in that sweltering heat, it would have been suicide.

And it was also the heat I blamed for my sweaty forehead and panting mode. I was exhausted and could feel my face muscles pulling in every direction but the right one. I was an absolute mess compared to her cool, calm and collected demeanor. She was relaxed, friendly and rested although she'd just got off a plane. I wasn't feeling like any of those, but it was important to make a good impression on Julian's business associates.

I flashed her a smile. 'How nice to meet you, too,' I said,

recovering pronto as Julian bent to take the bags from me and she bent forward to retrieve the rice cakes at her feet.

'I hope you're hungry, because I've got a special dish in your honor tonight.'

If you were (like me) expecting her to say, 'Thanks, but I'm watching my figure,' I'm sorry to disappoint you. Her eyes widened even more, if possible, as her face lit up.

'I'm famished,' she said enthusiastically, 'and Julian's told me all about your famous cooking – can't wait!'

Not only could she not wait to eat, but she also couldn't *stop*. She ate like a locust. Gracefully, praising everything on the table, but *abundantly*. I watched, slack-jawed from behind my stingy string beans and solitary steamed sole, as she dug through the gnocchi with asparagus cream. Then she tucked into three lamb shanks, devoured a variety of vegetable servings (but mostly my rosemary roast potatoes). After that she polished off three different kinds of dessert, topping it all off with blueberry ice cream.

At the end of the meal, her cellphone beeped discreetly and she apologized.

'I wouldn't normally get it, but this is about you, Julian.' And with that, she pressed a button. 'Nina, talk to me... Right, well, you can tell them that it's either the slot before the eight o'clock news or nothing. And while Julian grants interviews to the rival channels, they'll be watching slack-jawed.'

Now if you knew me in my heyday, you'd see the similarities between us. Impressed, I eyed Julian, who winked at me.

'I'm not interested in anything less, Nina! Now get your

ass in gear and let me know!' And with that, she hung up and smiled. 'Sorry about that. Just give her an hour or so.'

'Nina is Sienna's assistant,' Julian explained.

'Not for long if she doesn't pull her socks up,' Sienna added, reaching for some more dessert. 'That was, Erica, hands down, the best meal I've had in ages. Possibly ever, come to think of it. Thank you.'

Now who could resist such a gracious compliment?

My smile ran from ear to ear, while inside I was already worrying how comfortable I would honestly be with my man working elbow to elbow with this total beauty. Next to her I looked like the maid, even though I'd managed to change into a nice dress (one of my best, actually) and put on some make-up. Which the waxing session had readily erased, what with my watery eyes.

After dinner she offered to help me clean up, but when I declined, she turned to Julian.

'Right, then! Shall we get this show on the road?'

'You must be knackered, though?' Julian asked dubiously.

And then I remembered I'd made up the bedroom next to Julian's study, so he and his publicist could work way into the night.

'Knackered? Nonsense! What do you think they call me Super Sienna for? Come on,' she coaxed, linking her arm into Julian's. 'I need a nice brisk walk to burn all those calories Erica has piled into me,' she added, flashing me a wink as I cleared the table.

How ironic that none of the food she'd just wolfed down would stick to her perfect body, whereas mine would hang onto every single calorie of my miserable string beans and sole like a drowning man to a raft. But none of that was her fault. She had a healthy relationship with food.

Me, not so much. After all these years, I still saw food as ambivalent. It was in my eyes both a weapon and an act of love. An enemy, but at the same time, my emotional crutch. Blame my stepmother if you want, for putting me on endless diets as a child. For demonizing my healthy appetite. For making me feel guilty for not being a size 4 like her. For not loving me enough because I wasn't her child, but at the same time being too strict with me.

According to my shrink back in Boston, withdrawing food from me had been her strongest weapon. Because to me, food was a comfort. Because my Nonna Silvia and my aunts had cooked for us as a sign of love. The love that I never got from my own mother. It was no wonder I was screwed up as a kid. As a grown woman, I realized I had to come to terms with all this. I had to learn to see food as a true Italian, part of life and one of its joys. Nothing to be punished for.

I had one hell of a journey ahead of me.

# 5

## The Erica of Yesteryear

It turned out, after all the initial niceties, that Sienna wanted to dominate, although she did it subtly. 'We're going to have some late nights of Atlantic phone calls in the next few days, Julian. Better go easy on the pasta from now on,' Sienna would suggest, and he'd instantly push his plate away, still half-full, not even giving it a second thought, while I watched, gobsmacked. How the hell did she do it? When I asked him to do something, he'd smile and then take days to do it. Did I mention he's the worst procrastinator ever?'

And then, the next morning, I realized Julian hadn't come to bed. *At all.* And he criticized me for burning the midnight oil trying to save our business? How long had that set of Atlantic calls lasted, for Christ's sake? Did they call every single reader in the North American continent? And what could be so interesting as to keep him away from our bed all night? I didn't dare imagine them, heads together, working away (one hopes) into the depths of the night on some hush-hush agenda I'd never be privy to because they weren't revealing anything until it was black on white. Not even to me.

And I only had to thank myself for putting Miss Sienna Thornton-Jones in the guest room next to his study. Where, by the way, there was a nice black leather couch. Which was probably the only stick of furniture we hadn't 'tried out' in the two years we'd been here. I wondered why.

Julian came into the bedroom with a yawn just as I was getting up.

'Morning, babe.'

He looked disheveled, his hair sticking out in every direction and unshaven. He also smelled like an inviting bed. I watched as he opened drawers, pulling out fresh underclothes.

'So, what do you think of her?' he asked over his shoulder as he headed for the shower.

*Never mind what I think. You seem to have taken to her like a fish to water.* And speaking of, this was *our* morning shower time. Why was he starting on his own? We always showered together unless he had somewhere to go early. Like New York. Or San Francisco. Ah. Another busy day with Miss Sienna Thornton-Jones. Apparently, if I didn't hurry, I'd miss my slot.

Yes, with all her promises of turning him into an international bestselling author again, Sienna Thornton-Jones was the woman of the day. I just hoped it wasn't going to be for too many days.

Yes, I know. I was being insecure and silly. But for a split second, I couldn't help those thoughts penetrating my mind.

Julian looked at me as he lathered up and I took off my nightie, anticipating some good ol' us time. I stepped in next to him and he grinned.

'So?' he said.

'So…' I grinned back, wrapping my arms around his neck, letting the water drench my hair as he lifted it off my shoulders. *Now* he was talking.

'What's your verdict?'

I groaned inwardly. I really didn't want to talk about her right now, but he wasn't letting go.

'Most important, what do you think?' I asked back, trying to hide my uneasiness and trying to avoid obvious truths like, She bosses you around a lot.

Julian wrapped an arm around my neck and gave me a peck on the lips. 'She's great, isn't she?' he prompted.

Oh, why were men so oblivious to reality?

'Almost reminds me of you in Boston, honey. Remember when your chef, Juan, didn't show because he was home with that prostitute? Remember how you kicked ass?'

How could I forget? Julian had come to take me out to lunch. Lunch that our guests wouldn't be having as our chef had been a no-show. And so Julian had driven me to Juan's house, only to find he was with a prostitute spread unconscious on the floor.

'Me? You're the one who saved the girl's life.'

'Ah, but you got your staff organized in a jiffy. I'd never seen such fast workers my whole life. You were amazing, Erica.'

Were being the operative word. Now, I couldn't even find guests if I paid them to stay. So much for owning my own business. Maybe I was over, slowly reverting to the simple role of housewife, something I was personally never cut out to be. And we weren't even married yet.

I thought it would be enough, to have my own business and be free to be with my loved ones. Be my own boss, live the simple life. But things weren't as peachy as I'd hoped. Julian was slowly becoming a ghost and as if that wasn't enough, whenever a smart businesswoman like Sienna appeared on my horizon, it was like seeing my ghost – the Ghost of Business Past. The woman he'd met only two years ago, who had already disappeared under layers of Tuscan pancetta and potatoes.

I missed that dynamic woman, even if I'd been suffering like a dog because of the divorce. And I missed… OK, here's the naked truth: I missed the effort Julian used to make to come and see me when we were still dating, the way he used to drop everything for me. It made me feel special. He'd show up in any given one of my darkest moments with a box of pastries or flowers to take me out. It had always warmed my heart. And thrilled me.

But now, because I was always around, the steady rock to come back to, it wasn't the same anymore. It was safe to say that the thrill was on the wane.

Damn this routine. A routine, however, that only I was living, because he was a free spirit, coming and going as he pleased. And then it hit me. Julian was now like I used to be, traveling around the globe for business. I finally understood how Ira must have felt, resenting my success and the fact that I managed to get away from home regularly.

And the scary part was that ultimately (besides the fact that Ira was a lying, cheating scumbag, of course), my absences due to work were what had driven us apart. We'd gone from being doting parents to ships passing in the night, and every trip I made pushed us further and further apart. Which was why now I was on red alert.

Here in Tuscany, Julian and I were supposed to live together in perfect harmony and have it all. Together, as a couple, although lately we weren't acting like one much. And now that Sienna was in our home, it was obvious how basic my role was in his life. Anyone else could have done the chores I did daily. All that was necessary was a cook and a house cleaner. Because that was all I was doing these days.

It was almost as if I wasn't even there, and all his attention was on Sienna and the career boost he was about to receive. The businesswoman I'd hoped to continue being after moving to Italy hadn't yet materialized. Of course I didn't want the office hours or the meetings or the suits, but was it asking too much to have a score of paying guests who would add to our income?

It was a good thing I had a plan. And it was partly hatched by watching the way Sienna worked. She mainly used her contacts. The people she knew. So I'd decided to email all my contacts from the Farthington Hotel which used to be my kingdom. I would shoot a blanket email to each and every one of the guests I'd become chummy with and who I knew for a fact had planned at some point or other to travel to Europe. I would tell them about my new life and include a link to our website and see what happened. If Sienna could do it, so could I!

'Good news, my man,' Sienna greeted us (well, him) early one morning as I was packing the kids' *panini* for a picnic.

Julian was leaning back against the counter as always,

barefoot in jeans and a T-shirt, sipping his espresso and immersed in the paper that our foreman, Aldo, brought him every day as I silently went about my business. The fact that Sienna hardly acknowledged my presence was nothing, despite the fact that I fed her at least six times a day, but again, I was only the help around here. She was the one making him a success. I was only taking care of his basic animalistic needs (such as meals, laundry – and, in case you were wondering, not much else, lately), while she, on the other hand, had his undivided attention. Because I may have only fed him, while she was going to turn him into a star once again.

'Yeah? What's that?' he asked, an anticipatory grin illuminating his face.

When was the last time he smiled at me like that? I couldn't help but think, trying hard not to squish Warren's muffin as I closed the ziplock and shoved it into his bag on the table.

'Can I have blueberry, please, Mommy?' Maddy asked as she came in, pulling on her sandals, her back folded forward under the weight of an enormous rucksack.

'Sweetie, this is too heavy for you,' I said, lifting it off her. 'I'll get you a wheelie bag today. You don't want to ruin your posture.'

'Chill, *Marcy*,' Warren said as he came in and poured himself some cereal.

I suppressed a gasp. He was right. I had just sounded like Marcy. Julian eyed me and screwed his mouth to keep it shut in front of Sienna. Family squabbles weren't classy, apparently.

But Sienna paused to observe them with an amused grin,

too classy to show they'd interrupted her precious work discourse.

'Morning, you guys,' Julian greeted, pulling Maddy into his arms and ruffling Warren's hair.

So, apparently I was the only one not getting any attention except for a 'Thanks, love,' when I'd poured him his coffee half an hour earlier.

'I've scheduled a meeting with some TV people. BBC, to be precise. They want to meet you,' she said.

'For what, exactly?' I asked. The news? An interview? His own show?

'When?' Julian cut in, and I heard my neck crack as it snapped round in his direction.

When? Was that all that mattered, running to the master like an eager puppy? What about building his brand – protecting his image, etcetera? Even I knew that.

'Tomorrow evening. I've booked us the 11 a.m. flight.'

'Wow,' I managed without sounding too shocked. At least I hoped so. 'So soon?'

Sienna smiled at me. 'We've got to strike the iron while it's hot.'

Julian's eyes swung to mine in a silent apology. *I know what you're thinking, babe,* those long-lashed babies said to me. *I know you think I'm too hasty, but I've waited so long for this. And besides, this was all your idea in the first place.*

I blinked. Well, I knew that.

Sienna lightly smacked his shoulder and I resented that she felt she could touch him so freely. How long had she known him – five minutes? And theirs was a business relationship, to boot. Unless... there was something I didn't know?

But of course Julian would never have brought an old flame into our home without telling me, that much I knew for sure. He just wasn't that kind of person. But still, the easiness between them bothered me, making it difficult to keep nasty thoughts out of my head.

'Pack your toothbrush, Jules,' she said.

Which is precisely what he did. And later, in the intimacy (scratch *that* word) of our bedroom, he kept going on and on about England being his trampoline, the country where he felt the most at home, and how happy he was about going back as a celebrity and not the young boy who had been bullied.

I could have said, 'What about the wedding planning? Paul needs you here to take your measurements and stuff.' Which was ridiculous, so I didn't. Besides, he trusted Paul and me to get on with it. And there was me thinking we'd be going to pre-matrimonial courses at the church and sharing decisions and planning what kind of couple and family we'd be, etcetera. None of it was going to happen.

So I listened in silence, proud of him and happy that his life had turned out to be a success, especially as he'd been abandoned on the steps of a church in Italy. He could have turned out a terribly lonely, broken boy, but instead he was doing well in life. So why couldn't I be completely, 100 per cent happy for him, just like he deserved? Why did I fear that something bad was about to happen?

The answer was simple. Julian had a heart of gold and believed, above everything else, in the good in people. He always gave everyone a second chance, even those who didn't deserve it. And he'd never suspect anyone of wrong-doing until it had been proven. It was like he had no sixth sense sometimes. And I was the one having to bare my teeth (and claws) to protect him.

This England thing would lead to France and Germany and Spain and so on. How did I know for sure that Sienna was acting in the name of his best interests and not, say, just to bum a vacation off him? He was so gung-ho about it, he wouldn't have noticed her sticking a stiletto in between his ribs, while I would have seen her way before she even reached into her bag and, yes, I'd have pounced on her to protect him. But that's what you did when you were a mother – you became fiercely protective of your loved ones. There were limits to what I could do, but for now, I had to chill.

And the next morning they were gone, like thieves in the night. So much for him making an effort to stick around more.

# 6

## To Catch a Groom

Julian's US agent Terry Peterson and Sienna Thornton-Jones practically fought over who was going to have him first. London needed him. Dublin needed him. Berlin needed him. Amsterdam was storming for him. *Ah, but Los Angeles has dibs*, Terry would counter. It was one big tug of war where Julian was trying to juggle his commitments, not least the one to meet me at the altar at the end of September.

'I thought they were supposed to make things easier for you, not complicate your life,' I said to him twelve days later as I stared at the kitchen wall calendar I'd penned in with all his planned trips. Blue ink for him, pink for our wedding day, green for the kids' summer camp in Orvieto and black for Marcy's arrival on August 15th. Which was, by the way, Ferragosto, a national holiday during which the highways were crammed, if not dangerous. A day to stay home and chill, in my eyes. But did Marcy, a staunch Italian, even consider that? Of course not.

He looked up. 'It's hard enough traveling and smiling

and talking about your book a thousand times over to a thousand different faces when sometimes I don't even know where I am.'

Ah. So there was the chink in the armor. The words *you asked for it* came to mind, but I pushed them away. He needed my support now, not my mutiny. What was important for him should be important for me.

'Just work out a priority schedule and confirm as many appointments as you can,' I suggested. *Only don't forget ours*, I silently pleaded.

'But I can't,' Julian protested.

'Of course you can,' I assured. 'This is your chance of a lifetime. It's what you always wanted.'

'But what about the harvest – who's going to help with that?'

The harvest? Was he absolutely kidding me? I forced a nonchalant shrug. 'We can always get more help.'

He seemed to consider it. 'What about you being here on your own?'

Again, the amazing, magnanimous Erica rolled her eyes. 'The farmhands are perfectly capable of running things here, and the B & B booking ledger isn't exactly bursting at the seams yet.'

'And Margot? What if she starts having problems with her gestation?'

I swear he loves that mare as much as he loves me. But I can't fault him for it. Julian loves all living creatures and it's one of the many reasons I love him. 'Then I'll call the vet.'

He eyed me, still unsure. 'So it's OK with you if I go again? Just like that?'

'Just like that,' I said, trying to hide the fact that I wanted to grab him by his shirt and shake him while blubbering, *Please don't go! There are too many blue squares on my calendar that I'm so afraid we'll never make it to the pink square at this rate!* But I didn't, because I had to have some faith in the man I wanted to marry. Right?

'But what about the wedding?' he countered. 'If we start publicizing my book in Europe, this may easily protract into late fall…'

You see, just when I was about to give up on him, he'd completely melt me all over again. It really wasn't his fault if he was now part of a system that had snowballed. He'd been caught unawares. It was only Sienna and Terry's fault. They should get married to each other and bugger off to some distant PR planet.

'We'll postpone it,' I suggested, against any sense of self-preservation.

I could almost feel my own heart bursting while a shrill voice inside me screeched *Are you absolutely nuts?* But I shut it out. Because he was in this relationship too, right? It wasn't all about me. If I'd been the one to need this time, he'd have given it to me, no problem. In fact, he'd given me two years without whining. So yes, he deserved all my patience. Well, as much as I could muster, that is.

'Postpone?' he said, looking appalled. 'Absolutely not, Erica. We've been waiting for forever.'

I took his hand. 'It doesn't matter. I'll be here when you get back. Now go and get yourself famous again.'

He looked into my eyes and what I saw was uncertainty turning to hope. Because he *wanted* to go – I could see it in his eyes. And then I saw hope turn to gratitude and finally, unconditional love. It was worth every blow I'd previously received to my heart.

'OK,' he finally agreed, kissing me on the forehead. 'I'll go call Sienna.'

'You do that.' Once I was alone, I dialed Paul's cellphone.

'Hey, sunshine,' he chimed.

'Where are you?'

'I'm in Siena looking at invitations. Man, you wouldn't believe how cheesy they are.'

My jaw clenched. He'd be gutted, too, my Paulie. He needed to nail this wedding as much as I needed to nail (pun intended) my groom.

'Right. Paul, we might have to forget September for the wedding. There's a chance Julian might be away.'

'What? You're kidding me, right? We already have the late-summer fig antipasti and desserts! And the raspberry mousse. You can't just change everything like that! And what about the dress I found you? It's *sleeveless*.'

I could hear the panic in his voice. He wasn't used to things not going his way. Because most of the time, they did.

'Paul, chill. It'll be OK.' If I could say it, somebody had to believe it.

'I can't chill! I have to call all my contacts. The florist – you can't have local calla lilies in winter! And the invitations – you can't have a late-summer theme on your invitations if it's a Christmas wedding!'

'I never said it would be a Christmas wedding.'

'Then when is it, Erica? I need to know!'

Yeah. Him and me both. 'Listen, I'll get back to you as soon as I speak to Julian, OK?'

'Does he even remember you're getting married?'

I gasped. Of all people, he was the one who knew how important this was for me. I could have understood – and in fact expected it – from Marcy. But Paul? A bitter knot rose in my throat. He'd never spoken to me like that before. What was happening to us? Scratch that, what was happening to both my relationships? Could I not get one damn thing right?

'I-I have to go,' I whispered and hung up before he could hear the humiliation in my voice.

He was right, of course. At this rate, it really was going to be a Christmas wedding.

When Paul got home two hours later, he looked at me with spaniel eyes and spread his arms to hug me.

'I'm sorry, sunshine. I panicked. I was a jerk.'

'Yes, you were. But you were also right. I seem to be the only one wanting this wedding, after all.'

'Don't say that. Julian loves you.'

I huffed. 'I know. But he sure has a weird way of showing it lately.'

'The poor guy's stressed. He has a million things on his mind.'

'And I don't? I run this place single-handed. All he does is come and go, talk to strangers about his books and smile into cameras. I'd gladly trade. Plus, he's always with that… *Sienna*.'

I knew I was being unfair. He'd never said or done anything untoward that could remotely make me worry. It was just my old insecurity demons playing with my mind.

'Aww, come on. None of that self-doubt again. How many times do we have to do this? He loves *you*.'

I bit my lip, then eyed him. 'Yeah. I know.'

'And if anything, please be kind to her for *my* sake at least?' Paul pleaded. 'Sienna has amazing connections. I should get on her good side to see if she can hook me up with prospective clients.'

'And I'm the one who needs an honesty check? Could you sound any more utilitarian?'

He shrugged. 'That's how business works. You know that better than me.'

'Right.'

'So you promise to be diplomatic with her and get me in there?'

I huffed. 'Promise.'

And it turned out Sienna Thornton-Jones didn't simply have connections. She *was* connections. A real jet-setter. Word had it she'd been involved in some sort of politico-sex scandal as a teenager – something about a much older man, an MP – but I wasn't supposed to know. As if I didn't have fingers to surf the net like the rest of the world.

And now she was already dazzling Julian with talks about a movie option for his first comeback book, *Stepping Up*.

'Of course, we'll have to go straight to the USA, which means that you won't be here for Thanksgiving and maybe even Christmas. Sorry,' she said, eyeing us both.

She was no idiot. She knew what this was costing us relationship-wise. But did she care? She was just like Terry. People were secondary to her own needs. I guess, at the end of the day, most of us were like that. I wanted to put the wedding day before Julian's career. But – and therein lay the difference – I never had. Because I loved him and wanted

77

him to have everything he'd never had before. Even if now I was starting to think that she was milking it a bit too much.

*Ease up on him*, I wanted to say to her. *We're trying to keep our family together and your schedule isn't helping.*

'What do you think?' Julian asked me when we were alone in our bedroom. 'A movie…'

'It sounds like a wonderful opportunity.' Gawd, could I have been any more lame? *Support your man in all weathers*, I told myself, although it was storming brutally on my part at the moment.

'Geez, Erica, a little less enthusiasm or you'll go right through the roof.'

I stared at him. 'I'm being very enthusiastic and supportive,' I argued. 'I just don't want you to get hurt. Do you know how many times a movie option dies into nothingness?'

'I won't, but for now it's a nice thing to hang onto, isn't it?'

'Is that what you're doing? Hanging on? Is that what your life has become?'

He groaned. 'That's not what I meant, and you know it.'

I sidled over to him, taking his hand. 'Julian, you're a beautiful writer. Your stories are raw – honest and uplifting. Keep your feet on your writing path and let your people worry about Hollywood.'

He flinched. 'Why should I if there's more to life than writing a book?'

I dropped back, stunned. Is that what he thought his life was about? Writing a book? What about owning an agricultural business, a B & B, horses and oh, by the way, being a stepfather and, while we're at it, a future husband?

Obviously these things, these dreams no longer carried as much weight with him as they used to. Or maybe they were weighing him down too much...

'I didn't mean it that way,' he sighed as I turned away from him.

'No, of course not. I'm sure our family is at the top of your list of priorities,' I snapped, unable to help myself.

I knew I was wrong and in the darkness, I sincerely dabbled with an apology. But then I thought that if I apologized and by chance did it again, I'd look like a fraud. Better to let off steam and go back a little calmer tomorrow. Tomorrow, I'd apologize and start afresh. Maybe I was just tired and stressed.

'Goodnight, then,' he answered simply and turned out the light.

I barely even crossed Julian in the hall nowadays, so the hope of walking together down the aisle was becoming a bit far-fetched, because at times like this I wasn't so sure anymore. Not about wanting to marry him, of course, but actually catching him and keeping him still long enough to slip a ring on his finger.

So as far as the actual wedding preparations, Paul and I decided to keep the date vague. Say sometime in the new year. I promised not to declare war on Sienna Thornton-Jones and Paul promised to keep his contacts sweet and ready at the drop of a hat – flower people, invitations and, above all, the stormy Chef Veronesi. Who hadn't, as we all expected, dropped him. How the heck had Paul managed to keep him good?

I, too, was trying to stay good, but I wasn't a patient woman at the best of times and it was all taking its toll on me. For days I went to bed later than Julian (when he was home), corresponding with my former Farthington guests who had answered my blanket email. They all were delighted to hear from me and promised to book next year as they had already made plans for this summer. For which I'd expressed enthusiasm, and proceeded to highlight the beauties of Tuscany.

I even pre-booked a few meals for them (yes, I know, a year in advance but I'm not second-guessing myself) with an unsuspecting Renata who, at the end of the day, had a whole year to get organized. I told them about how her food was home-grown, and wouldn't it be fantastic to go and see the beautiful fields where your food had sprouted from, thanks to a great dose of love and dedication? I also promised them cooking and baking lessons from yours truly, including my famous lasagne. I also pimped our beautiful horses and a romantic carriage ride through the town. And, for the single ladies, a few nights out on the town for a chance to meet some charming local men.

All this, while gnashing my teeth at the thought of Julian and Sienna together, whether downstairs or abroad. It was official. He was spending way more time with her than with me. And to think I'd been the one to push him to write again in the first place while she was now getting all the credit for discovering his talent. I was the one who had read his manuscript, pulled it out of that old drawer and badgered him practically every day to finish and submit it, when he'd been doubtful about his talent. I was the one who had exhumed the gem.

Don't get me wrong. Sienna was a great girl and worked round the clock for him – even I could see that. And I knew she didn't do it on purpose to ignore me, but a little more consideration for the cook and cleaner of the house was always considered a special touch of class.

And she looked every inch the relaxed guest. Next to her I really did feel like the help. No matter what she wore, even tatty jeans and her hair up in a ponytail, she always looked sensational. She had the perfect complexion that only youth and good genes could give a girl. I'd never looked like that, not even after I'd lost a colossal amount of weight after college and was strutting it in England.

Sienna was what I've never been: fine-boned, perfect, balanced and, most importantly, un-temperamental. Almost bloodless. Come to think of it, I couldn't imagine her in the throes of passion. She never got angry. She simply told this or that contact to bugger off and to pray they never needed a favor. But when she did it, it sounded musical, like she was chiming away at her favorite tune. Maybe it was the British accent. And what pissed me off most was that I actually really, really liked her, dammit. When I didn't envy her, that is.

Because when I got frustrated and/ or angry, the whole household (including the workers out in the fields) could hear me. I could never hide my disappointment or be delicate and graceful. People knew when I was upset or happy. They wouldn't need a crystal ball to figure me out. I could definitely never play poker, that was for sure.

Just like every morning, Pino, the mailman, was coming up our road on his moped with his yellow-and-blue basket marked *Poste Italiane*. Like a real gentleman of old, he tipped his hat while he sauntered up the steps and I poured him his favorite drink – a tall glass of cold lemon and mint iced tea, with a shot of Sambuca, of course.

'*Ah, grazie, Eri-ha,*' he said as he placed an ominous-looking envelope with all sorts of stamps and seals into my hands before throwing back his head and gulping down the drink in one snap of his neck. He then wiped his hand on his uniform sleeve and shot to his feet, waving goodbye. '*Ciao, a domani*!'

'*Ciao*, Pino!' I remembered to call back, but he was already chugging down the hill.

I looked down at my scary letter and carefully pried the seal open, like a corpse during an autopsy, the sweat already pearling on my forehead. What could it be? It looked official and experience told me that, in Italy, official was hardly ever good.

So I skimmed over the typed letter and felt my knees buckling. It was from the NAS (*Nucleo Anti-Sofisticazione*), namely, the Health and Safety Department. Which never took prisoners. I scanned the text and sucked in my breath. And then, my ears buzzing, I sat down and read it again, concentrating on each and every word lest I'd misunderstood.

But I hadn't. They were threatening to revoke our B & B license on the basis that they'd been sent a picture of one of our rooms with an enormous rat on the bed. Which they'd included in their letter to us.

Rats? Were they crazy? We had no rats here! If they took away our license, A Taste of Tuscany – everything I'd worked for in the last two years – was a complete goner. They couldn't do this to me. I'd worked my ass off and saved for years just to be here in Italy and now that I finally had my own business, they wanted to take it away from me? A Taste of Tuscany was like my third child. I kept it well-maintained, up to code and spotless – there was no way a rat could have made it here. Even flies had a tough time here. But a rat in our home? And no one even mentioning it? Highly unlikely.

I would have understood if the NAS had arrived upon the departure of the Peggs family last year. In their case, they'd have been right to revoke our license. I personally would have handed it over to them myself, so disgusted we'd been by the absolute filth they'd left behind.

If there hadn't been a rat during the Peggs' stay, then we'd never in a million years ever have had to worry about having one. Man, you'd never seen such a mess. At first, we thought they were OK people. You know, the average British family with three kids, all in school, one awaiting their GCSE results, etcetera. The wife, Amanda, was soft-spoken and kept to herself. The husband was more of a clown. Decent people.

Or so we'd thought.

They left in the middle of the night (we wondered why, as the bill had already been settled) and found the keys hanging on the front gate of the property for just anybody to snatch and help themselves to most of the furniture. Ah. Did I say furniture?

When we got inside, the bloody bureau was missing! It hadn't cost much, as it was just a nice piece I'd bought at the Saturday antiques market, but what the heck would a family flying to London Gatwick do with an Italian Rococo-style bureau on their shoulders?

And then my clever Julian put all the pieces back together. Literally. The bureau had been in the room with the bunk bed. Too lazy to use the built-in ladder, they must have got into the habit of climbing atop the bureau for a boost. According to Julian, they must have broken it and rather than pay for the damages from the deposit (I can see the dad, cheap little bastard), decided to hide the evidence and throw it into some skip on the way to the airport – although not too far, given the bulk of the thing. I could almost imagine the three kids squeezed in and complaining in the back seat.

But that's nothing compared to what else we found.

'Easy, honey, you're going to have a kitten,' Julian had said as he always did before I lost it.

I stepped into the front room and, I swear, I felt faint. It wasn't just the smell. It was the seven family-sized garbage bags, open and tipped over (in their haste to escape, one assumes) and strewn across the floor. Including, for everyone's joy, coffee filters and something that looked like the remains of a chicken curry.

But the joy didn't end there. The kitchen sink was full of scraps of food (I did tell them we didn't have a built-in incinerator in the sink) and dish towels stained with everything from tomato sauce to… ice cream? I had to stare at the towels for a few minutes before I even recognized them, for all the patterns had been blotted out by filth.

Shall we move on into the bathroom? Damp towels in the shower, in the sink, under the sink, more garbage bags absolutely bursting with vacation goodies. I won't even mention the rest, because even if you did believe me, there's no way I could begin to describe it to you without passing out at the memory.

The true apotheosis of filth. To me, common sense, or courtesy, dictated that you don't leave the place looking like ground zero. You leave it as you found it. Whenever we go away to a self-catering place, we leave it spotless by practically mopping ourselves out of the place backward.

I remember ringing Rosina for some help, thinking that I'd give her one hell of a bonus even for showing up.

'Bring some gloves and a box of garbage bags – and all the bleach and cleaners you can carry,' I said and closed my cellphone to pull on a pair of new rubber gloves from under the kitchen sink.

I shook the memory out of my mind and looked down at the letter again. It had to be a joke. *Please, God, let it be a joke...*

There was a telephone number and an email at the bottom of the sheet, which was about the last thing I saw as the room swayed before me. Breathing hard, I whipped out my cellphone and stabbed in the number.

'Yes, hello, this is Erica Cantelli from A Taste of Tuscany...' I said in my very best Italian.

A long pause, then, '*Sì, signora?*'

'I received a letter from you about... about a... r-rat?'

'*Sì, signora.* We're going to have to shut you down. We suggest you don't take any more bookings for this summer.'

As if. 'But there's a mistake. We don't have any rats here and we never have, I can assure you.'

'Well, a former guest of yours complained.'

A former guest? Who? I wondered. They'd all left glowing reviews. 'Impossible.'

'I'm sorry, but we can't ignore the complaint.'

'I see. So what happens now?'

'We shut you down.'

I almost cried out. 'Shut me down?'

'Yes. Until further inspection.'

'Which would be when?'

'I don't know, *signora*. One of our agents will be in contact with you as soon as possible.'

And before I could take my next breath, they hung up. So much for Italian bureaucrats.

They were taking our business from us. Before we even had a chance to set roots. Before I could even breathe the Tuscan air properly. Years and years of wishing and dreaming a place of my own and now we were facing the danger of losing the business.

'Honey?' Julian called from the door, and I looked up from the letter at the wall opposite me, unable to focus. 'Are you OK? What is it?'

Numb, I held out the letter to him. Taking his work gloves off, he sat down and silently read, a deep frown of concentration on his face.

'The jig is up!' I croaked. 'A Taste of Tuscany is no more...'

'Nonsense. Just translate this very last bit here for me, honey, will you?' Julian said as I struggled to breathe.

He was calm and collected, just like he always was, and for a moment I wondered if he hadn't understood at all – we were losing our livelihood!

I breathed again. In. *Please, God*. Out. *We can't lose all this*. In. *This is all we have*. Out. *What are we going to do?* My voice shaking and my body like jelly, I translated, word for word, the contents of the foul document that was ruining our dream – our lives.

Julian frowned and folded the letter. 'Rubbish.'

'We can't lose this place! We just can't!' I cried.

'Sweetie, we won't.'

'How can you say that? How can you not be worried?'

Julian shrugged. 'Because no one can take your license away without any proof. That's just a photo of a rat.'

'Yes, but taken by who? Who would want to do this to us?'

'We'll soon find out,' he promised as he pulled his phone out his back pocket and dialled a number off by heart.

'Who are you calling?'

He wrapped his arm around me and squeezed as he spoke. 'Marco? It's me, Julian. Can you call your lawyer cousin and ask her to come over here tomorrow? We have a problem. I'll explain it to you later. Thanks, *amico*…' He looked down at me. 'He truly is a good friend. Now just try to relax and not worry too much. Tomorrow is another day.'

'But I can't sit around while someone's trying to destroy us! I have to do some investigating, gauge the damage…'

'Sweets, this isn't The Farthington, where you kick ass and it's done. This time you're going to have to sit back and let someone else do the work for you.'

As if I'd ever been able to do that. I was a natural problem-solver. A serial trouble-shooter. It was my nature and what I did best. But when my own family's well-being was concerned, it was hard to be as lucid.

'Are you sure a lawyer can solve this? We both know how the Italian law and bureaucracy work. Look how long it took us just to get residency.'

'Erica,' he said, taking both my hands. 'It'll be fine. But you have to stop worrying.'

I studied him. Why did I get the feeling he wasn't as emotionally involved as I was?

At precisely four o'clock the next day, Laura Magri, Marco's cousin, drove up to our front door in a Lamborghini. She was tall, just like his side of the family, commanding and beautiful. She knew what she was talking about and I liked her on the spot.

'I've spoken to the NAS in person. They knew nothing about it, so someone is just playing a horrible joke on you.'

'Thank God,' I exhaled.

'But I've asked around. These people, whoever they are, have done it before – to restaurants, B & Bs, hotels…'

'But why?'

'Tuscans are insanely competitive,' she answered.

'But we are in good relations with hundreds of colleagues all over the region – the entire B & B association. Who would pick on us in particular?' Julian asked.

'Can we sue them when we find them?' I asked.

Laura looked over at me, saw a kindred spirit and smiled.

'You could, although I'd wait to have absolute proof of their identity and see what it is they really want. I'm guessing they want to see you closed for good.'

'But this is our livelihood!' I cried.

'Honey,' Julian whispered, taking my hand.

'I'm sorry,' I apologized. 'I'm upset.'

'Don't be,' she said. 'Usually these things go away with very little money.'

'But we shouldn't have to pay anyone anything,' Julian reminded her. 'This is absurd.'

'It's all about who you know here, isn't it?' she said. 'A friend of mine in Milan needed information about her pension plan and couldn't get any for weeks. Then her cousin started working there and used her connections to get the information.'

'You see? She shouldn't have to be related to someone just to get the job done. This is ridiculous.' I wanted to tear my (or rather, someone else's) hair out.

Laura observed us for a moment. 'Let me make a couple of calls. See what I can do. I have your numbers.' And with that, she climbed back into her Lamborghini and disappeared in a cloud of summer dust.

'Let it go for now,' Julian said. 'We'll block the availability calendar indefinitely while she does her work and just concentrate on our wedding.'

'And get married where, exactly? Under a bridge? Or on a park bench? Because we won't even be able to serve lunch to our own kids if the NAS shut us down. Bam! Did you hear that sound? That was the sound of our doors closing forever...'

He laughed and caressed my hair. 'Silly sausage.'

'How can you not be worried?'

'It'll be OK. Trust me.'

It'll be OK, he said. What would it take for me to believe it and relax? Simply wanting to? Oh, how I wanted to. I took a deep breath and against all my instincts, forced a nod as a myriad of new plans started shooting before my eyes like meteorites. Or perhaps it was just me seeing spots because I was sure my blood pressure had raised the roofbeams.

'OK.'

But it was far from OK. Somewhere some sicko was

playing a cruel joke on us and had even gone as far as giving us a fake number to reach them – straight into the lion's den. A cruel joke with the intent of ruining us. And then I got a flash of a memory of a similar attack on The Farthington Hotel when I used to be the manager. Someone had put a mouse in one of the beds – neatly tucked it in and taken photos.

It had been our rival chain, I'd discovered. But here in Tuscany, especially in the province of Siena, there were hundreds of B & Bs. And I was going to find out who had a beef with us. Who would go so far as to collate false evidence against us? In whose interest would it be to bring us down? Did it have anything to do with that bus company, Etruscan Tours?

Besides, all our guests had always left positive feedback. And then a glimmer of a memory. All of them… except for one couple – an Italian couple – who hadn't left any feedback at all. I remembered thinking it was odd at the time. It had to be them. Most of our families were English, so this couple had stuck out because Italians normally choose B & Bs with Italian owners. We catered mainly to foreigners.

I remembered them observing the place, taking pictures of themselves in every corner of the property. Julian and I had laughed about it for weeks, posing just about everywhere. Even in front of the kitchen sink, saying, 'Take one here! This angle is spectacular!'

And now it all finally made sense. They'd been casing the joint before they struck.

I raced up to my study and searched frantically through our records until I found them: Marzia and Davide

Casciani. I copied their names onto a Post-it note and ran back downstairs to the kitchen where I'd left my laptop.

'What did you find?' Julian asked, the letter back in his hand.

'The Cascianis!' I cried, banging their names into the Google search engine.

Julian's eyes narrowed. 'The Cascianis? Oh, yeah, I remember them. The selfie couple. Weird, weren't they?' He came to crouch over me with a kiss before he reached into the cabinet for a cup. 'Coffee?' he asked.

I shook my head, waiting for results to pop up. And when they did, I almost fainted dead away.

'What…?' I croaked. 'It can't be.'

'What is it?'

'They… they own a new bed and breakfast near San Gimignano. And… and…' If I hadn't been sitting, I'd have fallen flat on my face. '… it's called… it's c-called… *Tasting Tuscany*…'

Julian stared at me over the rim of his coffee cup, then slowly put it down and came to read over my shoulder as I scrolled down to the description and my heart gave a knife-like sideways beat. I recognized every single word of the spiel. Not because it was typical hotel business jargon, but because I'd worked so hard on it.

'They're copying us word for word,' I whispered.

'Bloody hell. Check their availability calendar.'

I checked and they were booked to the hilt. The opposite of us.

'Now do you believe me?' I cried.

Julian had that pensive expression on his face, the one he got when he was on the verge of figuring something out. Which was lucky, as I was on the verge of a nervous breakdown.

'Erica, honey, I have a sinking, *stinking* feeling. Remember the bus tour in Castellino?'

'Oh my God, yes, I knew it,' I whispered. So *there* were all our customers. All those Brits from the bus tours were staying there. 'They want to wipe us off the map.'

'And the dead rat,' Julian added. 'They must have planted it when they came to stay and took a picture of it.'

I rubbed my face briskly and pondered and considered. And then, as the fruit of years and years in the business tackling anything that had come my way, I made my most important marketing–management decision ever.

'I'm gonna kill them. Drive straight up there and punch the first face I see.'

Julian's eyes widened. 'Erica, you'll do nothing of the sort.'

'You expect me just to sit around and do nothing while we lose our business?'

'We're not going to lose the business.'

'Damn right we're not,' I vowed. I had a plan. A mission.

# 7

## No Turning Back

As you can imagine, I spent the day stabbing at my laptop by the edge of the pool, trawling for more info on the Cascianis as the kids wrapped up in terry towels to dry off. I'd made sandwiches for dinner and declared an early night for them so I could concentrate completely on this. As if they sensed something was wrong, they kept quiet and didn't put up a fight when I sent them to bed, poor darlings.

I'd barely spoken to them all day. What kind of a mother had I morphed into? But I couldn't bear to tell them what was happening, not now. How could I ever explain to them that Mommy was flailing?

'The kids are settled,' Julian whispered, kissing the side of my face, but I barely noticed, pounding away on my keyboard and looking for anything, anywhere, that would clear things up.

'I've called Laura and explained the situation to her,' Julian continued.

I looked up. 'Who?'

'Marco's cousin, the lawyer? She'll be back first thing tomorrow afternoon,' he explained as he put a mug of chamomile tea on the table. 'Drink. It'll steady your nerves.'

'My nerves are steady,' I said and sipped gratefully. How well he knew me. This was the time to calm down and meditate on my next move. Although murder was what I really had in mind.

How dare these people attack us! Was there no one in this godforsaken country monitoring such unethical behavior? Were small family businesses simply left to their own devices? What if we couldn't have afforded a lawyer? How would anyone else with lesser means have coped? This was bullying – mobbing – and completely unacceptable.

And then I had a terrible thought. What was going to happen to us if Laura couldn't help? What if they weren't technically breaking any laws? There was no law against being obnoxious. It looked like my plan wasn't going to work. Learning as much as possible about them to counteract whatever they planned against us simply wasn't enough.

And then a sudden urgency filled my heart. I wanted to enjoy as much of Tuscany as we could before disaster struck and we'd have to leave. Just like when on your last day of a fab vacation you realize it's over and you start scurrying around for last-minute souvenirs as proof and reminders you actually had a great time, which was now rapidly – inexorably – coming to an end. We might as well get as much as we can out of this short, short stay in our land of dreams. Maybe visit every place we haven't seen yet. We'd see, eat and drink the whole region out before we had to go.

Huh. I hadn't thought of that. Go where, exactly? Back to Boston, where smug, smug Marcy would be ready to pounce on me and say I should have listened to her and never left in the first place? Or back to The Farthington, even though I knew there would always be a job for me? The feeling of failure would permeate my very soul for the rest of my days.

And imagine my kids going back to Clifton Street School... They'd be at the mercy of everyone, especially the moms who would gladly have murdered me when rumors about Julian and me had started.

I didn't care about myself, but Maddy and Warren would become the target of everyone's scorn. I could already hear the vicious digs: *Have you heard? Principal Foxham and that quirky woman who dragged him off to Europe? They're back! Only there's no way he's ever getting his old job back, what with sleeping with a school mom. Shameful!* (Never mind that they'd been practically lining up at his office door with lame excuses on a daily basis just to gawp at him.)

No. Never. No way was I going back to Boston to live. Or to die. After a lifetime of dreaming about a new life in Tuscany, I couldn't just give up and leave. Like Scarlett O'Hara from *Gone with the Wind*, I'd defend my Tara plantation tooth and nail. I'd eat dirt and roots, too, if I had to, but I wasn't budging from here.

'You OK, love?' Julian said.

'I can't believe this is happening to us,' I huffed, rubbing my hands over my eyes.

Julian lowered himself onto the seat next to me and in one glance, we surveyed what we owned and were about to lose – the rolling hills, now purple in the falling darkness, the vineyards, the fields, the swimming pool – everything we'd always wanted. He took my hand.

'I promise you it'll be OK. By this time tomorrow, things will be clearer and at least we'll know what's what. Just be patient and optimistic, honey.'

I snorted. 'Patient and optimistic – have we met? But I will get to the bottom of this, Julian. You mark my words.'

He chuckled. 'That's my girl – stay angry, Erica – it's our only weapon tonight.'

'Angry? I'm terrified, Julian.'

'Don't be. All will be well.'

'You keep saying that, but you're not reassuring me in the least.'

He flung his hands in the air, now frustrated. 'What do you want me to say? I just know that people don't get scammed out of a license without any proof. It legally just can't happen. You have to have official surveys and reports.'

I thought about it. Maybe that was so in England or the USA, but in Italy? I had my doubts. And something else was bothering me.

'You put a lot of your own money in this, Julian…'

He rubbed my bunched shoulders, pulling me back against him. 'Don't think about it. Just relax. Come here…'

I shook my head and buried it in my hands. 'I'm sorry – I'm too upset. I can't think of anything else.'

'Don't be, it'll all be fine, you'll see. Now stop worrying…'

I wished he understood. Julian had a habit of trying to cheer me up. Which was a great quality. But sometimes I just wanted to be listened to without him swooping in with his cape and saving the day. Because when I opened my heart to him, it was to make him understand how I was feeling. Not necessarily for him to solve my problems. Some men just don't get it.

He sighed, pulling me up. 'Come on – let's get you to sleep. Remember, you have a big morning tomorrow.'

Damn – Paul and I were going to check out my wedding gown. I'd completely forgotten. What a bride-to-be I was.

'I can't go to sleep. I have to shoot another blanket email.'

'I thought you'd done that.'

'I did, but only to my test-group.'

'Why not to all of them at the same time?'

'Because I was waiting for feedback from my test group. In case I'd forgotten something or presented it in a way that lacked something, they would have mentioned it and I could fine-tune it to my next batch.'

He looked at me with a strange light in his eyes. Was he beginning to recognize the old Erica? I sure was!

'We'll do that tomorrow. I'll help you.'

'You will? Don't you have to write?'

'I do,' he conceded. 'But this is important. Plus, you need your sleep before tomorrow.'

'Oh, crap, tomorrow! I can't go wedding dress hunting— we've got Laura coming.'

'Sweets, let go. I'll deal with it. Just go and get yourself a wedding dress, OK?'

I huffed. Let go, he says. As if it were that easy. The minute I let go, things always fell apart.

Julian, on the other hand, was as calm as pea soup. If any foreigner could live in Italy without killing anyone, it was him. It was as if nothing could touch him. I'd never ever seen him sad or worried about anything. He loved the kids and me and had done everything in his power to keep us safe, and I knew he'd continue to do so. So I followed him to bed, cuddled up to him and tried to think happy thoughts.

'OK?' he soothed, and I nodded, grateful to have him by my side, on my side.

'Better,' I conceded. For now.

'Oh, by the way, I've called my parents to tell them the wedding's postponed for now. Have you told yours yet?' he asked.

'I hope they weren't too disappointed?' I loved Maggie and Tom. They never interfered, never made suggestions unless I specifically asked them. The exact opposite of Marcy, they knew their place. I just hoped they wouldn't have to witness our downfall.

'... family?' I heard Julian say, and a twinge of panic pinched me.

'Er, what?' I said.

'You have told your family, right?'

Oops. 'Of course I will.'

He sighed. 'Your family is coming on August 15th and you haven't even told them our wedding is postponed?'

'I will.'

'When? After they get here?'

'ASAP. Promise.'

'Why not now?' he insisted. 'It's only 6 p.m. in Boston.'

Boy, could he be a pain sometimes. 'Because... because... I hadn't exactly told them about the wedding yet...'

'What?' he groaned. 'Erica, do you mean to tell me that you've said absolutely nothing to your parents about our wedding plans?'

'But it turned out to be a good thing, see? Now I don't have to answer any of Marcy's questions...'

'That's not fair. They need to know we're getting married, sooner or later. You need to give them a heads up.'

'Why don't we just elope?'

Julian stared at me for a moment, and then threw back his head and laughed. 'When *I* wanted to do it spur of the moment, you insisted you wanted the whole family here, and now...? What's changed?'

'Nothing. Let's do it. Let's just disappear, get hitched and come back as Mr. and Mrs.'

'No,' he said.

'Why not?'

'Because you were right. We're not two teenagers. Because Maddy and Warren need stability. They need to see us getting hitched and doing it the proper way, like two respectable adults. What if Maddy pulls something similar on us when she's older?'

'She wouldn't. I raised her, not Marcy.'

'Honey...'

'I know Marcy. If I tell her we're getting married in the new year, she'll insist on helping Paul with the wedding planning and I don't want her here longer than necessary, Julian. First, she'll try to brainwash you out of marrying me...'

He grinned. 'Impossible.'

'... and then she'll try to get me back on the operating table and show everyone pictures of me when I was...' I bit my lip.

When I was *enormous*. And when all she did was humiliate

me. I should call her and make sure she postponed her flight to only maybe a couple of days before the wedding. If I only knew the date. And then I could handle her a couple of days before. One single day more than necessary? Not happening.

He took my hand. 'No one's ever going to make me change my mind about making an honest woman out of you.'

I turned to look at him. 'Promise?'

'Cross my heart.'

'OK. In that case, I'll call tomorrow. But I'm warning you, it'll get pretty ugly.'

He slapped my thigh. 'It'll be fine. Now get some sleep, love, and dream of how awesome things will be when I can call you wife.'

I caressed his head and shoulders, enjoying the feel of his rock-solid body. 'Aww, I'm touched, Julian.'

'Go to sleep now. I'm exhausted.'

I fell back into my own space. Huh. And we weren't even married yet. We really were an unorthodox couple.

The next day, as I was debating whether or not to pick up the phone and inform the dysfunctional Cantellis about my equally dysfunctional wedding plans, a dark blue official-looking car with the letters NAS pulled up in our drive and I almost fainted on the spot – the Health and Safety Department! These were the real deal this time, not a prank.

'Erica Cantelli?' the bigger uniform (and paunch) asked.

'Yes?' I answered, swallowing.

'We received a phone call from Laura Magri's office? About a rat?'

'Oh, that.' I giggled nervously. 'No worries – someone was trying to play a joke on us.'

'That may well be, *signora*, but as it's been flagged up, we have the duty to carry out an inspection.'

'But it was just a joke, I tell you. Someone wants to shut us down. Why don't you investigate that instead?'

Mr. Big Uniform shrugged. 'That's a separate department. We're NAS. You want to sue someone for slander, you call a lawyer first.'

'But I already did…' I faltered, thinking that Laura had caused us more damage than the Cascianis. At least they hadn't made any official calls. But Laura? She'd brought the bloody NAS down on us.

'You're welcome to inspect us now,' I offered. 'Be my guests.'

Albeit my only ones. The place was always spotless. Let them inspect the hell out of us. Let them do it now and get it over with.

'No, we've just come to warn you, seeing as you're friends of Laura's. We'll come back in the future.' The threat in his voice was tangible.

'But I'm ready now! Go ahead,' I insisted.

But The Paunch lifted his hand in sign of 'we're out of here'. And in a flash, they were. Now was that not enough to send you over the edge?

'Hello!' came Marcy's voice over the phone the next day as Renata, Paul, Julian and I were having coffee on the terrace.

A loudspeaker squawked in the background as if she were at a soccer game. Crap – I'd totally forgotten to call her after all.

'Marcy? I can barely hear you. Where are you?'

'In Milan. I'm landing in Pisa at two thirty. Surprise!'

Surprise? Surprise was the least of it. Horror was more like it. She wasn't supposed to be here. Not for another two months. Not until I'd armored up first! If she found out about the wedding she'd never leave now!

But I was quick to recover. 'Oh, wow!' I managed, rolling my eyes and giving my gang the slice-my-throat gesture. Which would have been a great idea, come to think of it now. 'Great. So I can give you the good news in person.'

'What?' she called. 'I can't hear you. Did you say good news? Are you moving back to the States?'

'No, Marcy, we're not. I'll tell you when I see you this afternoon.'

I put the phone down and stared at the three stunned faces around me.

'Marcy?' Renata whispered.

'Here?' Paul groaned.

'*Mamma mia*,' Julian choked. 'I'd told you to call her...'

'I'm sorry, I forgot.'

'Absolutely brilliant,' Julian groaned. 'How long is she staying?'

I shrugged. 'How long is a piece of string?'

Marcy's plane was two hours late and despite the air con in Arrivals, I was self-combusting on panic fumes, sweaty and exhausted from waiting on the hard wooden chairs and the drive all the way to Pisa, which was on the other side of Tuscany. I'd told her that the closest airport was Sant'Egidio in Umbria, but did she listen? No. Hence the sweaty butt stuck to my car seat and the foul mood. And when she saw me, she'd certainly have a dig about my weight, my hair and the childish color of the nail varnish on my toes.

But when *she* appeared, one of her Chanel silk scarves wrapped around her head like a Fifties Hollywood star, shades as big as bug eyes and some poor airport guy lugging her cases, she looked fresh and radiant. How the heck did she do it every single time? Trust Marcy to piss me off before she even opened her mouth.

'*Darling!*' she called – a term I'd become familiar with when people were watching.

I pasted a smile on my face and opened my arms... only to see her head for Julian. Puzzled, he hugged her back, slanting me a questioning but resigned look.

Marcy was like that, staging these little scenarios in public. Today, she was Beautiful Businesswoman (notice the Blackberry and briefcase, probably full of *Vogues*) reuniting with her younger lover. Hopefully, she'd be too full of herself to concentrate on me.

'Julian, you look amazing. As fit as the day we met!'

'And you, dear Marcy, look like a schoolgirl. How do you do it?'

'Oh stop,' she said, hugging him to her again, and he sent me a wry, resigned grin over her shoulder.

And then it was my turn.

'Erica?' she gasped. 'Oh my God, what's happened to you? And why on earth aren't you wearing a bra?'

I folded my arms over my breasts as she briefly hugged me. 'I am,' I shot back.

'Well, then, we need to get you some new ones. They

aren't working anymore. Come on –we don't want to be standing around here all day,' she said as she passed her wheelie suitcase to Julian and linked her arm through his.

Julian's eyebrows shot up into his hairline as he looked back at me. I rolled my eyes and shooed them ahead. Two minutes in and she'd already shown her true colors.

'Paul, you look grand!' Marcy exclaimed when we were back at the house, giving him an even warmer welcome than Julian's.

'So do you, girl!' he chimed, and I groaned inwardly. .

But I had to admit, it was true. Marcy looked ten years younger. And faker. Me, all I wanted was to be ten years happier.

'Botox?' I asked, and she darted a glance at Paul before shooting me a chastising glare. How was I supposed to know I'd guessed right?

'It worked better for you than me,' Paul informed her. 'I couldn't open my mouth for a week.'

Now that was an uplifting thought. Imagine, Marcy unable to utter one single word the whole time she was here…

She turned her adoring eyes back to him, visibly more relaxed now that the cat was out of the bag.

'Really? That's a shame. I'll give you my doctor's name back in Boston.'

Yeah, next year, I thought. When she goes home.

'So, what's your good news?' she finally asked as we all sat round the dinner table, having made a theatrical fuss of Maddy and Warren, in one giant cliché.

She never really gave a crap about anyone but herself. I was surprised she'd even remembered their names.

Julian shot me a smile and took my hand. 'Well, Marcy, Erica and I are getting married.'

Her head snapped up and she almost dropped her fork. 'Married... *well*. Have you thought it out carefully, both of you? Marriage is a big step. Though once you're in, it's not so painless to get out. Although Erica's already done it once before.'

Julian eyed me and cleared his throat. 'Oh, we're both in all the way and we don't want to get out, Marcy. I've already adopted the kids and they now carry my surname.'

At that, I cringed inwardly and even Paul lowered his head into his hands. Anyone who hadn't known The Complete Cantelli Family History had no idea what Julian had just stirred.

Marcy sat up. 'You mean to tell me they're no longer *Lowensteins*?' she squeaked.

This time, I put my own fork down, eyeing Maddy, who was staring at her grandmother, wide-eyed, while Warren continued to eat, but I could see his cheeks growing crimson. He remembered all too well what Ira had done to him and Maddy.

I patted his knee under the table and pulled Maddy closer to me. I could stop a bullet like this, but not Marcy's words.

'Marcy, they've never really been Lowensteins. And Julian loves them like his own. You know that.'

But Marcy was shaking her head.

'I don't see why you have to get married, though. That's exactly when the fun ends and the trouble starts.'

'Oh, come on...' I said.

'Marcy, please don't ruin a perfectly good evening,' Julian pleaded.

'I mean it,' Marcy insisted. 'What happens if and when, with all due respect to you, Julian, the two of you split up? Do the kids go back to being Lowensteins again?'

Julian wiped his mouth and put his fork down, too. 'Marcy, we're not going to split up. Erica and I are solid.'

Marcy snorted. 'So were Erica and Ira.'

'That's not true!' I turned to Julian and whispered, 'I mean… I did my best to-to…' I bit my lip for the kids' sake. How to downplay what was the worst time of my life? 'We loved each other in the beginning, but it just didn't work out. It was no one's fault…'

Well, the truth was that Ira had discovered he wasn't attracted to me anymore. So he'd left me. Well, sort of. He'd been playing with two decks of cards, as Italians say. You know, the usual cliché – the young, sexy secretary. Which was, in the end, lucky for me, because, as unhappy as I was, I would never have cheated on him or left him because of the kids. Killed him, maybe, but left him? No.

I don't believe in half-baked situations. It was either black or white for me. In or out. And Ira hadn't left me any choice – nor much money. Only a head full of dreams for a better life in Tuscany. Still, I couldn't do it on just my budget.

That's when Julian had appeared in my life, decided he was in love with me, swooped in and saved the day. After less than a year together, we'd moved lock, stock and barrel to Tuscany. Where he'd proved himself to be the best man a gal could fall in love with. But still today, whenever Ira was mentioned – and it was always Marcy who brought him up – my blood boiled.

'So where is our invitation?' she asked.

'Erm, I haven't sent them out yet...'

'And when are you getting married?'

'Some time in the new year...'

'That's pretty vague, don't you think?'

'Uhm, well, yes, but—'

'No matter,' she sighed. 'It's only June. We can still swing it if I pitch in. Honestly, Erica, why do you put yourself in these situations?'

At that, my heart began to kick at my ribs. 'Pitch in? Thanks, Marcy, but Paul is organizing it. He's just starting his new business.'

'Well, then you'll need all the help you can get,' she said, turning to him. 'It's a good thing I came here when I did. Imagine, planning a wedding in less than six months!'

Paul's face went white, but he composed himself, reached behind Julian for the dessert trolley and grabbed two slices of tiramisu.

'Come on you guys,' he chimed to Maddy and Warren. 'Whoever gets to the pool first gets the biggest slice! I'll talk with your mommy later!'

One quick look in our direction and when Julian and I nodded, they jumped out of their seats and chased Paul – plus desserts – out and down the staircase to the ground floor, happy to get away from The Cantelli inquisition. Or should I say slaughter?

'Come on, Marcy, be happy for us,' Julian chimed. 'Your blessing is important.'

Man, could my guy act.

Marcy looked up at him without resentment. With affection, even, but her nostrils were pinched. And then, without another word, she shook her head and went back to picking at her food. And that was the end of that.

The next day, as I got up to pour Maddy a glass of juice, my back twinged dangerously. I moaned involuntarily, clutching at the table to steady myself.

'You OK, honey?' Julian said.

'Yeah, it's just…'

'It's because you weigh too much,' Marcy admonished me with her lacquered finger, and my skin suddenly went clammy. 'I knew you'd piled all the weight back on. You should have listened to me and had that damn stomach bypass when I told you to.'

*I did listen to you,* I wanted to retort at the mere thought of how she'd badgered me into the op alongside Ira. *And that's exactly when I found out Ira was having sex with Maxine Moore – stilettos and no panties – if you remember…*

But having matured (somewhat) over the years, I refrained from wringing her neck. No more arguing with her like I used to. No more getting lost in yet another kerfuffle with her simply because she pissed me off. No. I'd be cool, calm and collected from now on. I grinned my new I-can-do-this grin as I felt a major migraine coming on. Marcy was here for who knew how long. She had an open ticket, which to me was worse than having open-heart surgery. How the hell was I going to survive her until our wedding? And then my sudden brainstorm. Why hadn't I thought of it sooner?

I picked up the phone, groaned at the sound of his voicemail and left a message. 'Hi, Dad, it's me. Marcy's driving me nuts. Plus, I miss you. Call me.' *Preferably with your flight schedule if you ever want to see her—or me— alive again.*

That afternoon Renata, who had become my number-one supporter in my anti-Casciani campaign, came by with a copy of *La Nazione* newspaper, the Siena edition, under her arm.

'You're not going to like this,' she warned as she put the paper on the table and turned on the kettle.

I eyed her and unfurled the harbinger of bad news:

Tasting Tuscany (not to be confused with A Taste of Tuscany, a second-rate B & B in the same area that's recently closed for health and safety issues) is a new hotel in the Siena province that's ousting all others that dare to compete.

'*What?*' I boomed.
Renata shook her head in disgust. 'Read on.'
I read on:

The inauguration alone boasted a presence of 500 participants on the first day. The consensus is that Tasting Tuscany is undoubtedly the leader in the hotel business and is here to stay.

'What nonsense. Who do they think they are? How dare they cite us, after copying our presentation, our photos *and* our website.'

'There's more,' Renata said, pulling out a couple of mugs from the cupboard. I looked down to finish the article:

Tasting Tuscany has purchased a coach to take its guests – *free* of charge – on day trips to both the most famous sites and the hidden gems of our beautiful Tuscany, including San Gimignano for its majestic cluster of medieval towers, Montepulciano for its heavenly wine and Arezzo for its wonderful goldsmith shops and bottegas.

'Unbelievable,' I managed.

'There's still more,' Renata said in disgust as the water boiled and the kettle clicked off.

Note: day trip, tour guide in several foreign languages and seven-course meal at a luxury restaurant all included in the booking price. We'll keep you posted on Tasting Tuscany's next promos.

I rubbed my forehead. At this rate, they'd soon be burying us into oblivion. Every business had a right to exist and compete, of course, but these people were completely dishonest and morally unacceptable.

Renata poured hot water into the mugs and reached for the sugar.

'What other miracles are they going to perform?' I snapped as I slammed the paper shut.

Renata shook her head, presenting me with a steaming chamomile. 'Drink this. You need it.'

Need it I did. These people were on a mission, kicking us when we were already down. But we weren't all the way down. Not by a long shot. Because I had reached the point of no return.

'Mom!' called Warren from the front door the next day. 'There's a busload of guys outside – they're singing in English!'

Julian had returned earlier that morning and was in the fields as I lounged alone by the pool, fully dressed and feet dangling in the water.

'What are they singing, Warren?' Maddy asked as I pushed my feet into my flip-flops.

'You don't want to know,' Warren said.

Singing English men? Unless they were from the choir of Saint Paul's Cathedral, it usually meant trouble. In a town like Castellino, where the cops amounted to one, his deputy, the dog and its fleas, you couldn't count much on their intervention. There was no crime or violence, thus no means of preventing it. This was definitely going to be a problem I'd have to solve. And it was a problem. I could smell it from miles away.

I shooed the kids back inside. 'Warren, go inside and lock the front door.'

Unfortunately, he'd heard those words from me before and memories of his psycho father must have flashed before him, because he swallowed and asked, 'Are they trouble, Mom?'

'Of course not. Now go. Don't forget to bolt the door.'

He nodded and went, and in the corner of my eye, I saw him look back at me over his shoulder as he did so.

Straightening my back, I strode over to meet the posse, who were waving their arms out the windows of the bus, looking like beef spilling out of a meat grinder. The driver of the bus was Italian and shaking his head.

'*Mi scusi*,' he apologized. '*Non so dove vogliono andare.*' I don't know where they want to go.

One look told me it was an English stag party. There were about a dozen of them, mostly blond, long dirty hair, all dressed in variations of English soccer gear. And the stink of beer was unbelievable.

''Allo, love!' one said, jumping out the bus to the spot right in front of me.

I resisted the urge to step back. I was familiar with this kind of animal. Better show no fear.

'Hello, may I help you?'

'Yeah! We was overbooked at the Senese Hotel, yeah? No place to go now. Got rooms?'

I had loads of rooms, in fact. But that was none of his business.

'I'm so sorry, we're fully booked.'

'Aww, c'mon, love – just a few rooms. You won't even know we're here,' he coaxed as one of his buddies leaned out the window and threw up on the cobblestones.

And that was when bad-ass Erica of yesteryear was instantly back with another brainstorm idea. Ignoring the wino, I feigned real concern for their predicament.

'Gosh, I'm so sorry, some big rich guy just booked the whole place for a business conference.' Then I leaned in and whispered, 'But I do have a solution if you don't mind me suggesting one?'

'Hell no,' he said, and I grinned, turning him round to point north.

'I'll give your driver the directions, but right down in the valley there's an amazing place – very similar to this – with lots of rooms. It's called Tasting Tuscany. I think they're actually hosting a beauty contest for the local TV or something,' I added for good measure.

'Cor, super,' the Brit cheered, followed by the other hoodlums hanging out the windows.

I grinned amiably and pulled out my cell. I knew the bloody number by heart. 'Let me book for you.'

'Yeah, super.'

'Tasting Tuscany, *buongiorno*?' came Marzia Casciani's familiar crow voice.

'Yes, good afternoon. This is Erica Cantelli from A Taste of Tuscany.'

A long silence. 'Ah. What do you want?'

*To wipe you off the map, of course.* 'Ah, I'm standing here next to a group – the South London Male Voice Choir. Classical music…'

The yobbo next to me sniggered and I raised my hand to shush him.

'We have an overflow and simply don't have the room. Can we send them to you?'

I wasn't about to admit to her what she already knew – that she'd managed to put our business on hold for the time being. Better to seem pathetic for now if I wanted to reel her in.

Another suspicious pause and I found I was holding my breath.

Then, finally, 'Oh, yes, absolutely,' came the snidey voice. 'And thank you.'

Don't thank me yet, I thought, glee pumping through my veins. 'They're on their way,' I said and hung up.

The yobbo was already getting back onto the bus.

'Cheers, love!' he shouted, raising his thumb at me, and the herd inside roared in chorus, chanting all sorts of things that made me hope my children were out of earshot.

'Just ask for the old Bettarini farm,' I said to the poor bus driver. 'The place is called Tasting Tuscany.'

The driver looked at our own sign reading A Taste of Tuscany and then looked back at me, confused.

I sighed amiably. 'Long story. Here – for your trouble,' I said, opening the larder door on the ground floor behind me and pulling out an entire cured prosciutto. 'Take this for your family.'

The man's eyes popped open. '*Grazie, signora.*'

'Oh, you'll be earning it, don't you worry.'

He grinned. '*Sì, signora.*'

I smiled at him, stepped back and waved at the rowdy bunch. 'Right, boys, off you go! Have fun. Happy holidays!'

South London Male Voice Choir, my foot. These boys were Neanderthal soccer hooligans and going straight to the Cascianis. I sagged in relief as they hit the horizon, a trail of dust in their wake, and I could only imagine the havoc they'd wreak once they were on our rival's property. Did I feel guilty about it in the least, you may ask? Absolutely not. That's what they got for trying to ruin our livelihood. Karma's doing – not mine in the least.

A few moments later, Julian drove up in his tractor, all sweaty and shirtless, his body glistening in the golden light, his face a mask of danger. He jumped off the tractor, looking for all the world like a fuming cowboy, a rifle over his shoulder, taking long strides toward me, his eyes scanning his surroundings.

'Where are they?' he demanded.

'Who?' I asked innocently.

'The thugs.'

'Thugs?' I laughed.

Warren must have called him, bless his little soul, just as he'd done the last time I was in danger, under the threat of

Ira's baseball bat, and Julian had come running, breaking my front door open like a real hero.

'Oh, they were just looking for a place to stay. The South London Male Choir Voice, I think they said. I sent them to our rivals, of course.'

Julian grinned and wrapped his arm around me. 'You little schemer.'

If only he knew. Better let sleeping dogs lie.

'Where did you get that rifle?' I asked just as Marco and Giacomo brought up the rear, sporting a rifle each, their eyes glittering. Men and their tribal instinct. 'Never mind,' I said, exhaling.

Back at The Farthington, if there had been a problem, all I'd had to do was call security. Here, my security was Julian and our friends. Julian scooped me up in his sweaty arms, his T-shirt hanging from his back pocket, his jeans having seen better days. He kissed me thoroughly, like he always did when we were apart.

# 8

## The Miracle Maker

As I was furiously slapping something together for dinner or, rather, pureeing anything that got between my fingers, Julian came into the kitchen with his laptop.

'OK, listen,' he said. 'I've just received an email from Laura Magri.'

Our lawyer. Laura the lawyer, my mind wandered. Fat lot of good she did us, attracting the attention of the bloody NAS.

'Our pictures are being deleted from their website and the same goes for the description.'

I blinked. 'Is that it?'

Julian dipped his head. 'For now. It's still a good result, though, don't you think?'

Result? I'd give him a good result.

'What a waste of time that is,' I shot back, putting dinner in the oven and grabbing my car keys from the counter. I was sick and tired of flailing despite my best efforts. I'd tried everything in and out of the book, but the Cascianis seemed immune to honesty.

What a crazy country we lived in. Was this the way it really was, only I hadn't seen it behind my pink La Vie En Rose designer lenses? A country where rules are bendy-bendy and didn't even apply to everyone – was it supposed to be a joke or something?

'It won't be very funny if we lose our business,' I whispered to myself to cover my trembling lips.

Time to get off my ass and fight my own battles.

'What? Hey, where are you going?' he asked, looking up from his screen.

'I've got some investigating to do.'

At that, Julian smiled. 'Easy, champ. We don't want any broken bones.'

'Not at all,' I smiled as I walked out the door. Just a few minor purchases.

The Cascianis were absolute fools if they thought I was packing up and leaving without a fight. I'd chain myself to this place before I left. Better, I'd nail them to their own bloody front door.

As I wound my way through the Tuscan hills, concocting my homicidal plan where I emerge victorious, Renata called my cell.

'Erica, you're nuts,' she said when I let her in on my thoughts. 'How on earth are you going to bring them down? They're one of the oldest and richest families in the region.'

'You know them?'

'Everyone does. They own a chain of restaurants across the Chianti area. They're infinitely too big for you to scare.'

'Oh, I don't want to scare them. Never mind Tasting Tuscany – I'm going to give them a taste of their own medicine. Gotta go.'

'Erica—'

But I'd already hung up. There was no stopping me. So I dialed Julian.

'Honey, I'm not coming home tonight.'

'What? Where are you? Are you alright?'

'I'm going to get our business back, Julian.'

'In what way?'

'I booked Paul and me into the hotel for tonight.'

'To do what?'

'I'll think of something.' I had to, or it was our butts.

'Honey, we have a lawyer for that.'

'But she hasn't done anything. She's all… Lamborghini and no Casciani. I want justice.'

'No,' came Julian's voice. 'You want blood.'

'I thought you were mad, too?'

'I'm still mad, Erica. But I don't like your methods. I like to deal with my cards on the table, you know that.'

'So, what are you saying? I'm some sort of thug?'

'Of course not. But you always manage to get yourself into these predicaments and I always have to pull you out, some way or another.'

Which had, of course, been true in the past. But I was angry now and anger fueled me better than fear. It made me lucid. Like a sniper on a rooftop, ready to strike.

'Just let me deal with it, Julian. I know what to do.'

'Erica, no. I know you.'

'And I know the hotel business. Trust me.'

Julian heaved a sigh. 'I don't know. You're just asking for trouble. Let Laura deal with it.'

Oof, again with the fancy-pants lawyer. Julian was holding out on me because he didn't want to offend our neighbors, Marco and Renata. Better for me to change tactics.

'Just let me give it a shot, Julian. Please?'

Silence, and then a groan. 'OK. One shot. After that, you leave it to her. OK?'

Aargh…

'OK?' he insisted.

Laura Magri wasn't interested in doing the job properly. All she wanted was fast and good money.

'Erica?'

'Yes, Julian.'

'Thank you.'

'Dinner's in the oven. Kiss the kids for me.'

A sigh. 'Right…'

'Now, will you please pass me to Paul?'

Julian groaned, but I heard him mumbling, 'She wants to talk to you. Convince her to come back home. I sure as hell can't.'

'Sunshine,' Paul said, and I automatically grinned. My partner in crime.

'Paulie,' I said. 'Pack an overnight bag and have Julian drive you to the bus station. I'll meet you in San Gimignano.'

And as I hung up without giving him a chance to argue, I saw it, down in the valley – Tasting bloody Tuscany, its sign very similar to our own logo: four blue cypress trees on a green hill, while ours was three green cypress trees on a blue hill. They'd even copied that. I looked around, fuming, like an angry bull before a taunting red cape.

Seen from afar, even the structure looked similar. Of course they'd think they could get away with our pictures on their website! Because they hadn't yet met angry Erica Cantelli, former manager of a luxury hotel. This was one of the meanest businesses around and I was geared for blood. Pools and pools of it. And speaking of…

'And this is your idea of an evening out?' Paul hissed as, two hours later, we huddled in the dark on the ground beneath the bushes separating the swimming pool from the patio at Tasting Tuscany, The Enemy's reign. We'd checked in, me wearing a blonde wig (not that it could hide my big butt), had dinner and were now taking our evening stroll as I reached into a massive handbag.

'As I said, this is war. Hold this jar.'

'What's in it?'

I scrambled to my feet, surprisingly nimble for one with a back like mine, but you know determination moves in mysterious ways. I poured the red liquid into the pool with a relish that was beyond gleeful. It was sinister. Malevolent, even. But they had it coming.

'Dye,' I rasped as if issuing a command and unscrewed the first lid.

'Erica, no! It could be dangerous for their guests.'

'It's only food coloring. What do you think I am, a monster?'

'And a vindictive one at that,' he groaned.

'And don't you forget it. Unscrew that one, too.'

'Is this really necessary?' he hissed.

'How would you like it if a rival company just round the

corner called itself Menus and Venues and suddenly started stealing your business and contacts? Starting with Chef Alberto…'

Paul's face transformed back to his usual bitchy stance. 'Gimme that jar.'

I grinned. 'Attaboy.'

And with that, he unscrewed the lid and poured the contents into the water with an almighty woosh. Immediately, it turned a dark red, swirling, and I remembered the scene in The Ten Commandments movie when the waters of the Nile turned to blood. Oh, yeah! That would teach them.

They'd really need Moses to fix things up around here by the time I finished with them. Served them right for trying to mess with my business and my family's happiness. The wrath of Erica Cantelli had just been unleashed. And I hadn't even started yet.

That night, I slept as soundly as an innocent babe in a basket cradled by the Nile river.

The next morning, the owners of our rival B & B, Mr. and Mrs. Copycat Casciani, came to a skid by the pool to join the wannabe swimmers with towels flung around their necks staring down in disgust. Blending with the other guests, Paul and I, hands on hips and tsk-tsking like the rest, stole a glance at our enemies, who were scratching their heads in dismay.

Within the next five minutes, the hotel would empty completely. Better get a move on and beat the crowd out of here.

'And our work here is done,' I whispered in triumph.

But to be totally, completely honest, I did feel a twinge of guilt. I never meant to hurt their business. I was only trying to protect mine. After all, they were the ones who had attacked us. Personally. Viciously. Come on, even you… Would you just stand by and do absolutely nothing, with a lousy lawyer and the Health and Safety Department on your back through absolutely no fault of your own? No, I didn't think so, either.

We turned to go, but a shriek stopped us in our tracks.

'*Il sangue di Cristo! E' un miracolo!*' Christ's blood! A miracle! a female voice cried and I whirled round, looking for the idiot who could say something so, so stupid.

No, no, no, you got it all wrong! I wanted to scream as people moved closer to the pool, some dropping to their knees and crossing themselves, murmurs and gasps now filling the area. It's supposed to be blood, yes, but not Christ's!

My plan had backfired catastrophically. It served me right, in a sense, but now it was too late for repentance, so I grabbed Paul's sleeve and we split the scene, and in five minutes we were in my Fiat 500L on the way home.

'And stop laughing already!' I growled as Paul wiped his eyes.

'Man oh man! Only you could think of something so crazy.'

'It's not crazy. My plan was good. Great, in fact. It simply backfired and blew up in my face. Now, everybody thinks that the place is blessed or holy.'

Paul made an effort to put on a serious face, but the mirth was still there, under his facial muscles, threatening to take over again. He always had a great sense of humor, my Paulie.

'So, what are you gonna do?'

'I don't know yet, but I'm nowhere near done, I promise you.'

Thanks to my idiocy, a recalcitrant ally, a bit of food coloring and a thirst for vengeance, Tasting Tuscany had now actually become holy ground. And I'd been the one to consecrate it in two seconds flat.

'Who's going to tell Julian now?' I muttered.

'I sure as hell ain't,' he said. 'How did you think that you could sabotage a business with a little food coloring?'

I glared at him. 'How was I supposed to know I'd be consecrating the damn joint?'

Paul lifted his hands and sighed. 'It's too late now. No point in fighting. The damage is done. But you have to tell Julian.'

'Why? I thought you were my partner in crime.'

'I am. But only against the bad guys. Julian is a saint.'

'Please don't say religious words,' I groaned.

Paul made a face. 'Well, he is, to put up with you.'

'Why have you turned on me so suddenly?'

Paul giggled. 'Because, my dear, you are the work of the devil.'

'Paul!'

'You have to tell him.'

I knew he was right. So I braced myself for what I knew would be – and this is the only expression that suits the situation – his *biblical wrath*.


'You did *what*?' Julian boomed.

'I know, I know,' I moaned, burying my head in my hands as Paul skulked away. Judas.

Julian paced the kitchen floor, his hands in his hair. 'Erica'—he never called me Erica unless I really put my foot in it—'do you realize what you've done? This is a criminal offence! Trespassing and damaging someone else's property?'

Was that how he saw it? Damaging someone else's property? I'd do much worse to anyone trying to harm our well-being. What was the matter with him? Didn't he care about the business anymore? I crossed my arms and gave him one of my special hairy eyeballs.

'First of all, I wasn't trespassing – we booked a room. Second, I didn't damage the property – I actually gave it a one-way ticket to being canonized. Before you know it, they'll be known as Tasting Tuscan Miracles!'

But he stared at me, opening and closing his mouth like he was going to have a stroke.

'I swear I don't recognize you anymore, Erica! You've changed, and not in a good way. Whatever happened to the kick-ass hotel manager who had it all together?'

I eyed him sulkily. Good question. What had happened to me? Back in Boston, I ran the place like a dream – the whole shebang. And now I couldn't keep a small B & B booked for three consecutive months?

In the past, the Cascianis would have been nothing but a tiny blip in such a big scheme, but here and now, we were talking about our livelihood. I needed not to be a failure. Because next to Julian, who was a major celebrity all over again, what was I, besides a mother? I'd left an amazing career behind and I wasn't about to be ruined by two mean crooks who called themselves hoteliers.

And the injustice of it all. Living out here sometimes

seemed like trying to survive in the Wild West, where just about everything goes. Here, I felt that there were no rules, no laws. So I'd created my own justice system. Yes, I'd acted the fool. I understood that now. But I had my reasons. Which Julian should have supported. But he just shook his head, studying me, and I felt the weight of his judgment. Never had he been this angry at me before. Never had I felt so misunderstood by him.

'What am I going to do with you?' he asked quietly as I sat there, like one of his former students in his principal's office as he gave me an almighty masterpiece of a lesson.

Julian never yelled, never got angry. But he sure had a way of making me feel awful. Unworthy. I wasn't so sure that this was better than being yelled at. I might have respected the yelling more, but this? This was destabilizing and did absolutely nothing for our relationship.

'Why can't you play fair and square?' he insisted.

'Because this isn't a sport, Julian,' I suddenly flung at him. 'This is business, and there are no umpires to put you back in your place and protect the other team's rights.'

'Erica, this has to stop. Your obsession about the lack of guests in the B & B is taking over your life. Didn't you want to be a stay-at-home mom for them?'

A stay-at-home mom, sure, but with an income. I wasn't depending on any man, ever again. Memories flooded back of how Ira had chastised me for my working hours (the only thing that had kept food on our table), of leaving him to take care of the kids rather than bugger off to his lover's place. A place that he'd bought with money stolen from my account, leaving my Tuscan dream in shreds. And all the tears I'd shed, humiliated by his physical repulsion for me. It was a situation I'd barely escaped with my sanity intact.

No. I couldn't go back to living a life that I couldn't control. If our competition was dishonest and bent on ruining us, food coloring in their swimming pool was the least I'd do to get the business up and running again. Because Julian just didn't understand. Adopted at birth by a rich couple, Julian had been born with a silver spoon in his mouth and a natural talent for sports. With his looks and money, he'd never had to fight for anything, be it opportunities or love.

Everything seemed to come so easy to him, while I'd had to fight for everything my whole life – my mother's approval, my job at the hotel and even to keep my first marriage afloat. That alone was a war, where I had to fight a gazillion battles a day, not knowing if I'd even make it to the next without capitulating. And apparently now, even though I thought I finally had it all, I still wasn't done. It hurt to be seen by him as the flailing woman. I used to be successful when he met me. And that was how I want him to continue seeing me. But at the moment, I wasn't successful. If anything, this was a fight to the end. Something Julian needed to understand if we were going to be together.

'This is part of my life, Julian. My new life. I failed the first one. If I fail this time, too…' I bit my lower lip, my eyes burning from unshed tears of frustration.

He pulled me into his arms. 'Shush. You didn't fail anything. You worked miracles. Any other woman would have capitulated ten times over.'

I snorted and blinked hard to stop the tears. 'Who says I didn't capitulate?'

'Stop, now. You can't right the world's wrongs or teach other people honesty.'

'Then what else is left?' I mumbled, and he lifted my chin with his index like he used to long, long ago.

'To live, love and be happy?' he whispered.

To live, love and be happy...' I sniffed, nodding. 'That actually sounds like a nice idea.'

He grinned, back to his calm self. 'It is. You should try it sometime.'

Julian was right. I couldn't continue bearing the weight of the world on my shoulders. Nor could I change people who didn't want to be changed. Maybe it was time to let my hair down and truly, as he said, abide by our motto. Take care of myself more. Not worry so much about looking ten years younger but actually try being ten years happier.

And so I let Paul drag me out for a light afternoon to Fiorella's Bridal Salon, where I must have tried on a gazillion gowns. Many of them I wouldn't be caught dead in. Besides, they were almost all too small.

'We can order your size,' Fiorella assured. 'This is just to see what looks good on you.'

I swallowed back a snort to hide the hurt that was my lifetime companion. Humiliation. Nothing looked good on me. I was still far from my ideal weight. Slimmer than the meringue disaster of my first wedding, granted, but nothing like how I wanted to look. Like Sienna Thornton-Jones. She was slim. Sleek. Effortlessly elegant.

I stared stonily at my reflection, not seeing much of a

difference from my teenage days when Marcy used to drag me to Macy's for Humiliation Week. If I didn't lose weight pronto, I'd call the bloody wedding off myself. It was now officially time to lock the refrigerator and throw away the key.

But who was I kidding? Every time I even looked at a pastry, I put on weight. Was it my fault if Tuscany was teeming with succulent food of every sort? Everywhere I looked, from the bakeries to the street food stalls in the piazza, delicacies of every shape and form ambushed me. Every café was an excuse to get away from everyday life, sit down and try something new.

And then our motto floated back to my mind. Live, love and be happy. Yes. I needed to focus on the good things in my life. Never give up on being a mom and wife. Because spending time with my kids and Julian was like a breath of life. How had I managed to chain myself to my laptop when I had these three miracles by my side?

'Are you happy today, Mommy?' Maddy asked.

I stopped. 'I'm always happy when I'm with you, sweetheart.'

'So you've solved the B & B problem?' Warren wanted to know.

'I've solved the B & B problem,' I lied.

'Good. Because we don't like you cranky and neither does Dad.'

Oh, I'm sorry, I'm sorry, I'm *so* sorry, I wanted to say, but it was enough to pull them both onto my lap, even if Warren was already a strapping young lad of fourteen. A moment of weakness with mom wouldn't hurt him, right? So I smothered them both with repentant kisses while Maddy giggled and Warren yucked and feign-wiped his face. But neither of them moved away. If anything, they hung on and I don't know who clung harder, them or me.

'Can we watch a movie all together?' Maddy asked, happy that things were finally returning to normal and that Mommy wasn't batshit crazy, after all. (Well, maybe just a little.)

'Of course. I'll make some popcorn. What do you want to watch, Maddy?'

Warren rolled his eyes. 'I'm not watching *The* bloody *Mermaid* again.'

'Yes, you are,' I said, giving him my world-famous hairy eyeball.

'Fine,' he huffed, back to his old self. 'But I'm watching *Gladiator* after she goes to bed.'

'Deal,' I said and got up to make the popcorn.

'Don't move,' Julian said to me. 'I'll get the popcorn. You stay put.'

'Don't mind if I do,' I said with a grateful grin, sandwiching myself between the kids, already much happier than I had been in a long time.

# 9

## Wedding Bells

It was mid-June and waiting for the impending NAS inspection any day now was like being on death row. Every day, I whizzed round the property to blitz and blast any specks of dust that had managed to form in the twelve-hour time frame that I'd been away, in my own house, trying to live, love and be happy with my family.

'Life is like a mirror,' Julian always said. 'If you smile into it, it'll smile back.' So I did my damned best to follow that simple formula. And, apparently, sending out positive vibes had produced an effect.

'Hey,' he whispered as he came out of his study and into the kitchen where I was preparing dessert. 'Chin up. I have good news.'

I looked up from my chestnut, chocolate and rosemary *castagnaccio* batter and he grinned.

'I have a huge staying-home window in July – three weeks. Maybe we can avoid postponing the wedding.'

I gasped.

'Really…? You mean get married in July?'

'Let's say mid-July. The earlier the better. It would leave us more time for the honeymoon.'

That would mean marrying this wonderful man, the love of my life, in four weeks? Where do I sign? But, hmm that also meant that Marcy would stay the four weeks until the wedding. But, on the other hand, it would also mean that she wouldn't have to come back in September for what was the original wedding day. Which was a huge bonus in my book. I was already mentally paper-whiting out all those big black Marcy squares from my calendar that had practically blotted out the entire summer and making room for the big pink one. There was a God after all!

'I'd love to! I do have to check with Paul, provided we do a small wedding. Would that be OK with you?'

'Dum, dum, du-dum…' he sang as I launched myself into his arms, getting batter all over his face and in his hair.

'Oops, sorry.'

He grinned his sexy look, the one he only gave to me. 'Time for a celebratory shower?' he whispered, his lips caressing my ear, making my skin tingle.

When I called Paul, he was with Chef Alberto and having, it sounded, the time of his life. Good for him. I explained the situation. 'Can we do it?'

'If we work double time and hire someone with incredibly good taste and organizational skills to help, i.e., not your stepmother, I think so,' he answered.

Good taste? Organized? Easy-peasy. 'I have three someones.'

So I called my zia Maria in Boston to tell her the good news and actually felt her grin across the Atlantic Ocean.

'That's amazing news! I'm so happy for you! But… all three of us in the same building as Marcy? Are you sure, Erica?'

Good question. Was I really going to start World War Three with this ceremony, just when Julian and I had reached a sort of even keel and things seemed to be going better? Now, if you think I'm exaggerating, you need to know that every time Marcy encountered her sisters, there were fireworks. Although, my aunts were the least intrusive, the classiest and most upbeat people in the world. There was no problem they couldn't face. And they were a laugh – a real pleasure to have around, always telling me stories about my real mom. As opposed to Marcy, who hadn't been much help – or for some reason preferred not to be – with her vague memories and I don't knows whenever I happened to ask her a question.

All I personally remember is that my grandmother, Nonna Silvia, had been my rock in the storm during my childhood, followed by my aunts in ranking. And when she died, my three aunts all did their best, leaving us wanting nothing in terms of affection and attention. Homework, advice, making us pretty dresses and good old sturdy support through our (mostly mine) growing pains. Judy, Vince and I adored them shamelessly.

All I had to do was convince them to leave Boston for a bit and be in the same country with Marcy. Which was a tall order.

'Absolutely it's a good idea,' I answered. 'I've got a plan.'

'Oh?' She sounded intrigued.

'I've asked Dad to come down and take Marcy away

until the wedding day. That way, you guys can come over and help Paul and me organize beforehand. The wedding is in four weeks. Can you do it?'

I knew I sounded crazy. No bride would act this quickly unless she was trying to bag her groom before he escaped. Which wasn't all that far from the truth.

'Four weeks?' Zia Maria said. 'We can organize a war in that time, don't you worry.'

'You might have to if Marcy doesn't collaborate and buzz off.'

'She doesn't scare us. Plus, we get to spend some time together. We miss you and your family so much.'

I sighed in relief. Notice how she didn't say you and the kids but also included Julian in the equation. Because they understood he was my family, too, and not just some guy I'd run off to Italy with on a whim, as Marcy claims. But it's fair to say Marcy adores him for all the wrong reasons, while my aunts love him for making me happy.

'We miss you too, Zia Maria.'

'I'll have Monica email you the flight details,' she said, blew me kisses and hung up, most certainly to speed up her own chores in preparation for the big day.

If I knew my aunts, they'd have me covered.


One of the biggest responsibilities of running a farm is taking care of the animals. Our vet visited on a regular basis and assured us we and our farmhands were doing everything right. But when Margo, Julian's favorite mare, was nearing the end of her gestation period, she became listless, until one night she was downright moaning in pain. After the vet had been and gone, we didn't have the heart to leave her all alone in her stall, so Julian and I spent the night with her, rubbing her huge belly. She was sleeping quietly enough, but every once in a while she would huff when the pain got to be too much and her suffering hurt my heart. Julian kept whispering soothing words to her, and I marveled at the fact that animals may not understand every single word you say to them, but they understand your tone and feel every ounce of your love for them. If she could make it through the night, the vet would return at dawn. Only a few more hours to go. If not, we'd have to rouse Marco and some of our neighbors to help.

'Are you OK?' I whispered to Julian in the dark so as not to stir Margo.

'She should be alright,' he whispered back, his voice raw from fatigue. We'd been there all evening with the kids who'd wanted to stay longer, but we'd drawn the line at their bedtime. It was going to be a long night. A night spent amidst doubts and fears of every nature. At dawn the vet arrived as promised, informing us that she would be okay. Julian and I went inside for our morning shower, trying to wash off the sense of helplessness, but I sensed that he was still very worried. The downfalls of not being able to protect everything you love. As a mother, I would know.

When Dad's taxi pulled up a few days later, I cried. He hugged me fiercely, his own eyes moist.

'How are you doing, princess?' he said coolly, but I could read him like an open book.

'Great,' I said and laughed, unable to believe he was standing right before me in the flesh. 'Just great.'

But he could read me too, apparently.

'Not so great if you need the cavalry,' he answered with a wink. 'How is the old battleaxe? Still mad at me?'

I stopped. So *that* was it. They'd had a fight and she'd flown direct here, just to teach him a lesson. I nodded up to the stick figure sitting under the pergola eyeing us.

'What the hell are you doing here? I told you I wanted to be alone!' Marcy squeaked, making to collect her magazines and her Martini pitcher.

'Still downing them like there's no tomorrow, I see,' he whispered under his breath, and I looked up at him. Poor Dad.

'Come down, Marcy,' he urged. 'I've got a surprise just for you.'

'Surprise? What surprise?' Her eyes lit up as she jumped to her feet.

Now we were talking. And apparently, so were they. Finally.

Dad took his cue like a professional actor.

'I'm taking you away, just you and me, to a luxury spa resort on the island of Elba. I missed you, sweetheart...'

To her credit, Marcy wasn't quite sure. It was only when I started oohing and aahing about how lucky she was that she decided she'd won a battle – and he, brownie points.

Julian came down to give my dad a welcome hug and collect his suitcase, and I followed him inside, hoping whatever it was she'd done this time, she'd forgive him. Because that was the way it worked between them. She made the mistakes and he asked for forgiveness. I wondered if Dad was weak or simply a genius of a nature I'd never be able to understand.

'They *sound* OK,' Julian murmured as we climbed the stairs to Marcy's bedroom.

I heaved a sigh. 'For now. He's taking her away for a bit. And when they get back, Marcy will have to be on her best behavior with her sisters. Even she can do it for a short period of time, I hope.'

Julian chuckled. 'What happens when Marcy finds out they were here all the time she was away?'

'She won't, unless you or the kids blab, but I've trained them perfectly.'

'I'm sure you have. But secrets always come to the fore, you know that.'

Did I ever. I shrugged, too happy and relieved to question my luck. 'I like to live on the edge. Speaking of, let's get back downstairs. And, oh! Please disregard any of her comments on me whatsoever.'

Julian grinned, wrapping an arm around me. 'I won't believe a bad word about you,' he promised.

So we now had less than four weeks to prepare a wedding, two of which, if I was lucky, Marcy would be happy and out of my hair.


With my parents gone off on holiday, three days later the taxi bearing my aunts pulled up into our drive and they piled out as we all flew down the steps, Maddy and Warren in the lead. Soon, there was a jumble of arms and legs and kisses everywhere along with many *Mamma mia*, look how you've growns, to which Maddy curtsied and Warren stood ten feet tall, grinning shyly, not yet used to female attention.

'Alright, everybody,' Julian said, taking their suitcases, helped by the newly strengthened Warren. 'Let's get into the shade. You guys must be exhausted from your flight.'

My aunts fussed some more over the kids on the way up and I knew everything (well, almost everything) would be alright. At least the wedding plans would be going smoothly.

In the space of an hour, Paul and Zia Monica were on their PCs under the pergola and Zias Maria and Martina worked their magic on the phones, all around the same table, wheeling deals while Renata worked on the seating plan. There was nothing left for me to do but choose between options presented and feed my mini army some good old Italian goodies, so I rustled up some snacks.

'*Quanto? How* much?' Zia Maria shrieked over the phone at the poor guy from the printing company in Siena, making us all jump.

So much for poise and class.

'*Sei pazzo? No, grazie.* Are you nuts? No thank you!' She slammed the receiver down.

I'd never seen her do that before. Zia Maria was a concentrate of class and cool. She lifted her eyes and grinned.

'That's the first time I've ever heard an invitation costing as much as the dinner itself. *Banditi!* Boy, that felt good.'

Paul suddenly looked up at her, his face bright. 'Honey, you want to come work for me? We'll split the profits fifty-fifty!' he offered, and Zia Maria blushed.

'No, thank you. I have Le Tre Donne to get back to.'

'And two sisters to boss around.' Zia Monica mumbled through the pen in her teeth as she surfed the net. 'You'd think she owns the restaurant all by herself.' She looked up at me. 'Are you sure you want calla lilies and not white roses, honey? Callas are expensive.'

'Absolutely. I already did the white roses on my...' I stopped, remembering that farce of my first marriage. Everything, from the dress to the cake to the meal, had been an absolute disaster and Marcy had only made it worse, as usual. But that was another story.

To fuel my miracle workers, I brought out another tray of food: *focaccia*, with tiny ham *involtini* parcels, sesame breadsticks, *torta Cecina, which is a kind of savory pancake made with chickpea flour. And don't forget the* eggplant, mint and pine nut pockets, all washed down with lemon-mint iced tea. They jumped onto the tray like schoolkids at a picnic outing.

Without Marcy we were all serene and relaxed. Julian was out in the fields while Warren and Maddy were with Renata's kids in the back garden. And it was pure heaven, like I'd always dreamed. I had my favorite people under my roof and in three weeks, Julian and I were finally getting married. I closed my eyes and breathed a contented sigh. Live, love and be happy. The rest we'd simply have to figure out as we went.

'Good, huh?' Paul sighed after a moment as we all savored the food mixed with the fragrant summer air.

'Fantastic,' Renata agreed, closing her eyes and letting the breeze caress her skin.

'Peaceful,' Zia Maria added, and we all giggled, knowing she didn't need to explain why.

We polished off our food and sat there, all content in

a typical tranquil Tuscan summer afternoon. Oh, if only Marcy had been different. She could have been a part of this all, I thought, wishing Emanuela, my real mom, had lived to see us grow up. She'd have loved the kids. And they'd have adored and looked up to her.

'I just don't understand why she won't talk to me about my own mom,' I said, following my own train of thought, and they all turned to me.

'Oh, sweetie, forget about Marcy,' Zia Martina said, her hand on my shoulder. 'You know she's Miss Drama Queen. And all your dad has to do is take her on vacation and he's forgiven.'

'What exactly did he do?' I asked.

'That's the thing. The poor guy did nothing wrong.'

'Except marry Marcy.' Zia Monica giggled. 'Ah, my heart goes out to him.'

'She's always been jealous of our friendship,' Zia Maria explained. 'Even when we were young. And of course the guys we dated were all, according to her, *morti di fame*, dirt-poor losers.'

Renata and Paul giggled. I couldn't help myself and grinned. It was typical of Marcy, bringing someone else down when she felt she was nowhere near their level.

'She's always accused us of having an affair, all together, of course, with your poor father! Can you imagine that? And he puts up with her!'

It wasn't the first time I'd heard it, so it didn't bother me in the slightest. Dad was a lamb.

'But why did she hate my real mom so much? Why won't she tell me anything about her? What's she hiding?'

'Absolutely nothing,' Zia Martina chimed. 'She's always been odd. And they never got along, you know that. We told you everything there is to know, *cara*, dear.'

I huffed. 'I wish I knew more about the family's past. I wish… I wish Nonna hadn't left Tuscany in the first place.'

'You know,' Zia Martina said as if she'd had a brainstorm, 'we were thinking about riding out to San Gimignano to see if we can find our old home.'

I felt my eyes pop open. 'The *casolare*? Nonna's *agriturismo* that she sold to make the money to go to America?'

Zia Monica grinned. 'Think you can tear yourself away from wedding planning for a couple of hours?'

Zia Maria nodded excitedly. 'I'm sure I can find it. It has an amazing view of the town.'

'Wow, that's so exciting. Go, go, go!' Renata said. 'Paul and I'll hold the fort.'

'Are you sure?' I asked. 'We're expecting a few follow-up calls.'

Renata and Paul both shot me a look.

'Go already, before we change our minds,' Renata said, shooing us away.

So the five of us climbed into my blue Fiat 500L and I punched San Gimignano into the satnav with Zia Maria, who was the eldest and thus remembered best, sitting up front with me. We took off, over auburn hill and luscious green dale, past majestic cypress trees that seemed to guard the landscape since the beginning of time, me in search of my origins and my aunts in search of their past.

I could almost see my nonna Silvia come alive from the faded sepia pictures with her long hair pinned up as was the fashion, rocking it in a stylish dress with a red-lipsticked half-grin, half-scorn as she defied the camera to judge her. Silvia had never cared what others thought of her. And that was what had made her the coolest grandmother in the world.

'Are we there yet?' Zia Monica wanted to know after twenty minutes.

We were so high up that puffy white clouds wafted past us and in the distance I could see several towns dotting the green land, an intricacy of white and terracotta knotted in small bundles scattered here and there haphazardly. Here in Tuscany, although every corner was unique, it was easy to get lost in the fairy-tale landscape of the cypress trees and hills that abounded, so much that you could get lost, thinking you were in one place rather than the other.

'Just a few more minutes. It's on a hill covered with cypress trees,' Zia Maria said.

'Hello? Have you looked around you? Every hill is covered with cypress trees,' Zia Monica pointed out. 'How are you going to find it?'

Zia Maria smiled smugly. 'I have my landmarks. Go down this hill into the village and come out the other side, Erica.'

Following Zia Maria's directions past the town, then up again over a hill that seemed never-ending, Zia Martina, the second eldest, chipped in with a 'Yes, yes, down this road. I remember now. Look, that's it! That's Tenuta Bettarini, our old farm!'

I instinctively braked and we stared at the property nestled at the top of the highest hill overlooking an immense reddish-brown valley, dappled with several minor and greener hillocks. It jumped out at us, like straight out of a fairy tale. A thick white mist swept around the base of the Bettarinis' hill like a cat's furry tail.

And I stared in stunned silence. It was impossible. It couldn't be. We might have come a different way, but my satnav confirmed it. I stared at the computer screen and then out beyond the windshield to the B & B that had tried to shut us down. The bloody Cascianis. What the…?

And to think that I'd always promised myself that if I ever set foot on my grandmother's land, I'd run rings around the place, embrace the high stone walls and cry, 'I'm home! I'm home! I'm finally home!'

But nothing could be further from the truth. Because the reality was that Nonna's farmhouse, the place I'd dreamed of all my life, was now the bane of my life.

'Erica? You OK?' Zia Maria asked.

'That…' I stammered. 'T-that's Tasting friggin' Tuscany…'

'What, you mean your rival company?' Zia Monica gasped. 'The ones who tried to shut you down? Erica…?'

I pulled myself together. 'The very ones.'

I'd kept my promise to Julian that I wouldn't interfere with the snail-like course of justice anymore, but family history and fate had brought me here once again. What was I to do? Wasn't this a sign or what?

'Let's go down,' I croaked, shifting into neutral and rolling down the hill. This was unreal. How could my family's ancestral home be the very B & B that was trying to ruin us? And yet there it was. Dazed, we all stared in stunned silence.

'It's changed so much. Now, it looks like… *your* place,' Zia Monica said, and I nodded, still slack-jawed as I drove through the open gates and parked.

As we walked round the property walls, Zia Maria craned her neck and softly exclaimed, 'Look – the courtyard!' and 'Look – the tobacco tower! It looks completely different.'

'Are you sure this is Nonna's farmhouse? Most *casali* look very similar...' I asked hopefully.

'Sweetheart, we grew up here. And look! See?'

We followed her hand as she pointed to a vaulted archway, so similar to ours, only this one was inscribed with the lettering: Bettarini, 1789.

'Oh my God,' Zia Martina cried. 'Yes, I remember!'

And then I thought about my nonna and whether or not her spirit had wafted back here, to the place she loved so much but had been compelled to leave for her family's well-being, just as I'd left Boston for my children. Was she, in effect, still here? If I closed my eyes, I could almost see her, walking around on the dusty gravel in her pretty dress, her hem just the right length, her heels just the right height, her hair long and wavy as had been the style.

I wondered if she still lingered. Also, if I could cheekily ask her for a little intervention-cum- upgrade of her ghostly presence on the premises. You know, a few screams in the night, objects being thrown around in broad daylight and some rattling of chains...

'No, it can't be!' Zia Maria cried and took off like a shot.

In unison, we followed her round the back, where she halted with a skid, just like a little girl, right before an enormous oak tree.

'What? What is it?' Monica wheezed as we caught up.

But Maria paid no attention, running round the tree, caressing it, her eyes narrowed until she shouted, 'Look! Oh my God, look!'

We scanned the tree trunk. It had a heart circling two letters: M and G.

'Who's that?' I asked, and Zia Maria blushed.

'Maria… and Giovanni.'

My eyes popped out of my head. 'You had a Giovanni?'

She blushed an even deeper red as Martina and Monica nodded in unison.

'He was gorgeous,' Martina swooned.

My aunt had a secret love? Who knew? 'What happened to him?'

She sighed and shook her head. 'He moved to Argentina with his parents when I was a girl. I still miss him…'

'Oh, Zia Maria,' I moaned in sympathy. God knew I'd had my share of unhappy loves, but to think of my aunts as women who had loved and lost like me… that made me feel even closer to them.

Monica turned. 'Wait – there must be Martina's around here somewhere.'

Zia Martina shrugged. '*I* can't even remember the boy's name. We were so young when we moved to the States.'

'And I was the baby.' Zia Monica sighed. 'No Italian love for me. Oh, well…'

'What *are* you talking about – you've still got Father Frank lusting after you, haven't you?' I said, but Martina's face told me the subject was taboo, so I dropped it like a hot potato.

'Oh my God! Look at this,' Zia Maria cried, her fingers touching an incision in the tree. 'This is new – it's still green!'

We all moved in closer for a better look: E+E=E circled by a heart. I looked up at them blankly.

'Emanuela plus Edoardo... equals Erica,' Maria sighed, swiping at both eyes. 'He said he was going to come here and do that one day.'

'And now he's done it,' Zia Monica whispered. 'The poor man. He'll never get over losing your mother, Erica.'

I stared at the simple mathematical equation that was meant to be my family. It was too beautiful to be true. The testimony of my dad's love for both my mother and me. All this time Dad had held a candle for my real mom. And harbored a special place in his heart for me. All this time and for years I hadn't known. And somewhere deep inside me rose a wave of sympathy for Marcy for never having the chance of being first in his heart.

You couldn't beat the sweet memory of your first love. My mom and Marcy had been practically identical on the outside – I'd seen it in the pictures Nonna Silvia had left me. But on the inside, they were worlds apart. And this hatred Marcy had felt for her twin that was my mom had somehow transferred onto me, like a cheap decal that you scrub and scrub but simply won't come off, as if I'd personally done something wrong to her.

'Why?' *Why, oh why couldn't she just forget the past and love me as her own?*

'Because she'll never forgive your mother for having you,' Zia Maria explained simply. 'You were what got in her way. And then she had to raise you as her own if she was going to have any chance of him marrying her. You were her only shot.'

'And her only burden,' I whispered. 'Do I really remind you of her – my mom?'

Zia Maria chuckled. 'Oh, yes – tremendously! You have the same eyes and the same stubborn streak. Your mother was the most similar to Nonna Silvia. They'd die rather than admit they were hurting. Rather fail than ask for help. Remind you of anyone?'

'Yeah,' I sighed. 'It sure does.'

'I wouldn't worry about Marcy too much. She's always been a bit unstable,' Maria said softly.

But deep down, I knew there was more to it. Something bothering her tremendously. Something no one else knew.

# 10

## Madonna Mia

The next morning, I got a call from Renata to tell me she was on her way over. Funny, considering she almost never called – and because she was a three-minute drive away.

Only this time she made it in two minutes flat.

'Hey, what's up?' I said as I opened the door to her grave face, and my stomach fell. This was not going to be good – I could already tell.

'Well… remember when you were wondering about Tasting Tuscany's next miracle?'

'Ye-es…?'

'They've done it.'

'Done what?'

'Their next miracle.'

'What did they do? Lower their rates even more? Hire dancing naked ladies? Hot virgins?'

Renata shook her head. 'Only one virgin. Seen, or rather, filmed, wandering listlessly around the grounds, blue veil and all.'

'*What?*'

'There's been,' she snorted, 'an apparition of Mother Mary. She appears to be attracting people in droves.'

'For the love of God! Ooh, what they wouldn't do for an extra euro.'

'And what's worse?' Renata dared, cringing.

I grunted. 'Just spill it out.'

'They're even selling T-shirts and videos of the apparition.'

'Talk about milking it.'

'I'm so sorry, Erica.'

'Yeah, thanks.'

I had to see this for myself. Our rivals had accomplished the miracle of miracles, and people believed it. Because of what I'd done, not only were they getting more guests, but even the attached bar was also teeming with patrons. You could almost hear the *ka-ching* of coins dropping into their laps and euro notes flittering down copiously upon them straight from – to the point – the heavens.

So I checked YouTube and stared at the footage on the screen. There she was, the Virgin Mary, wandering listlessly, just like Renata had said, down the road leading to the entrance. She looked pensive, sad. She looked... *familiar*.

'Holy shit!' I shrieked, flying out of my seat and falling back down with a thud, too shocked to breathe. There it was – the key to the mystery of Mother Mary's apparition.

With her hands laced over her trim waist, she was not, in fact, Mother Mary but Mother *Marcy*. In one of her silk scarves – a blue one. She must have convinced Giacomo to drive her all the way down there for her own bout of reminiscing. There was no other explanation.

And now that everyone had taken her for the Virgin

Mary (I know, you gotta laugh), she'd inadvertently (one hopes) given the competition something they could use as leverage to increment their business exponentially. Or, better yet, miraculously. I couldn't believe our rivals' luck. Just a couple of coincidences had led people to believe the place had been graced by the presence of the Madonna.

While I respected every religion, I just wished that those worshippers hadn't instantly dropped to the ground as if they'd been shot in the knees without even suspecting that it wasn't the real deal. But then I suppose that's what they mean by blind faith.

Only this religious fervor, which was based on a false apparition, was ruining my family's business. But I had a plan. After the miraculous apparition-cum-miracle play, they were in for a mystery play.

'Dammit, Erica, when you asked me to dress up like Madonna, I actually had something else in mind!' Paul hissed as we descended from my Fiat 500L onto the dusty, deserted road just about one hundred meters from the turn-off to Tasting Tuscany. By now, I knew my way around blindfolded.

At this ungodly hour, when everyone else was having their siesta to stay out of the sweltering heat, we were the only ones around. Julian would have said 'Only mad dogs and Englishmen,' while I'd have said, 'Only provoked kick-ass businesswomen determined to get their lives back.' And determined I was, to give the security cameras – and the Cascianis – the show of their lives. Because so far, my marketing strategies had managed to only bring a few guests in. If I could have a full occupancy for the summer, it would have paid for part of the wedding. Not that it was anything fancy. Just a small ceremony with our closest and dearest, a priest, a few flowers and a great dinner. But after this little foray, I knew I had to get back to proper strategizing.

'Oh, come on, Paulie. You always wanted to dress in drag. So what are you complaining about? Here's your chance. Now put these on and listen to me. All you have to do is lope down the hill with your hands joined as if you were praying. Clear?'

Then, at home, all I'd have to do is add a dissolve effect on him as if he'd vanished into thin air.

Paul mumbled something that sounded like 'blasphemous bitch', but I was on a mission.

'Are we clear?' I insisted.

'Yes!' he hissed back, snatching the virginal clothes from me as I filmed him while he pulled them on. Which was, if you'll pardon the pun, the whole *crux* of the matter.

I paused my camera. 'Now say your lines,' I urged, and he obediently delivered them in an authentic Tuscan accent.

'And cut!' I said, beaming. 'You should be in pictures.'

'Yeah. If I get into trouble, you're paying bail,' he muttered.

'The original image is fuzzy and this will be a match. No one's going to recognize you,' I assured. 'But the whole region is going to find out what scammers Tasting Tuscany are.'

'Are you sure you know what you're doing?' Paul asked. 'Why won't you just let go of it – let bygones be bygones and all that kind of stuff and concentrate on your wedding instead?'

'Because this is just as important to me.'

'Well, that's a mouthful. If I had a guy like Julian who

wanted to marry me, I wouldn't worry about anything else.'

I huffed. Why did my Paulie, my very BFF, not understand? 'If I let go, the Cascianis, or anyone else around here, will think they can treat our family like that and just get away with it. This will teach them a lesson once and for all.'

'I think you're tempting fate. I hope you're right and that it all doesn't come back to you as bad karma.'

On the evening in honor of Mother Marcy's appearance, the original video featuring Marcy was scheduled to play on mega-screen at our rival B & B. Believe it or not, even the local press was there. So I had Giacomo's cousin switch tapes at the last minute and stick around to watch people's faces while I watched it from home on the news.

Knowing what was coming, I felt a pang of guilt, but then I squared my shoulders. The Cascianis had been the ones to come here under the pretense of being paying guests while instead spying on our business. They'd taken pictures of every nook and cranny, copied every said nook and cranny in their own farmhouse, copied our logo, copied our name and planted a rat on our property, to boot. They'd even taken pictures of the rat and pretended to be the Health and Safety board threatening to close us down if we didn't surrender spontaneously. I was only fighting back.

As we watched the footage, me from home and all the faithfuls from the Casciani grounds, the screen lit up and someone whom only I knew was Paul yanked on a blue frock and a veil, grumbling, in perfect Italian: 'With all the money Tasting Tuscany is making out of this scam, if they want their third video, they'll have to cough up at least double the price!'

There. A taste of their own medicine. Served them right for messing with me.

The result of my bit of film editing was, as you can imagine, *biblical*. Camera crews, newspapers and anyone with a digital camera gathered at the entrance as the frontliners pounded at the doors that the Cascianis had run behind and bolt-locked.

The management wasn't making any comments and only the guests – very few, at this point – were allowed to come and go by displaying a special pass. Even the local *Carabinieri*, who carry out domestic policing duties, and the financial police, the *Guardia di Finanza*, and my NAS buddies from Health and Safety were involved as the angry Catholics wanted their pound of flesh from the Cascianis, who had dared mock their faith.

Just so we're clear. I am a Catholic. And although my first husband, Ira, is Jewish, I'd managed to have the kids christened at one point. And in the worst moments of my life I've found myself praying and it's helped me no end. This had nothing to do with mocking religion. If anything, this was a defense of what was most precious to me. This was, in the style of Vito Corleone in *The Godfather, strictly business. And in the style of Erica Cantelli, They want to mess with me? I will mess with them.*

'You son of a gun,' Paul breathed, slack-jawed as we continued to watch. 'You did it again, Erica.'

Yep, I sure had. Now, the Cascianis would be a bit too busy recuperating their own reputation to continue messing with ours. Now, we were even. Good thing Julian was away until tomorrow. I knew he'd eventually find out and then there'd be, if you'll pardon the pun, *hell* to pay.

But please don't get the wrong idea. Julian and I always told each other everything. But this time, I thought he wouldn't understand just how important it was for me to defend and hold my own. He'd never been in a situation where he was financially in danger. So I'd had to do my bit.

As expected, the Cascianis claimed they'd had no part in it (except for milking the 'miracle', I thought with a snort) and that, to demonstrate their good *faith* and that they had nothing to do with the hoax, they'd host religious gatherings at a 50 per cent discount. But my experience told me that they'd ruined their reputation and that from now on, they'd have to tread very carefully. Mission accomplished. They'd think twice before financially ruining a family who had done nothing wrong but try to earn their bread honestly by offering wholesome family vacations.

The next morning, without any fuss at all, Margo delivered a beautiful chestnut foal which Julian, upon Maddy's suggestion, named Gracie.

She was smaller than expected, but the vet said she would be just fine. Julian and the kids spent the entire morning in Margo's stall fussing over the pair while I returned to my laptop and continued my research. Things were finally on the up and up again!

Having been a kick-ass hotel manager half my life, I refused to be stumped by my own B & B. I had done everything according to the book (heck, I had written that book!). My communication with our guests before, during and after their stay was spot on. The interior design was superb by the highest standards, as were the mattresses and bedding. We were friendly and available round the clock without being intrusive.

We provided treats and essentials like boutique-brand toiletries. We supplied a bottle of our own (amazing) wine with every booking. We provided free picnic hampers. Huge breakfasts. Blended mixes of coffee.

As far as the heart of the trade was concerned – reviews – our website was packed with them, and they were all five-star. Just like those VIP hotels. And that's when something inside me clicked and the cogs in my mind started spinning. That was it– a new version of A Taste of Tuscany that would distance us miles from our rivals. A deluxe version.

I sent Julian a text.

'Honey, get your little black book out.'

To which he immediately answered. 'I threw that away when I met you, love.'

'Aww, that's so sweet. But I've got an idea that'll put us back on the map with a vengeance.'

Two seconds later he videocalled me. It was early morning and his hair was a mess, but he still looked divine.

'Julian,' I breathed like a love-sick teenager. Who, incidentally, had plans to run the most successful, former B & B. Which would become a boutique hotel. And the best in the entire region. Possibly by noon, or sooner, depending on the recipient's internet signal.

'Hi, love! What's cooking in that beautiful head of yours?'

'Hi honey! Can you do me a favor? I need you to text your jet-set buddies this message: *Exclusive Tuscan farmhouse lettings only for the filthy rich who want total privacy*. We'll be totally elitist and affluent. No more families with six kids swinging from the chandeliers and crawling up the walls. Just your rich friends who can spread the word to even richer friends.' Our rivals would be eating our dust.

'I like it!' Julian agreed.

'Tell them we are open for bookings starting from today.'

'Will do, sweetheart! What a great idea!'

'Thank you! And oh! Tell them, BYOH.'

'BYOH?'

'Bring your own housekeeper. For free. The filthy rich are just looking to spend their money in ways that show just how rich they are, but they never want to spend a dime on their staff.'

Julian laughed. 'I know, what's with that! Erica, honey, this is going to work big time!'

'Of course it'll work. From now on, we'll be all about exclusivity. As Basil Fawlty from Fawlty Towers put it, "No riff-raff."'

'I am so proud of you, Erica.'

'Oh! I totally forgot to tell you,' I blurted. 'Tasting Tuscany? I went there!'

'What, again? Oh, honey, you promised.'

I shook my head. 'No, you don't understand. My aunts and I were looking for Nonna Silvia's farmhouse.'

'Ri-ight…?' he said cautiously.

He knew me well by now, I had to give him that.

'Well, we were driving along because obviously, Zia Maria, being the eldest, remembers how to get there and bam – it was the same bloody place!'

Julian's eyes widened. 'Tasting Tuscany is the old Bettarini Farm?'

'Yes! I mean, what are the odds, right?'

'And knowing you, this actually means something, right?' he ventured.

I shrugged. 'It has to.'

He snorted. 'Of course.'

I ignored his sarcasm. 'Although I haven't got a clue what it means.'

'Maybe it means nothing, Erica, and it's just a coincidence.'

'A coincidence? You know I don't believe in those, Julian.'

He cocked his head. 'You sound like a cop.'

'In this day and age, I've had to become one,' I defended myself, but Julian kept watching me, shaking his head, knowing there was more but afraid to find out exactly what. 'And you know what the climax of the afternoon was?'

'You bumped into the Cascianis and kicked them all the way down the hill?'

I wish. Although they should be just about going nuts.

'No, of course not, silly. We found something my dad has recently carved into a tree trunk. E+E=E. Edoardo plus Emanuela equals Erica.'

Julian grinned at me. 'Romantic and nostalgic.'

'I know!'

His face softened at my joy. 'You should never doubt how important you are to your father, sweetheart.'

'I know he loves me, but I never knew just how deeply, you see? Anyway, we had a look round for old times' sake…' And then I'd hatched my plan.

'You had a look around and…?' he prompted, fearing the worst.

How well he knew me.

'And that's it.'

He visibly relaxed. 'Good girl. I'm proud of you. So from now on, no more stunts, right?'

'No more stunts from now on. I promise you, Julian.' Meaning, what I'd done was done, and no one really needed to know except for Paulie and me.

'I trust you, sweetheart,' he whispered.

And that was that. I really meant it. From now on, no more stunts. It would be just like before: me and my incredible business acumen.

My super brainstorm saw results in the time it took for Julian to send his blanket text to his jet-setter friends dying to spend their money on the best that life could offer them. I had asked him to omit the names of the other recipients for privacy.

Operation Boutique Hotel had an immediate effect, as within ten minutes, booking requests started pouring in like a sudden rainstorm. Eva Santos, the famous tennis champion. Eric Bradley, the Hollywood action movie star. Amina Woodruff, the famous novelist. And at least five of Julian's former team mates, all requesting a minimum stay of three weeks each. I dashed to my laptop, answered the requests with a warm welcome letter containing a link to the website and pulled up the calendar to do a dummy run with the dates. We were now a few confirmation texts (and deposits, thank you very much) from being fully booked all summer and well into October. Thanks to one simple but brilliant idea, and Julian's contacts, we were already back in the black! Erica Cantelli, ass-kicker extraordinaire, welcome back!

# 11

## Biblical Vengeance

The next day, Fiorella of Fiorella's Bridal Salon greeted us at her door and my aunts started talking to her in Italian, to which she almost freaked with joy, telling them how beautiful I was (did I tell you I loved her?) and how the dress I'd chosen suited me and they should wait and see.

They fell into an instant understanding and I could hear them chatting on endlessly while I changed into my stunningly beautiful wedding dress. It was even more enchanting than I remembered. I piled my hair on top of my head and tiptoed out, exhibiting myself in a slow twirl.

'Well?' I asked. 'What do you think?'

Three sets of jaws dropped as Paul grinned.

'*Mamma mia, sei bellissima!*' Zia Maria cried, coming to hug me while Zia Martina and Zia Monica oohed and aahed about it to Fiorella.

She shook her blonde bob enthusiastically, going into a fit of tight dialect even I could barely understand. (Maybe that one half workout at the gym had begun its magic.

Maybe by simply surrounding myself with skinny people, by osmosis I, too, would become skinny. Fat chance.)

Paul lifted my hair further, showing them how he envisioned it, and they all launched into a festival of '*Sì, sì, bellissimo! Perfetto!*'

'You look amazing,' Paul beamed, his eyes glistening. 'You're going to be a gorgeous bride.'

I felt my own eyeballs water. My Paulie, my lifeline, who has seen me through everything after all these years. This was just as much his victory as mine. 'Looks like we made it,' I whispered, trying not to blubber. This was a good thing – no crying from now on, but just happiness and love.

If you're a karma-type of person and haven't been on my side all this way, you might think I deserved what happened thereafter for getting my own back with the Cascianis (when really I was just defending what was mine). You might think, if you're so inclined, that it was God's wrath that descended upon us. I still can't make any sense of it.

It was the end of June, i.e. two weeks to target and the hottest summer yet, with scirocco winds arriving all the way from the Sahara Desert, bringing the typical yellow sand that stuck to your face and neck and any other parts exposed. And somehow getting stuck into the parts that weren't. The skies were yellow and even the streets were coated in sand, cars overworking their windshield wipers just to get rid of the stuff. If this kept up we'd have a very yellow wedding.

Martino looked up at the sky and pointed south.

'Bad,' he said in his broken English, shaking his head.

'It's too hot for the crops, isn't it?' I asked.

'*Sì.*'

But there was nothing we could do, save pray for the reprieve of some rain. Not enough to spoil the tourist season, but just enough to cool the earth even slightly. Normally, we'd have received a few light showers, nothing major, in view of a healthy harvest in September. I remember reading that entire crops had gone to waste for excessive heat.

Later that evening, as we sat down on the patio to an early dinner, my eyes went to the horizon where clouds were gathering.

'Look.' I pointed past Julian. 'There's a storm coming. Seems our prayers have been answered.'

Julian turned and frowned as a low rumble filled the air. He rose to his feet, reaching for Maddy on his left.

'That's not a storm!'

'*Al riparo!*' Run for cover, shouted a voice from below. It was Martino, our vineyards foreman, racing up the stone staircase.

'Inside, now!' Julian yelled as my aunts jumped to their feet, pulling me and the children along.

Julian pushed us inside and followed us before he and Martino drew the heavy chestnut doors closed over the sliding glass doors, sliding the bolt into place. Whatever it was, it was swarm-like – huge bugs, loud and determined to get into the house.

'The windows!' I cried. 'Everyone, help me close all the windows!'

My aunts and the children raced ahead of me as Julian grabbed my large wooden kneading board and shoved it up against the fireplace opening, securing it with the couch.

'What are they?' I cried.

'Locusts!' Martino answered. 'They eat anything that will stay down long enough!'

Locusts? They were going to ruin everything! Our crops! The landscaping! It would all be ruined, from the lawns to the orchards and even the pool area! I would have to cancel my guests!

'The horses!' Julian cried, but Martino grabbed him.

'*Troppo tardi,*' he sentenced. 'Too late.'

'I can't leave them – they'll be terrified!' Julian yelled in dismay, and my heart went out to him. He'd built a strong bond with those lovely creatures.

'Terrified, yes. But also safe. They're all inside. I'd already closed them in for the night.'

We all fell silent and listened to the deafening sound against the windows and shutters as the locusts tried to get in, beating themselves against the shutters. Never had I experienced anything so horrifying in my whole life, bar Ira wielding a baseball bat over my head.

In my arms, Maddy trembled. 'Are we going to die, Mommy?'

I looked down into her green eyes, wide with fear, and I hugged her, ruffling her hair as I smothered my own fear and desperation. 'Oh, no, sweetheart – of course not! It's like... the rain. Tomorrow, it'll be sunny again, you'll see.'

Julian, who was by the window, fists rolled up in anger, turned to us, his eyes softening.

'Come here, sweetie.'

He beckoned and Maddy left my lap to go sit on his. When she nestled up against him, he stroked her head.

'Listen to me, Maddy,' he whispered, and she looked up

at him solemnly. 'It's only nature playing a little joke on us. The... uhm, storm is loud but really, it's nothing. You mustn't be afraid. This is a solid house. You'll always be safe here. OK?'

She nodded and wrapped her arms around him.

'What about the crops?' Warren asked, and Julian shook his head.

'The harvest is going to be ruined,' Martino said. 'The grapes, the olives, the fruit – everything.'

'Are we poor now?' Warren asked.

'Of course not, lad,' Julian answered, but in his eyes I could see dismay.

The amount of damage and recoup work were already incalculable, even without considering the loss of the guests' income. This was an absolute disaster!

My cellphone started ringing on the counter. It was Renata.

'Are you guys OK?' I heard her shout over the loud rumble.

'Just made it inside,' I answered. 'Does this happen often?'

I knew about flooding, strong winds, droughts, but all the months I'd spent on researching Tuscany, nothing had ever mentioned this kind of phenomena.

'I've never seen anything like it before,' she answered. 'I'm afraid to see the damage tomorrow morning. Marco's practically in tears.'

'Yes, Julian, too,' I whispered for Maddy's benefit. 'He's worried about the horses, especially his foal, Gracie.'

'They're safe, Erica,' Renata reassured. 'The stalls are sturdy.'

'You're not scared?' I asked under my breath.

'Nah, it'll be OK. Just stay shut up for the night and you'll be fine.'

'OK,' I said. 'Thanks, Renata. Call me if you need anything.'

'You too, sweetie. Stay safe.' She hung up.

Paulie. I had to call Paulie.

'Hey! Where are you?' I yelled down the phone.

'I'm at a friend's house. I was just about to call you. Everything OK?'

'We're coping. Stay put and don't go out until morning. Can your friend put you up for the night?'

A silence, then an amused, 'I think so.'

'Paulie, you little devil!'

'Might as well make the most of it, right?'

'I want every little filthy detail when you get back,' I said and hung up, turning to my housekeeper. 'Rosina, please prepare rooms for yourself and Martino – you're not going anywhere in this mess.'

Rosina nodded and shuffled off.

Having left our dinner on the patio table on the terrace, we all now sat down at the table in the kitchen, where I hauled stuff from the refrigerator and pantry and my aunts busied themselves slicing crusty bread, *parmigiano* (Parmesan) and pecorino cheeses, and prosciutto and *finocchiona*, my favorite type of fennel salami. I fished inside the refrigerator and brought out my *panzanella* dish and rice salad. And why the hell not? A huge tiramisu I'd been saving for the weekend. This was, in one way or another, the end of something, so we might as well face it on a full stomach.

As we sat and munched away without any appetite,

Martino and Julian giving each other slight shakes of the head and sighs, my aunts and I did our best to cheer up the kids and Rosina, who knew that tomorrow there would be one hell of a clean-up to face.

But that was not the only thing that had been destroyed in the blink of an eye. My bookings would now have to be canceled and totally refunded, because thanks to the hunger and devastation of the locusts, our property, Colle d'Oro, looked like the surface of the friggin' moon.

As we chatted away, a loud bang shook the kitchen, and the board covering the opening in my pizza oven shook as Maddy screamed.

Julian jumped to his feet and with Martino's help, pushed it back into place.

'It's OK, sweetie,' I assured her as she climbed up my lap like when she was younger. 'It's just the wind. Tomorrow, it'll be over.'

'You promise?' she squeaked.

'I more than promise. I cross my heart. Now, let's finish our dessert, OK, sweetheart?'

Zia Maria looked at all of us around the table and topped everyone's glass up with wine. We drank in silence, fortified by the warmth it gave, and by the strength that can only come in numbers.

'Don't worry, Julian,' I said when we were alone for a brief moment. 'Everything will be OK.' If he was down, it was up to me to put aside my fears and doubts and pull him up, no matter what was going on in my mind. The devastation, my fear, my sorrow had to wait.

He exhaled deeply, as if he'd been holding his breath all evening. 'I know, love,' he said, patting my hip. 'It's just that... little Gracie – there's no way I can even get to her. I hope they're all OK.'

'I'm sure they are. The stables are secured. Everything will be fine, you'll see. Tomorrow morning we'll get up early and check the situation. There's nothing we can do now and worrying yourself sick won't help.'

I was right in theory, but images of the damages hurt my heart. Julian had put his whole life into the property.

'The crops – the vineyard was so promising...' he continued, and I held his shoulder.

'Julian, it's not the end of the world. Most people will fare much worse than us. Look at Renata and Marco. At least we have assets to fall back on.'

He exhaled again. 'You're right. I should stop being so despondent.'

I studied him. Had he suddenly tired of being strong and depending on nature for his livelihood? After all, he'd never been a country boy. Was he tired of what I'd called The Good Life?

'It'll be OK,' he agreed finally, and I realized I'd been holding my breath. 'Let's be upbeat about it. Actually, tomorrow I'll go see if Marco needs a hand.'

'Good man.'

But all the same I wondered if, besides an unexpected swarm of insects feeding on our crops, there was something else – something he didn't feel comfortable telling me.

After an almost sleepless night, the next morning the farmhands came in extra early to assess the damage. Julian had run out across the derelict, once verdant fields to the stables just before dawn and was relieved to see the horses were perfectly fine, if a little rattled. He nestled on the floor and let Gracie, the newborn, nuzzle his head while he wrapped his arms around her midsection, talking to her softly. For a moment, just a fleeting moment, I got a view of the tender boy he must have been.

Luckily, Marco's crops weren't that affected. Ours had taken a bigger hit, having been practically decimated. We surveyed the lands by jeep, taking the time to check everything and take stock. Almost everywhere we looked, the crops had been razed to the ground as if an invisible acid had dissolved everything in its wake. How were we going fix this? The crops were not only ruined, but they'd also… disappeared almost completely.

And so had Julian's serenity. I could see it in his slower gait, in the clenching of his jaws. Read it in his eyes and on the contours of his lean face. It was going to take a lot of work to replant everything.

In the last few decades all over the globe, nature had gone completely berserk; almond trees blossoming in December, hailstorms in July. But this could have happened anywhere in the world. It wasn't Tuscany's fault. So why did I feel I'd personally broken Julian's heart?

And then it dawned on me. For him especially, our Tuscan dream was not only a burden, but it was also slowly turning into a nightmare. A nightmare that he was silently enduring for my sake. But what could I do? We were in this together, right? In sickness and in health.

But – and here's the catch – we weren't married just yet. If he was unhappy with me, he could still back out. I knew he wouldn't, probably out of sheer decency, and I knew that he loved me. But he'd have to be a fool not to think long and hard before he committed to this life completely, right?

This morning, it was all hands on deck. Paul, who got in later, my aunts, our farmworkers and even Marco's family and staff, all clearing away the damaged crops, first on our land and then on Marco's. It was a time that had brought us all even closer, if possible, our families lunching and dining together practically every day for a week. It was the adversities that brought people together. But every day of it, Julian got gloomier and gloomier.

Luckily, Maddy and Warren shared the same kind of affinity with Renata's kids and spent these hot summer days absorbed in their friendships, safely biking on the paths between the two properties when they all got bored with one or other house. I was so lucky to have Renata as a friend. I was surrounded by people I loved. Maybe Julian would realize how lucky we were, after all. Things just had to turn out fine.

A few days later, as we sat down, just the two of us, to a lunch of veal and grilled vegetables, Julian put his hands together and sighed. He bore the traces of the hard times in the new lines around his eyes.

I reached out and took his hand. 'What is it, honey?' Was he as despondent as I was about having to postpone the wedding again?

He stared into space for a moment and then shook his head as if to shake off a horrible thought. 'The town won't give me a license to open the riding facility. Not with the land looking like this.'

Which was a big blow. We'd been banking on the school. I poured some of my special homemade iced tea with fresh mint and lemon. 'Who did you speak to?' I asked, passing him the cool glass.

'The secretary of a certain Leonardo Cortini, head of the council for Tourism. He's a real piece of work. I can never get a hold of him on the phone but I see him around town in a Ferrari acting like he's God's gift to women.'

'That's impossible,' I grinned. '*You* are.'

Julian smiled weakly but said nothing.

'Tell you what. Let's go to the town hall tomorrow, see what we can do,' I suggested, but Julian shrugged and then yawned.

We'd barely got over one hurdle and here was the next already. And he was tired of it, of course. I could see it. I wondered if I hadn't been pushing him along too hard.

Who was I kidding? I'd dragged the man of my dreams to a beautiful country where things worked at a very slow pace. Most of the time, getting past bureaucracy was an uphill battle. How much longer could Julian handle being a foreigner in Italy? How long could he bear the cross of a different life?

I pushed the ridiculous thought away. Yes, times were tough, but Julian was an extremely intelligent and resourceful man. Up until two years ago, he ran an entire school. Trouble was, he didn't seem to want to run A Taste of Tuscany anymore. Or had he ever? Granted, we'd agreed on the fact that I'd run the B & B and he'd take care of the horses and write. But the demands of running a farm merely messed up his career plans. The more time he spent on the farm, the less time he had to globetrot and PR his work. And that was a fact.

He yawned again. 'You know what, Erica, don't bother.'

I eyed him. 'What do you mean?'

He shrugged. 'I've worked my ass off for the past two years – not that I didn't want to – but already with the rebuilding of the vineyards and the olive groves, I'll hardly have time to write.'

Maybe it was his polite way of saying a riding school had never been that important to him, after all.

'OK.' I shrugged.

His eyebrows lifted. 'You don't mind? I thought you wanted a riding school.'

I shrugged. 'I want what you want.' It was true. I wanted him to be happy. 'We'll hire more farmhands. You *should* write more. You'd be crazy not to. It's virtually the royalties that are keeping us afloat,' I acknowledged, not without a shade of misery. I hated that A Taste of Tuscany wasn't helping out one bit.

He nodded, relieved, and again I wondered if Julian hadn't made a mistake following me to Italy to run a farm and a B & B when what he thrived on was literary recognition.

'Fine, then,' I concluded. You write your books and oversee the produce, and I'll take care of the business. Maybe hire a couple more farmhands.'

'Are you sure you don't mind?' he repeated.

'Of course not. You do your job, I'll do mine.'

'Brilliant,' he said, beaming, the weight of the world (or simply of the farm) off his shoulders.

'Brilliant,' I repeated, and we clinked glasses.

But deep inside, I couldn't help notice how our dreams were going in different directions.

# 12

## Brides Past and Present

July started with the task of pruning all the damaged olive trees, replanting all the flower bushes and re-landscaping the grounds of our property. But the lunar landscape left behind by the locusts was taking much longer than we'd expected. The damage had extended to the neighboring towns, making every venue in the area unfit to host anything except for a Star Trek convention.

As far as the wedding was concerned, we could have settled for a civil marriage at the town hall, but even that had to be booked months in advance, and besides, it that was not what we wanted. Our wish had been to get married in our own home, surrounded by our friends and family in our own, beautiful home.

Julian's three-week window that had been allocated to the wedding and honeymoon was soon over and the calendar filled once again with all his blue squares that had kicked my one pink square's ass to the curb indefinitely. But Paul insisted on not losing momentum as far as planning was concerned. He was convinced that the land would be restored in time, and that everything would be fine. That was Paul for you, the eternal optimist. Personally, I didn't think it was going to happen anymore, and it was driving me crazy. I needed a break from it.

My VIP boutique hotel was a dead duck. But I was going to come up with a definitive solution, once and for all. I needed to prove to myself – and Julian – that I hadn't lost my drive. That I was still Erica the Ass-kicker.

I was five minutes into my one-woman war council when my cell phone rang.

'Hello?'

'How ya doin', boss?'

Only one person had that lilt. Jackie, my Number Two when I worked at The Farthington. 'Oh my God, Jackie! How are you?'

And then she laughed her nervous laugh. 'As stressed as ever, thanks, and you?'

Ditto. 'Everything's fine,' I lied. Why make the poor girl even more miserable? 'You do sound stressed, what's up?'

'Up? Only that it's The Farthington's 100th anniversary and Mr. Farthington asked me to invite all of our past guests for a huge shebang.'

That was old Harold for you, doing things in style. I learned all I know from him. 'Great idea. So?'

A huge sigh. 'The system's completely crashed. I have a guy working on it but he said it's not looking good and even if he could find any data, it would only be very recent, due to our updated system...'

'How recent?' I asked.

'Two years, tops.'

Yikes. That was a proper pickle to be in, as Julian would say. 'Is there no other back-up system? One that you've implemented since I left?'

'It's the back-up system that's crashed.'

'Ouch…'

'I've tried remembering all their names and I've even got people on Linked In and Facebook to track them down, but so far we've only found twenty-odd people. Erica, if I can't pull this 100th anniversary off, there goes my bonus, if not my job.'

She was most definitely right about that. Harold Farthington took absolutely no prisoners. One mistake and you were out, no matter who you were. A few years ago he'd even fired his own nephew for not recognizing a famous guest.

*Think, think, think, Erica! Hotel crises, this is what you're good at! This is where you shine!* 'Why don't you start with the big clubs and associations that you remember? That would give you hundreds of member names,' I offered.

'That's a great idea! Now why didn't I think of that?'

'Thinking outside the box is an occupational hazard.' For me, at least. Something that machines can't do. It's a good thing that I depended so little on them. I even used to copy all the important info into a ledger in case— Holy shit!' I blurted.

'What? What's wrong?'

'Uh, Jackie! Hang on a minute, will you? I might lose you, so I'll call you back, okay?'

'Why, where are you going? Erica, I need you, please don't hang up! Erica? What are you up to now?'

I ran down the stone steps as fast as I could and to the cellar where we kept all of the junk we didn't need anymore but hadn't had the heart to throw away. Like old sports equipment, the kids' old textbooks and such. And my Farthington ledger. Where I had copied the names of every guest, and I mean every single guest that had come through the lobby doors.

Due to the width of the stone walls, there was no signal down here, and I felt for Jackie whose life must have flashed before her eyes several times by now, probably on a loop.

If only I could find it in this mess. I waded my way through Julian's mountain of sports equipment, from the canoe he hadn't used in ages to the paraglider he found on Ebay. Maddy's very first pajamas, Warren's first baseball outfit, and even some clothes I still hoped to fit into one day. (I'm sure you tell yourself similar jokes, too?) Old bags that were barely keeping together via the rotting stitching and shoes that not even The Wicked Witch of The West would be caught dead in. You gotta love the cockroach killer toes! And there, right around the corner, was my stuff, all neatly labeled.

But no Farthington box. Wiping the sweat off my face and lifting everything in my way, I stopped only when I hit the stone wall at the very back. And there it was, labelled Farthington. My little baby. The light of my former life. I hefted it onto my hip and, huffing and puffing, emerged from the cave-like depths of the cellars and into the sunshine, wiping my brow and then reaching into my pocket for my cell phone. I hit the Call-back button. Jackie answered immediately.

'Please tell me you have a solution,' she begged.

'I have THE solution,' I replied, feeling my face stretching into the hugest grin ever.

'What do you mean?'

'Just the names of every single person that has booked since I started working there.'

'What?' she shrieked. 'Are you serious, Erica?'

'Is your email address still the same?' I asked. 'I'm going to scan these pages over to you right now, OK?'

'Erica, I don't know how to even begin thanking you.'

'By keeping this a secret.' I was not supposed to take this info off the premises, but my little ledger was a work of art.

'I'll keep this a secret until my dying day! And beyond!'

'Thanks, Jackie. I appreciate it.'

'You just saved my life. Oh, Erica, why did you leave me alone in this office?'

Because I wanted to be my own boss. If could solve a problem of that entity, I could sort my own measly B&B out, for sure. I turned on my printer and began scanning the documents, my mind already cast forward to my next effort to save my business.

'You'll be fine, Jackie. You're a tough cookie. Good luck for that raise.'

'God bless you!' she called and hung up before the tears came. The perks of being in a stressful job. Glad I had got out of it in the end.

So, taking stock: it was an undeniable fact that this summer we were in no shape to offer guests a place to sleep. So what could I offer? I could offer food. Not on the property, granted. I didn't want to infringe on Renata's business as she catered meals. But I could offer another kind of food— cakes! Was I not a damn good baker? I would bake American-style cakes! Italians loved them, and yet, hardly anyone I knew here could quite replicate them. I already had all the right baking utensils. And I could operate from my own kitchen. All I needed at this level was word of mouth. I'd start slow, use a couple of friends as guinea pigs. I'd make birthday cakes, wedding cakes, divorce cakes, baby shower cakes, communion cakes, confirmation cakes, college degree cakes, coming out cakes. Any kind of cake! Without realizing it, Jackie had given me the one thing I'd lost. Confidence in myself. Once again, The Amazing Erica was back, only this time, she was back to stay for good!

July 15th, our intended wedding day, had come and gone, and where was Julian? You guessed it, away. And instead of cutting my own wedding cake, I was baking like there was no tomorrow while my aunts and Paul continued with the planning in my office. In the space of two weeks, the word had spread and I had cake orders up the wazoo. To Maddy's utmost delight, I let her choose the color schemes and she watched in rapture as I carefully placed the decorations she handed me; beads, pearls, baby slippers or bride and groom, whatever the occasion was.

'You're a natural, sweetheart,' I said, kissing her forehead. 'Mommy could never have done this without you.'

'You can do anything, Mommy,' she breathed as I added the final touches to a baby shower cake.

'So can you, Maddy,' I assured her. 'If you want something badly enough, you can do it. Just believe in yourself.'

As I had. The cakes flying out of my kitchen so fast that I didn't have time to deliver them, so I had to have someone to do it for me. Was this how easy it was?

'I can do anything? Like being a ballerina at the La Scala? Mila says it's hard.'

'Your ballet teacher is right. It is hard. But you can do it if you really, really want it. But always have a Plan B.'

'What's a Plan B, Mommy?' she asked.

'It's your second-biggest dream. In case the biggest one doesn't work out. It keeps you happy.'

'Are these cakes your Plan B?'

'That's right, Maddy. Always have plans. Always have hope. You might not get exactly what you want, but you can always do something else. That's what life is for. Making decisions. Good ones.'

'Do you always make good decisions?' she asked.

'Most of the time,' I said, dotting her cute little nose with pink butter-cream.

A week later, Marcy and Dad returned from their trip to Elba. And, as you can imagine, she wasn't happy with what she found on her return – her three sisters.

'What the hell are *you* three doing here?' she snapped.

'Marcy, don't start now, honey,' Dad urged, as gently as ever, while Marcy jumped to her pretty little feet.

I looked down at my size nines. It was hard for me to believe that I took after Marcy's twin, yet I didn't look an iota like either of them.

Dad put a hand on her shoulder. 'They're here to see their niece. Behave yourself.'

But she was way beyond behaving. Ho, boy. I should have known this visit would bring no good. Who was I kidding? I only wanted the attention focused away from me. But it really wasn't working, because I was caught up in the oncoming storm and there was nothing I could do to avoid it. Oh, to be with Paul in Florence for the day, looking for wedding tableware!

Marcy's chest puffed out, like a bird ruffling her feathers to look bigger and menacing. Julian slanted me a preoccupied glance and I almost snorted. He hadn't seen anything yet.

'Oh, honey,' Dad said. 'Never mind them. You know I live for you and only you.'

And that was exactly what Marcy had needed to hear.

'You do?' she asked, then got a hold of herself in front of her audience. 'Of course you do. Damn lucky to have me, that's what you are.'

We all glanced at each other furtively and busied ourselves with our chores. Her insecurity was at sky-high levels lately and I wondered why. Was it because she was back in Tuscany, where she'd lived in the shadow of her sisters, particularly my mother? I knew that there had always been bad blood between them, but, putting myself in her shoes, I couldn't help but wonder if she and I really were that different, after all. But what was eating at me most was why she thought it was even remotely necessary to go to our rival B & B. Dressed as the Madonna to boot.

So, later that afternoon, I asked her. In a non-aggressive way. Politely, while she lounged by the pool, her favorite place.

'Marcy, what... uhm, were you doing at Tasting Tuscany?'

She looked up at me from her magazine, her lithe form hugged by the luxurious hammock. Her eyes darted away from mine – just one fraction of a second.

'What *are* you talking about?' she asked innocently.

Oh, so we're doing it that way, as usual, are we? You see? Even if I was as non-threatening, as non-confrontational as possible, she'd always clam up. Never once would she admit to anything.

The only thing that she and Mother Mary had in common was that they'd both ended up with a baby they hadn't banked on. Only Mother Mary's was cool, became a cult and performed miracles. Me, a little less…

So, done with the humble stepdaughter who always walked on eggshells so as not to annoy her, I crossed my arms and flashed her my famous hairy eyeball.

'Well, hard to deny it, when the entire province of Siena thinks you were an apparition of the Madonna. Only we know who you really are.'

She sighed. 'Oh, alright. Yes, it was me. It wasn't planned or anything. I didn't know anyone was filming me. I just wanted to see the place where I grew up.'

My eyebrows rose. 'I thought you hated it and never wanted to go back.'

She shrugged. 'I do. But I wanted to see something with my own eyes.'

Now that got my attention. 'What? What did you want to see?'

Silence, then a soft puff of breath lifted a strand of her soft hair off her cheek. Why, oh why, couldn't I be as delicate as her? And why, most of all, could I and this woman whom I did love at the end of the (very long) day, never build a lasting relationship of some sort? Why did we always have to keep starting from scratch every single time?

'Marcy? What is it you wanted to see?'

Again she huffed and shifted slightly on the lounger. 'I-I wanted to see the tree where your father carved his three Es.'

How had she found out about that? 'Marcy, that was such a long time ago,' I lied for her benefit.

She smirked. 'You're wrong. It's a fresh marking.'

Oyoy, I thought, smelling trouble. 'Maybe it's another E,' I suggested lamely. Who was I kidding?

She shook her head, tears streaming down her cheeks. 'Another E+E=E on our old property? No. All these years and your father is still in love with Emanuela. Even in death, she beat me.'

'Oh, Marcy, don't say that. He had two kids with you. He loves you. He even left his fishing trip to come and be with you now.'

'Really?' she asked hopefully.

OK, that was just me allowing myself a bit of poetic license. I had no idea what he had been up to, but this sacrifice, fictitious or not, would earn him oodles of brownie points with her.

She studied me and in her dubious expression, I could see my own insecurities and doubts about Julian's love and dedication toward me. That much my stepmother and I did have in common. Just like I wasn't the center of Julian's world, Marcy wasn't the center of my father's.

'Yes,' she admitted. 'But his one and only true love will always be Emanuela. Your mother. And there's nothing I can ever do or say to make him love me more.'

Could she be right, after all? Had my father answered my call of help to come out and fetch his wife just to revisit and reminisce at the scene of his love story with my real mother? Marcy had spoken her suspicions with such sadness, with such resignation that I felt it might just be true.

My father always had that sad look in his eyes, never wanting to talk about my mother, especially during the last two years after my aunts had told me the truth. It was as if he wanted to guard his secret love from prying eyes. And Marcy, like everyone else in my family, had been shut out.

But what could I do to help her? It had taken me more than thirty-five years to get my own love life straightened out.

'What was she like? My mother?' I asked.

Marcy sighed. 'She was... oh, I don't know. Ambitious. Always asking people for information on how to do things, how to get to places and stuff. A bit like you.'

'Driven, you mean?' I insisted.

She picked the magazine up again and speared me with a glare. 'Yes. She wanted her own business, just like you.'

I beamed, but then tried to hide my pride so as not to hurt Marcy. 'What about her grades – were they good? Did she paint? Did I take after her? Dad doesn't paint, so—'

'Erica, stop pestering me. I don't know all the answers to your questions. Emanuela and I were never close. I'm sorry.'

'But you were identical twins! Did you at least share any secrets?'

At that, she stared at me hard and I thought she was finally going to reveal something.

'No, we weren't close at all. Accept it and move on.'

*Move on*, she said. As if it were easy, not having answers to my questions. Like walking in the dark. And to think I'd banked on her cooperating. There was no way I was getting any more info out of her, now or in the future.

'And why are you making this about you?' she accused. 'I'm here fighting for my marriage and all you can do is ask about your mother.'

I felt my mouth drop open. But I shouldn't have been surprised. Because Marcy was just like that. She'd never really matured. And every time I told myself that we were finally on our way to being in an equal, balanced relationship, she'd blurt something as hurtful as that. It was always about her and what she wanted. Never mind that I'd been born practically orphaned. And that all I had of my mother was a pearl necklace and a few anecdotes.

So I turned to my father in the hope that he'd be more sympathetic and more open about his love for my birth mother. When I asked him about the tree, he let out a faint sigh, as if he could see Emanuela – his Manu – through the pages of his life right before his very eyes. And suddenly, in the way he was looking at me, I saw something – a link of some sort that he was acknowledging and that he'd never mentioned before. Not really. Yes, he'd always been closer to me than to Judy and Vince, but it was more of a distant kind of thing. We'd never really had a *relationship*. To us, Dad had only been Marcy's mild victim, who smiled at us benevolently from time to time. But nothing more.

Now, I saw it – all of it. His affection, his happiness in his memories. But also his loneliness. I don't think it was because he didn't care, but simply because I reminded him of the love of his life and his greatest loss. Just like I reminded Marcy, who instead dealt with it by being aggressive, or ignoring me at the best of times. But sweet old Dad didn't know how to do feelings and was content with just being in the background while the Cantelli women took over.

'I promised Emanuela I'd carve our names on that tree one day...' he whispered.

Now that was really romantic. I wondered just how much I'd missed out on regarding my dad. He was an entire universe of secrets and hidden love that he jealously kept close to his own heart, lest anyone should unwittingly damage them. I understood his selfishness. The memories of their love were all he had left. But somehow, today he did want to share something.

'And when she got pregnant with you,' he continued as if a dam had collapsed and he wanted me to know everything about them, 'she chose your name. Erica is the Italian name for the heather that grows on the highest peaks. That's what she thought of you as – her highest achievement. And so do I...'

'Oh, Dad,' I cried, scrabbling to hug him. 'I never knew that you felt that way about me! I...' My throat tightened, but I swallowed and choked the words out as my eyes misted. 'I always thought I was a burden to you...'

At that, he clutched my hands in his. 'What? No, my little princess. You're the best thing that's *ever* happened to us. When she told me she was expecting you, I knew my life was starting there and then. Your mom – wherever she is up in that sky – will always love you.'

The revelation of a father–daughter bond I hadn't been aware of took me by surprise. My father *really* loved me. And he still loved my real mother enough to carve our names into my mother's favorite oak tree – the tree she'd spent hours under, reading her favorite books. Although she was gone, I felt like I'd suddenly rebuilt my lost family. I could literally feel the million pieces of my life slowly reconvening, like stardust particles.

'Thank you, Dad. I guess I really needed to hear that.'

'Any time, sweetheart. You just call me when you need me. But I know you're in good hands. Julian really loves you.'

'I know.'

'I'm going upstairs to pack. God only knows Marcy has

purposely left half of my clothes behind.' He grinned. 'The half she doesn't approve of.'

The next day, the last day of July, with a heavy heart, my parents and my three aunts headed to the airport to go home. In separate taxis. But I would see them soon again for the wedding, whenever the grounds were presentable for a wedding do.

Despite all of Julian's reassuring words, I still didn't want to look like a piece of haggis-in-a-dress at my own wedding. So, after a great deal of research and introspection – and before I changed my mind – I found the only place that stayed open the entire month of August, changed into an old pair of sweatpants and dropped the kids off at ballet and soccer practice on my way to…? You guessed it – the gym! Yes! I was going to do this! I could do this. Shed the weight, build some muscle tone, and look and feel better.

When I got there, all gung-ho, I paid my seasonal package – 400 euros in one hit – and got a cardio detector strapped around me at heart level. I got the heart monitor in case I dropped dead, but a name tag? Suppose I didn't want people to know my name? Would *you*, if you looked like me? Wouldn't it have been better if it had been like… Athletics Anonymous?

*Hi, everybody, my name's Erica and I'm a gym-newbie.*
*Hi, Gym-Newbie…*

Laughing to myself, I pushed through the double doors off the main office and into the main gym hall.

At first I thought I'd got the wrong place. If I expected the place to be filled with hard-slogging people determined to get their figures back, I'd be disappointed. And I was.

It looked more like a disco, with low lights and music so

loud it practically pounced on me, making even the walls pulse in empathy. Not to mention the fancy skin-tight gym wear, earrings and make-up. And that was just the *guys*.

Everywhere I looked, multicolored arms and legs in woolen legwarmers of every pattern and color pushed up and down and out at me, like a huge motley centipede from the Eighties on psychedelic drugs. There was a booming voice directing them somewhere at the front, but I couldn't see its owner, so I just placed my mat before me and studied the others as they... jumped? Danced? Twisted? In a blind frenzy.

I couldn't make any sense of it, but it sure was fast – way faster than I could ever hope to move. By the time I'd figured out the beat and even *thought* of lifting a leg so as to get the gist of it, they'd already kicked out again, first one leg and then the other, and spun round, leaving me dumbfounded and fumbling like a child trying to learn to walk. If I tried any of this, I'd give myself a heart attack for sure.

Well, I had to die of something, so I moved my arms around and followed them in their stomp-act while yanking at my old bra, which did nothing to support my boobs in this situation and were, by the way, swinging heavily every which way as if they had a life of their own.

Even if I was practically standing still compared to them, a thick coat of sweat soon formed on my forehead, trickling down into my eyes and my cheeks, to meet the sweat on my upper lip, which splashed down to meet the sweat between my boobs and so on. (You get the picture.)

'E *uno, due, tre, quattro, cinque, sei, sette, otto!*' the invisible instructor boomed faster and louder, and I increased my fumbling speed, my heart rate out of whack in just seconds.

Just as I thought I'd collapse, the motley centipede picked up speed, the floors now vibrating with all the pounding going on. Not to be any less, I charged into a step that made me look like a huge-hipped grizzly bear on speed.

As the beat increased, so did the volume, proportionally to the stink of sweat (not mine, I hoped), and soon I was gagging for air, wondering what the hell had come over me when I'd decided to join this nuthouse.

I must have the wrong time slot, I told myself. Surely there was another group, one slightly older that didn't move at warp speed. These people were all way too young and nimble for me, thin as cheese slices which, by the looks of them, they certainly didn't indulge in, for everywhere I looked I saw tiny asses, narrow hips and inexistent thighs.

They all seemed to be dancing what I thought looked like the Maori ceremonial haka, such was the determination and the ferocity on their faces to eradicate their (invisible) excess fat, the demon that had possessed their bodies, their neck and face muscles stretching under the effort. *Demonic fat! Leeeave this poor woman's body nowww!* Well, I could certainly sing to that tune.

Before I could make sense of it, it all stopped – the music, the shouting, the pounding. At the end of the exorcism, the lights went on and peace suddenly fell, faces now shining and smiling, people shaking hands and hugging (yuck), basically clearing the decks now the devil had been defeated.

Once most of them were gone, I spotted a woman on the other side of the gym – huge, much larger than me. She, like me, was older and plainer than the mob who had just left and completely overwhelmed by it all. I smiled and there was a sense of familiarity for her that only lasted a second until I realized it was my own reflection in the bloody mirror.

I cringed and moved closer. Whoa. There had to be some mistake. That wasn't really me… was it? My ass was huge. Did it really look like that to the outside world? Yikes. I had no idea…

But wait – was I on *Candid Camera* or something? Maybe Renata had organized some sort of joke, having convex mirrors delivered to the gym. Or, more simply, the gym just had them to make you work harder and upgrade your subscription payment.

Pure horror seized me as I braved to move in even closer, twisting and turning, inspecting my ass again. How come it didn't look this big at home? Was it the lighting? The sweatpants? *What?* I wondered, checking out, while I was at it, a stray hair on my chin. Are you serious? And that face – pale and pasty – was that really me, with the purple smudges under the eyes, the tired face and the wrinkles? Jesus. When did all this happen?

'*Mamma mia*, we have a mountain of work to do here, I see,' came the boomer's voice across the gym hall.

I whirled round, giving him the hairy eyeball, and he literally stopped in his tracks.

'Ooh, we have a touchy one,' he grinned.

'I beg your pardon?' My arms were folded now.

'How much do you weigh? At least 85 kilograms, *sì?*'

A bit more, actually, but there was no way I was telling him.

Like a miniature version of Mr. Clean, he was half my height and circling me with a keen eye.

'But you're a tall girl. Big in the hips and the boobs.'

I opened my mouth to say something – anything – that would put him in his place.

'Narrow waist, though. Your tummy will be the first to go.'

'Really?' I said before I could stop myself. 'How long?'

He laughed. 'Depends on how often you come in, how much you eat. Do you do any walking?'

I thought of the antique markets in Castellino. 'Do Saturday morning strolls count?'

'Not if they're leisurely and lead to Fernando's bakery, no.' His eyes shone with good humor. 'Ever try to lose weight before?'

I rolled my eyes. 'Hasn't everybody?' I said, realizing my mistake.

He hadn't, obviously, with his wiry, toned muscles and washboard stomach.

He ignored my comment. 'Ever succeed?'

'Only a few kilos here and there.'

'What seems to be the problem?'

You see, this was why I shouldn't have come here in the first place. Normal people didn't understand people like me. They didn't understand the agony and the cravings and the immediate regret after binging – all the torture and the ecstasy thing going on. If he didn't understand my body that was plain and simple, how did he think he could navigate the nooks and crannies of my mind?

'I... love eating?'

'Yeah. That love has to stop now.'

Was he serious? Half the reason I'd moved to Tuscany was the food. And I wasn't going to feel guilty about it.

'I mean, you can still eat almost anything you want,

but you must avoid carbs at all costs, fried foods, fats and sauces.'

Which left only vegetables, protein and fruit. As if I didn't know the theory behind dieting. It was the practice that I was a little rusty on.

'And sweets, of course,' he added. 'You must avoid sweets.'

I sighed. There went my stash of Kinder chocolates under the bed (old habits die hard). And my homemade cupcakes in the top cupboard that Warren usually beat me to. Who am I kidding? He only got the dregs.

'And you must exercise portion control,' he concluded.

Portion control? It sounded like a form of capital punishment to me. If I couldn't eat to my heart's content, then how on earth was I going to fill the void? And why should I still have this void when I was happy? Because I was happy, right? Happy-ish? Jesus, I'd come all the way to Italy for a new life and still I wasn't satisfied? What did I want? 'A kick in the head,' my brother, Vince, would have answered.

'Do you understand portion control?'

'I understand instinct control.' The instinct to swat him out of my face. But he was right. If I could control myself in every other field, why shouldn't I be able to control my instincts and my portions? The next time I dished up the lasagne, I was going to make an effort to give myself a smaller slice. It might not have made a difference on a one-off basis, but if it became the norm to eat less, it had to work, right? Glad you agree.

'I make cakes,' I informed him. 'And I never lick the bowl. How's that for control?'

He grinned. 'That's a start. So see you next week?'

And make a fool out of myself again, not knowing which way was up or down while the haka relentlessly continued?

'I... uh... might be in the wrong group, though.'

He waved his hand. 'You'll get the hang of it.'

'But everybody else is so... slim...'

He laughed again. 'You'll get there.'

'Not alive, I won't.'

He laughed. 'What's your weight loss target?'

I hadn't thought of that. Enough to fit into a wedding dress? Enough not to have people stare in disbelief when they saw me at Julian's side? If anything, I didn't want to stand out anymore. I wanted to be normal.

'I'd need to lose 30 kilos to be anything like them.'

'You don't need to be anything like them. All you need is to be at your own best. *Sì?*'

I thought about it. It made sense. False promises were useless and harmful. '*Sì...*'

'And of course, don't think it's easy. It takes a lot of sweat and tears to lose weight. You'll have to come in for a couple of hours at least three times a week.'

Three times a week? For a couple of hours? Was he insane?

'I'm not going to lie to you. It takes balls to do what you're doing. Deciding to lose weight isn't for everyone. Only the strongest can do it.'

'Survival of the fittest?'

'Exactly. You a fighter?'

We obviously hadn't met. I'd survived worse than the gym. 'I'm a fighter.'

'Good girl. See you Monday, then.'

# 13

## Living, Loving and Being Happy?

As the many pieces of my life were still trying to find each other in all that madness, at least my conscience and willpower were revamped, as Mr. Clean's words had begun to sink in. It *did* take a lot of courage to overhaul my life completely with the decision to lose weight. But I had courage to spare. With all the changes I'd brought about in my life over the years, and all that had happened to send me reeling and landing with a painful thud on my ass, what were a few squats in comparison? And dieting? Nothing I hadn't done before.

To the point I went home, to where Rosina had made an exquisite lasagne, and fixed myself a tuna salad for dinner – no mayo, no oil, just tuna and lettuce. And no bread, of course. Maddy and Warren watched me as they chomped away on their glorious food, Paul's portion safely tucked away in the microwave for when he got back from Chef Alberto's. Even if I knew Paul wouldn't have any space (or inclination) left after eating Alberto's food. Just the thought of Alberto's goodies made me weak in the knees and I put my fork down, overwhelmed with a craving for real food and not this joke.

'Aren't you hungry, Mommy?' Maddy asked as she held out some of her lasagne for me, bless her generous little soul.

'No, sweetheart,' I said, caressing her pink cheek.

'Mom's got to lose some weight or she won't fit into her wedding dress,' Warren sentenced, and I flashed him a pox disguised as a smile.

'Is your wedding dress pretty, Mommy?' Maddy asked.

*The one in the shop was*, I wanted to say. *But in my size, it would look like a deflated hot-air balloon.* 'Very pretty, sweetheart. Almost as pretty as yours.'

Her face lit up. 'I get a dress, too?'

'Of course. You're going to be my flower girl.' Hopefully before she started dating.

She gasped in bliss. 'Flower girl...!'

'That's right, honey.'

Maddy thought about it. 'Then no pasta for you, Mommy.'

How right she was. I was on a mission now. Saturday was a non-fat day, as well, and even on Sunday I'd done myself proud with a long walk into town and back without even glancing at the eateries that dotted the *corso*. And on top of that, in the privacy of my bedroom I also performed fifty squats in my pajamas for good measure.

But, as it often happens, by Sunday evening I'd chickened out. The memory of all those skinny people whizzing around like jumping jacks while I could barely stand on one foot made me feel inadequate. I'd vowed to keep up with them somehow, but how? I wasn't so sure anymore.

I needed a push of some sort. Besides my reflection in the mirror, I mean. And then the light bulb over my head lit up.

'Paul, you absolutely have to come with me – I can't go back there alone!' I said as I cleared the table for his laptop.

'Go to the gym? With all those sweaty, stinking, grunting, leotarded losers? You must be joking. I'll sign up for dance classes with you, though.'

Dance classes with Paul was how I'd lost the weight the first time. But now I needed more. I needed a crash course, a crash diet and a crash helmet, because I was in for one helluva ride that would hopefully get things going once and for all. And I didn't want to do it alone. Besides, wasn't Paul my partner in crime?

'I thought gay men liked the gym?' I pressed, and he turned in his seat to look at me as I loaded the dishwasher.

'That's so biased! And politically incorrect.'

I shrugged. 'I just thought you might like some eye candy, that's all.'

He sat up. 'Were there any good-looking guys?'

A swish of purple legwarmers and carbuncular sweaty faces flashed before me. 'Uhm…'

'Right. I'll come to *one* lesson.'

'Yay!'

'Don't get excited. One lesson means one.'

As it turned out, Renata came as well, only she really should have stayed at home, because all her cackling and making fun of the crazy outfits was distracting me while Mr. Clean (I still didn't know his name) was explaining a new exercise.

'Will you shut up?' I hissed. 'Go home if you're not interested.'

'Are you kidding me? And miss out on all this fun?' she hissed back. 'Just look at that woman and that Brazilian outfit. Is she for real?'

'Can't you be more respectful?' I asked. 'That's just so mean.'

'Erica?' Mr. Clean called over the crowd who, like synchronized swimmers, turned all at the same time to look at me.

I swallowed, feeling two inches tall, an apology on my lips, when he said, 'Erica, I need you to stay behind today.'

Everyone continued to stare at me and at the ragtag trio I was part of: the obviously gorgeous and gay man on my right, and the tattooed, big-boobed, big-mouthed Marxist on my left.

Great – all I needed was for everybody to notice me. I'd spent all my life trying to fit in and not stand out, and now everyone knew my name. So much for Athletics Anonymous. It was like high school all over again, only I'd never got into trouble back then.

'See what you've done?' I hissed again, hiding behind a red-headed bombshell in front of me as the music resumed and an even more complicated series of steps and jumps and lunges started.

Paul did his very best and looked very much the part while Renata was doubled over in the corner, holding her sides and guffawing her ass off at the pseudo-haka number.

'That's it,' I snapped at her. 'You're out. Go home.'

'Aah… I had so much fun, Erica. Thank you for inviting me.'

'Actually, I didn't. It was all Paul's idea. Because he doesn't know you as well as I do. He thought you'd actually be able to behave yourself.'

She giggled. 'I'll have to come back for another laugh,' she said, drying her eyes as I rolled mine.

'No, you won't. Now go home and think about what you've done.'

But she just burst out laughing again while she collected her gear.

When the session was over, I waited for Mr. Clean to finish talking to someone.

'You, ah, wanted to see me? Sorry about that, by the way.'

'You mean Renata? Don't mention it. She could never keep a straight face in a gym.'

I blinked. 'You know her?'

'*Cara*, everyone knows everyone in Castellino, don't you know that by now? Plus, we used to be in the same class at school.'

'Oh.'

'Don't let her put you off, Erica.'

'Oh, it's not Renata,' I defended her.

'Then what is it?'

I shifted uneasily. 'It's just… it's too difficult. I feel big and slow and… awkward.'

He studied me for a minute. 'Tell you what. Why don't you stay behind for Pilates and a half-hour workout?'

'Now?' I had to go home, make dinner, supervise homework and, oh – strap on an oxygen mask pronto.

'Just this once. See how it goes. Pilates is nice and quiet and the workout is at your own pace. What do you say?'

'We'll watch the kids for you,' Paul, always a Judas in these situations, chimed in. 'Stay. I'll hitch a ride with Renata.'

I shrugged. 'OK, then.'

It turned out that, with fewer people in the hall, it didn't stink so much. The lights stayed on and the music was so soft I could actually hear him – and the others – breathing.

First, we quietly stretched and did all sorts of gentle movements that didn't make me feel like a two-ton elephant. Even Mr. Clean's voice had toned down. If this continued, I could actually enjoy it. I looked around, comforted by the presence of women my age and even older, some even pleasantly plump, clad in clean but no-nonsense sports gear that didn't glow in the dark or give you a wedgie. Their hair was tied up in scrunchies and, most of all, there was a lot of smiling and deep breathing going on. Yes, *this*, I could do. The haka? Not so much.

Sitting cross-legged on the floor, I studied my reflection. Next to my similars, I didn't stand out like a yeti. Actually, I kind of looked... normal, you know? I felt ten feet tall for fitting in.

And when Mr. Clean kneeled before me to check my position, he winked in approval.

'How was that?' he asked me at the end as I was putting my sneakers back on.

I looked up and smiled. 'It was good.'

'Excellent. And by the way, Erica, I used to weigh much more than you.'

I swear my eyes popped out of my head. This four-foot-nothing, lean Mr. Clean?

'Really? You?'

'*Sì*. So- see you on Wednesday?'

I nodded enthusiastically. 'Wednesday.'

'And, Erica? Bring your friend again.'

'You know she's married…'

He shook his head. 'The other one…'

'Paul? Sure.' Well, well, well…

When Julian returned, he marveled at how well I'd done with the cake business.

'I had to do something. I was going crazy,' I admitted.

'I'll make it up to you, sweetheart,' Julian promised, moving to stand behind me as I was changing into my nightgown, his reflection infinitely more pleasing than mine in the mirror as he wrapped his arms – his very long arms – around me, lacing his fingers over my levitating midriff and gently drawing me back against his chest. 'The wedding, my absences, the locusts, everything.'

Now that the decision to forgo the riding school had been made, he seemed much more relaxed. At least one of us was on the up and up.

'It's not your fault,' I assured him.

'How about we just go ahead and do it when I get back from my next trip?'

'What?'

'We'll just book a normal restaurant, get Padre Adolfo in and get it done.'

'Are you serious?'

'Of course. You already have everything else ready.'

'So you're ready to marry me, just like that? Anywhere we can find?'

'Of course. Who cares if it's a restaurant and not a fancy place? All I want is you, Erica.'

If I'd cared before, now I was past that. All I wanted was to marry the guy, already.

'So if I can book Padre Adolfo, we're in?'

'Absolutely.'

'You've got yourself a deal!'

Julian kissed my ear, nibbling lightly. 'Have I told you lately how sexy you are? Mind-blowingly sexy.'

'OK, you don't need to overdo it,' I warned with a resigned chuckle, placing my hands over his and craning my neck backward to let him kiss me in what could only be classified as a *Titanic* kiss.

If you haven't already tried it during the movie craze when people were re-enacting the famous scene and consequently falling off boats all over the world, try it now, even without the ship. You don't need it if you have a man who rocks your world and blows your insecurities way out the water.

'What?' Julian said. 'Why are you looking at me like that?'

'I love you, Julian.'

He reached down and pulled my hand to his lips. 'I love you more,' he whispered back. 'Now pull on some clothes.'

'Don't you usually say the opposite at this point?'

'Not this time, love.'

I shrugged. 'OK. Where are we going?'

Julian was grinning at me, his dark eyes mischievous, and something inside me twisted. God, I really did love this guy.

'To celebrate.'

'But, Warren and Maddy...'

'I've got a sitter.' He winked. 'I'm taking you to your favorite restaurant.'

'L'Archetto? The one that serves *pane Arabo?*'

'The very one.'

'Cool! Thank you!'

'You're very welcome, sweetheart.'

So after our meal of *pane Arabo* (which is basically a large pita bread filled with fresh ingredients like mozzarella cheese, *prosciutto di Parma* and rocket lettuce, with a drizzle of olive oil and grilled for a few minutes), I sat back with a sigh, content as I watched other diners laughing and drinking, glasses clinking and forks chiming against emptying plates. Even for a few moments, life could slow down if you let it. The Casciani issue now hopefully over, the wedding plans in Paul's hands, baking gave me the chance to spend more time with Maddy and Warren. Even he enjoyed watching (and licking the bowls). It was so nice to have them home and I truly cherished watching them growing up. Something which I hadn't been able to do in Boston while pulling eight-hour shifts (and traveling) for The Farthington.

As far as Julian was concerned, even when he was home, we rarely spent time together, immersed as he was in his career. And Sienna. Most of the time he worked with her over the phone (when she wasn't here) until way into the night, breaking into a hearty laugh from time to time. She apparently kept him well entertained. While I hadn't, being either asleep or too damn deflated by the time he turned in.

Not that he was offering, lately. And we weren't even married yet. I couldn't even remember the last time we made love. What with the stress of the locusts, losing the crops, replanting the crops, and everything else, I was just too exhausted – and fuming – even to lift a finger after dinner, let alone engage in some hot sex.

*Hot sex*. I couldn't even remember the last time I'd even longed for it. Were we aging too quickly? Was life passing us by so fast we'd forgotten to *live, love and be happy*? Had the thrill already gone? How could I make it come back?

Later that day, I got a call from Paul's amazing chef, Alberto.

'Can you meet me at my restaurant?' he asked. 'Paul's in Florence and I need some decisions made.'

Made for what, a wedding that may never, ever happen? I eyed the kitchen clock. My roast was in the oven. Not that I'd be partaking, but still, the family needed to be fed.

'Give me half an hour.'

As I pulled up to De Gustibus, Alberto's restaurant, or Bust De Guts, as I still liked to call it, he was waiting outside with a sheepish grin. At the question mark that must have blossomed on my forehead, he laughed.

'Come.'

'Where?'

'To a food lover's dream place – a farm in Pienza. They will, if they pass my test, be providing their cheeses and other kinds of produce for your wedding dinner. I told them you're a tough cookie and that you want nothing but the best.'

Which was true. 'OK,' I said. 'Hop in.'

'Or… we could go in mine,' he suggested, pushing a small remote.

Behind me was a thick thud. I whirled round to meet the blinking eyes of his famous black Ferrari.

Suddenly, whizzing off to Pienza for a food and wine afternoon with another man seemed odd to me. But I wasn't doing anything wrong, was I? It wasn't like I was going up into the mountains to a log cabin with the guy, right? So rumor had it he flirted a bit. OK, more than a bit. But at the end of the day, he was Paul's love interest and if I could do anything to bend Alberto's ear to Paul's fabulousness, I would. But, between you and me? I was *not* getting the gay vibe.

As we soared (there's no other word for traveling in a Ferrari) through the Siena countryside, I admired the backdrop of yellows, russets, auburns and greens and the winding paths guarded on either side by towering cypress trees. Before I knew it, the ride was over and Alberto parked under the medieval walls of Pienza.

I turned to look over the ramparts and almost died and went to heaven. Below us, as far as the eye could see, spread the breathtaking Val d'Orcia. I'd forgotten it was so beautiful.

'Up we go,' he said, putting a gentle hand at my back to push me forward onto the road weaving into town.

And in two minutes flat, I was struggling. Mr. Clean would be ashamed of me. I understand not being able to do the haka, but a tiny *Treka* up a hill? Was I that out of shape? Jesus.

Alfredo shot me an amused glance. 'Need a boost?'

'I'm fine,' I wheezed, trying to sound normal, my chest about to explode.

Christ, how much did I weigh again? Certainly more than eighty-six, judging by my wheezing noises I was frantically trying to smother behind my fake cough and throat-clearing.

Through winding paths (and me trying not to pant too loudly or sweat too profusely), we emerged through to Piazza Pio II and the cathedral. I stood in silence (also because breathing at this point had become tricky), absorbing the familiar and yet still astonishing site.

Alberto stuffed his hands in his pockets and stood back to admire what he obviously knew like the back of his hands. 'You know, Pienza is dubbed *La Città Utopia*.'

If there was anyone who had done their homework on the province of Siena, it was me. I flashed him a smile. 'The Ideal City.'

He made an impressed face. 'Ah, you already knew that. But did you know that it's the birthplace of Pope Pius II?'

I grinned and he grinned.

'OK, I can tell you know that, too. But did you know, my dear Erica, that Pienza has two very romantic roads?'

Romantic? That caught my attention. I could bring Julian here and maybe, with a bit of luck…

'Ah-ha,' he said, his amber eyes twinkling. 'Here, let me show you.'

And he took my hand and dragged me up another steep street as with my free hand, I tugged surreptitiously at my bra, which seemed to want to give up its fight. I could only hope that it would, if you'll pardon the pun, hang in there and not give up its fight altogether, especially now.

Higher and higher we climbed, my feet getting heavier and heavier, my breathing reduced to a strangled wheezing. Just as I thought I'd crash onto the cobblestones like a felled bull in a ring, he stopped.

'This, my beautiful friend, is *Via del Bacio*.'

'The street of the kiss,' I translated rather badly.

It sounded awful in English. Why did Italians make everything sound better? Look and taste better, too? Because Italians were people of love.

'Exactly. And did you know that there's also a *Via dell'Amore?*'

The Street of Love? Whoa.

I looked up at him and he nodded, not letting go of my (sweaty) hand and leading me through a maze of medieval paths (that gave no sign whatsoever of leveling out) winding through ancient stone archways. In two minutes, we were standing under a sign that read, to the point, *Via dell'Amore.*

He stopped and glanced at me. What? For real? Was he trying it on with me? What about Paul? Not that Alberto had mentioned him all afternoon and whenever I happened to slip in his name, Alberto chuckled and said, 'Please – no work this afternoon, *sì?*'

And now he was flirting with me? Had he run out of fodder? Paul would kill Alberto (and me) if I had proof he wasn't gay. Not that I ever suspected he was. He was just too manly and gruff, in a way. Nor was he the politest guy in the world (I'd seen the way he kicked his staff around). But there was something about him – his boyish arrogance, maybe – that made him almost... well, endearing.

Or, most probably, it was the fact that he'd whisked me away on a carefree day and begun to womanize me for a few hours while I couldn't get my own groom-to-be to pay some intimate attention to me.

So what if he was flirting? So I kind of flirted back, albeit subtly. Plus, I could handle him easily. He was a classy playboy, nothing like the town playboy, Leonardo Cortini. All they had in common was the type of car they drove.

No, Alberto was an interesting guy, a god in the kitchen. He had an under-the-skin sexiness that got into you after you spoke to him for a while and you realized how soulful he was, with that bitter sense of humor and the gaze that held much more than meets the eye. In another time, another life (and if neither Paul nor Julian existed), I'd have easily fallen for Alberto's enveloping, protective manner. Of course, I'd have much preferred to be with Julian, but as usual, he wasn't around.

Alberto ran a hand through the short hair at his nape and removed his denim jacket. Underneath he wore a black T-shirt revealing tribal tats. Oh, bad boy, was he, then?

'*Scusa*,' Alberto suddenly said to a teenager rollerblading by. '*Ci faresti una foto, per favore?*'

A picture? Here, in the Street of Love? Ho, boy. The man was sure pulling out all the stops. A soft thrill traversed me and I kept telling myself it was all in harmless fun. Tomorrow, I'd be back in my own frustrating reality. But for today, I'd sit back and enjoy some innocent banter. It had been such a long time since I'd felt this important in anyone's eyes.

The teen braked and shoved his cellphone into his back pocket as Alberto pulled out his own phone, pulling me back against the brick wall with the street sign *Via dell'Amore* above us.

As the boy waited for the right moment to shoot, Alberto casually put his arm around me, leaning in close to my face. Paul would absolutely kill me if he found out about this outing (or the lack of Alberto's outing).

'*Grazie*. And now,' Alberto said to me, his arm still slung over my shoulder, 'for the reason of our trip.'

'You mean you're finally going to feed me?'

He looked down at me, his eyes focusing on my face, then grinned. 'I'm going to feed you, yes.'

'Cool. Because I'm not on a diet today, in case you were

wondering.' Screw Mr. Clean. Today was a day away from reality.

He opened a door to reveal what looked like a hole in the wall. I shot him a glance before I peered into a large, dark cave, welcoming the coolness inside after my rubber soles had practically melted on the smoldering cobblestones.

'In there?' I asked, and he nodded, his eyes twinkling.

'After you, my lady.'

As we walked down a narrow corridor, he put his hand on my shoulder. 'You'll be blown away, trust me.'

He was right. What was supposed to have been a mere tasting of cheeses and cold meats for our wedding antipasto turned out to be a full-blown lunch. Parma ham, cooked ham, smoked ham, a type of salami called *finocchiona* seasoned with fennel seeds and an array of soft cheeses including the *Cacio di Pienza*, *Marzolino di Pienza* and the famous *Pienza Pecorino Toscano DOP*. All accompanied by an amazing focaccia drizzled with olive oil and oregano, olives, capers and every succulent Italian antipasto I could think of.

Sadly, it looked like Alberto cared more about my wedding day than Julian did. I knew it was silly of me even to think so and that Alberto was only doing his job the best he could (which included some very classy personal touches). If Julian could be here, he'd take more part in the preparation. Right?

As we sat down, he ordered a selection of Montepulciano wines. Bingo. No Italian meal was a meal without wine.

'I'm going to get you the best wine in Tuscany for your wedding,' he promised.

My wedding. Huh. I snapped my head back and glugged the contents like a Coke can and Alberto laughed.

'Well, I'm glad that you're on top of my wedding. Is work all you ever think about?' I said breathily.

Uh-oh. That was supposed to be me wheezing, but it came out a bit too flirty. But Alberto was man enough to ignore that little nudge, thank God. There was no way in hell I'd ever entertain a little foray into adultery and I wanted to make damn sure he got that much straight. But he reassured me with a smile.

'Yes, work is my life.'

'Don't you have a… companion of sorts? Seriously now.' A little digging for Paul to show him I was only looking out for his interests would maybe ease the blow of our little outing together.

Alberto laughed. 'A companion? Let's say I'm never lonely.'

Lucky you, I thought as I polished off the wine and stuffed a square of focaccia into my mouth, chewed and washed it down with some more vino.

'Are you happy?' I asked. 'With your life, I mean?'

He smiled. 'I have the best job in the world, I live in one of the most beautiful places on earth, and I'm young and healthy. Why wouldn't I be happy?'

Well, why not indeed… He himself had said he wasn't lonely. A slight shadow of envy passed over me. No, not envy. Just… wanting to be happy. Wasn't that one of the main goals in life?

The sun was low when he dropped me off at my car in front of De Gustibus. And speaking of Bust de Guts, as I called it, I was splitting at the seams from the gorgeous food and wine.

'Thanks for a great time, Alberto.'

He looked at me and squeezed my shoulder. 'Thank *you*, beautiful.' And then he let go. 'Take care.'

On my way home, he sent me a text with an attachment: the two of us posing like a couple in *Via dell'Amore*. I laughed and shook my head, humming 'Here comes the bride' to myself all the way home.

As I had an eighteenth birthday cake to start tomorrow, today I was pre-prepping some meals, particularly my *panzanella*, a summer salad made with stale bread dipped in balsamic vinegar and olive oil layered with sliced onions, olives, tomatoes, tuna or ham, corn and a generous dose of mint or basil, whatever you have in the house. This is because Tuscan cuisine is based on the ancient tradition of using whatever is left over from the previous meal to reinvent something new. It's called '*cucina povera*' and everyone in my house loves it. It's too bad you have to wait while it sets in the refrigerator for twenty-four hours.

'I just got a call from Sienna,' Julian said as he came into the kitchen. 'She wants me to do a photo shoot to promote my book.'

I looked up from my *panzanella*-in-progress. She really was seeing more of him than I was. What happened to halving the times he'd be going abroad?

I bit my lip. 'Right. When are you going?'

'Tomorrow morning. But I'm only going to Milan. Be back by the evening, sweets,' he promised, kissing the side of my head. 'And, oh, Terry's flying over to discuss a few promo ideas.'

I snorted. 'You mean like the last time, when he wanted

you on the cover of your book in a baseball outfit so badly torn there was more skin than stripes?'

Gorgeous skin, mind. Because he was such a beautiful man. As opposed to me, the grizzly bear with boobs who had to starve to death to look half-decent. How the hell had I managed to pull this guy in the first place?

'He's only trying to do my what's in my best interest, Erica.'

'Your interest – hah! I wouldn't be surprised if he asked you to pose in shredded briefs. Tell him you're not a fashion model like David Beckham.'

'OK, Victoria,' he said with a grin.

I speared him with an icy look. 'You think this is funny? Terry's not to be trusted. Somebody's gotta keep an eye on you.'

His eyes narrowed. 'What's that supposed to mean?'

'That if he told you all the pantiles on the rooftops in Castellino were made of gingerbread, you'd believe it.'

Julian looked at me and then went all stony and defensive like I'd never ever seen him before. The look on his face made me stop and think I was being a bitch. I shouldn't be so aggressive. This man had saved me.

'I'm sorry, Julian. I just don't want you to get duped.'

'I won't get duped,' he insisted.

'Oh, trust me, you will. You know I'm good at reading people and he… he scares me. He's not a friend of yours. All he wants is all the money you can make him. Every time he sees you, his eyes light up in dollar signs.'

Julian shrugged. 'That's what agents do.'

'No. There are agents, and then there are good agents. A good agent takes care of his people. But Terry only takes care of himself. Can't you dump him and just keep Sienna?'

Whoa, had I just suggested that? You see, I am a selfless woman who cares about her man's career, after all!

'Erica, I had three completely different careers before I even met you. I don't need you to worry about me. Besides, Sienna is my European agent. Terry knows the other side of the pond like the back of his hand.'

I glanced at him as I finished prepping my *panzanella*. What was happening here? Before Terry and Sienna had come into our lives we were just fine. I was his sounding board. I was indeed his Victoria Beckham, but now, apparently, he didn't need my opinion anymore. Now wasn't the time to drag out all my insecurities. I didn't want to seem needy to him.

I shrugged and with all the indifference I could muster, said: 'Suit yourself, superhero.'

He'd noticed the shift in my demeanor. And he didn't like it. So he tried a different tactic.

'Hmm, *panzanella* – looks great.'

'It's not for now. It has to sit in the refrigerator for a few hours,' I explained. 'I'll save you some for when you get back.'

Julian took my hand. 'And when I do, for your once-a-week reward, I'll bring back a nice dessert and we can have a late night, just the two of us, on the terrace under your beloved pergola, how's that?'

I turned to him, unable to hide my concern. He acknowledged it with a sweet, resigned smile that meant we were good again, that no one could come between us. And that, come hell or high water, we would find a way to get married.

I took his face in my hands and whispered, 'Hurry home, future husband.'

# 14

## Back to Back

After my final dress fitting at Fiorella's Bridal Shop and a few confirmations for the car, the flowers, a simple restaurant, Alberto, Padre Adolfo, we were ready to book a date—August 20th! This afternoon I'd shoot my family (now there was a thought) and my in-laws a blanket invitation and I was done! With one week to target, all that was left was getting the bride ready! As I was grooming myself for the return of my own groom that afternoon, I pushed an arm into the shower stall to turn the water on for my shower, twisting at the waist to avoid the jets, when I froze in that position, knives of pain shooting up my back. After several tiny warnings, this time my back gave out completely. Julian had warned me.

'*Owowowow...*' I groaned helplessly, afraid to move a muscle as water already rained down onto my head, through my hair and onto my face.

That's what an old bag like me got for soaking endlessly (and in my case recklessly) in the bathtub or in the pool and not changing into something dry afterward. Who did I think I was, the swimmer Katie Ledecky?

I reached out, grasping for the faucet only a few inches beyond my reach as a spasm rocked up my back from tail to neck, and I fell to my knees in agony, my upper body in the stall, my legs sprawled out behind me. And then I was like a larva, completely unable to move. Damn Pilates! Damn Mr. Clean!

I lay paralyzed by pain as the minutes dragged by and I was completely soaked now. I couldn't think of a single way of getting out of this predicament. Call for help? Never in a million years – I'd have to deal with a million I told you sos.

When I was floating, not only was I easing the weight off my back, but my mind was also at ease – way worth a few odd twinges here and there the next day. Had I inherited my Nonna's arthritis? Except this was unprecedented. Never ever had I been glued to the floor afraid even to lick my lips. Even my hair was starting to hurt.

But there was no way I was going to lie here for the rest of my days, so I attempted to wrench myself out of the stall and was stopped by my arm, which seemed to have lost any will to live. Or move. There was no more pain now so much as a strange numbness that had spread to my legs and arms. If I lay here, perfectly still, I was OK except for my throbbing headache developing due to the fact that I was under a freezing shower (I hadn't managed to turn the hot water yet).

With a deep, deep breath, I made another attempt to move, figuring if my whole body was numb, it wouldn't hurt, right? Wrong. Out of my entire body, the one part I needed to work, my spine, was the only thing that didn't even understand the concept of numbness. It was wide awake and howling in alarm, refusing to budge a single inch.

But wait – if I crouched like this, like a cat, arching my spine way out of whack so I looked like I was praying to a tiny insect on the floor, it actually didn't hurt *that* much. I tested my new position, managing to breathe even. Still with my back arched, I crawled backward, banging my knee, but the stars dancing in my eyes were nothing compared to when I actually, in the same breath, tried to straighten my back slightly because I was getting cramps. Now what? And then there was a knock on my door.

'Are you still there?' Paul said. 'Julian's going to be home in an hour or so. Chop-chop – let's get this beauty show on the road!'

Him and his makeover obsession.

I glared at him as he took a step into the room, taking one look at me. 'You don't look very good – what's wrong?'

'It's OK,' I wheezed. 'It's just my back. Turn off the sh—'

Another spasm caught me in mid-sentence and Paul gripped my arm.

'Do I need to call your doctor?'

'No, he'll just say to take a pain reliever.'

'Did you?'

'I'd shake my head, but…'

'Top drawer as usual?'

'Yes. But this is a different kind of pain, Paul. I don't think a pill is going to cut it.'

Half an hour later, I was still on the floor writhing in pain as Paul fretted over me.

'Don't you worry – I'll get you to the hospital.'

'How? I can't move.'

'Then let me call an ambulance.'

'And alarm everyone? No. I'll get to the car,' I promised as I pulled myself up – and I swear I saw my whole life flash right by me. But I made it to the landing, huffing and puffing so hard it was a wonder the house was still standing.

'Good girl. Easy – here's the first step.'

I looked up at Paul for reassurance as we made our way down, and I had to stop at every step, the pain getting worse by the second. Ho, boy. Had I underestimated the whole situation?

'And here we—'

'Yeowwh…!' I screamed helplessly as my feet touched the last step and the pain shot up.

I could feel it disc after disc, flooring me completely as my grip on the railing failed and Paul's hands weren't enough to keep me standing.

It felt like my spine was ripping from the inside out. I knew it. My back was always touch-and-go and sometimes, I'd end up in bed for days. All because I hadn't kept my weight down, as my doctor had warned. Damn my gluttony. I should have heeded the words of caution from Julian. If only I'd listened, I wouldn't be in this position – this *painful* position – now.

Paul looked about him wildly for help.

'You stay here – I'll go get the car. *Rosina!*' he yelled up the stairs as I rested my head on the railing, wanting to die but knowing the ordeal was all ahead of me still.

Man, I hated pain with a passion. How the hell did masochists manage to get a kick out of it?

I lifted my head to see where he'd gone as I couldn't sit anymore, my whole lower half screaming. What the hell was keeping Paul?

Luckily he came running back, but only to circle the space at the bottom of the stairs like a headless chicken. I lifted my eyes a fraction.

'Paul, stay calm. With the right massage and some rest, I'll be OK. I'm not going into labor, you know.'

'There are no cars!' he shrieked.

'What?'

'Not one! Julian's got the jeep, yours is at the mechanic's and I sent Martino off to town with mine to get me some stuff!'

Big gut-wrenching stabs of pain made me double over in a new kind of pain. If I didn't know any better, I'd think I really was in labor.

'Let me call Renata.'

'Don't bother. She's in Florence for the day with the kids.'

'So what do we do? I know!' he cried as I leaned forward into a feline position again, trying to breathe without collapsing onto myself.

He ran out the door, down the hill, disappearing out of my limited line of sight in literally thirty seconds.

The next thing I heard was the sound of a tractor and, believe it or not, coming up the hill was my glamorous wedding planner gay friend at the wheel, his face so white and stiff he looked like a dummy. If it hadn't hurt so much, I would have laughed.

'You can't drive that,' I moaned, but Paul jumped down to come and get me.

'The brake!' I moaned. 'Pull the brake first!'

'What? Oh, sorry,' he cried and scrambled back in before the whole thing careened down the hill again, deluxe wedding planner and all. 'You'll be OK!' Paul cried as he half dragged, half lifted me onto the cart hooked up to the tractor.

I wanted to lash out and kick him into the next field. Well, at least I'd be able to lie down on the soft hay. Only I couldn't lie down, either, so I sort of pretzeled out, clutching at his seat as he jumped back in and slammed on the gas pedal. Which made the tractor lurch.

'The brake. Disengage the brake!'

'How?'

'Push the toggle and then bring the lever down.'

He obeyed and we were off to a start and I couldn't help but yowl in pain.

'No more food – ever again,' I growled. 'I swear I'll go on a diet – lose weight – I promise!'

Paul turned to give me an amazed look, nearly missing a stray *cipresso* branch that was sticking out into the road.

'Watch where you're going or we'll both end up on a gurney,' I cried, already seeing the headlines in the news:

Tragedy Between Castellino and Siena: Mother of two and BGFF die in a self-induced tractor crash on a quiet country road.

Paul's face paled and he nodded again. 'Hang on, sweetheart. I'll get you there in no time.'

Who was he kidding? The tractor only did twenty kilometers an hour! It was built for strength, not speed, and the hospital was miles away. Although the roads were good and smooth, the hairpin turns, ups and downs, didn't do me much good.

'You better step on it, Paul!'

'I don't want to jostle you,' he argued.

'You'll be jostling a cripple if you don't floor it!' I argued back, taking a deep breath, trying to keep my cool.

In response, another gut-wrenching stab hit me, as if my spine were paper and someone was going at it with a Stanley knife.

'OK, got it. Sorry, hun, I forgot how vicious you get. Hey, look, there's Beppe! His car's broken down.' As we passed the poor old dairy farmer, Paul called out, 'Sorry, pal, not this time!'

'Stop!' I yelled, and suddenly, the tractor came to a screeching halt.

'What? What is it?'

'Let him in – he's old and it's too hot out in this sun.'

'Are you nuts!' he said and then turned to Beppe, who in the meantime had reached us.

Paul put the tractor into first gear with a few more screeches as Beppe hopped straight in the back, his hands searching mine.

'Don't worry, Erica. I'll help you. I have cows,' he muttered, and my eyes popped open in protest. 'I'm not in labor, Beppe, it's just my back!'

'Good enough for me!' Paul conceded as he took off with a screech and a halt that would have thrown me to the far end of the cabin if Beppe hadn't caught me.

The old man looked down at me, then shouted something in pure Tuscan dialect, which I completely missed but Paul, who barely spoke Italian, understood.

'Sorry for the bumps, sweetie,' he called back at me. 'You'll be OK, I promise.'

At this rate, we were never going to get to the hospital.

'Just pull over and let me die here,' I moaned. 'And tell the kids I love them.'

'Erica, sweetie, please. Hang on!'

'To what?' I barked back. Then, insanely, I snarled, 'Your driving sucks!'

It wasn't true. Or rather, it was, but I didn't mean to say it. It just came out, but he looked at me like I'd kicked him in the head, his eyes darting back to the road ahead.

'I'm sorry, I'm sorry, I'm so sorry!' I shrieked as another stab nearly tore me in half. 'I love you.'

That seemed to fuel him and he accelerated, thank God in heaven.

At that point, Beppe pulled out his cellphone and two minutes later Marco, Renata's husband, arrived in the car that he only used for special occasions. How sweet.

'Marco…' I whispered as he and Paul lifted me and gently put me on the back seat, where the pain slowly subsided and I closed my eyes for the rest of the journey, confident I was in good hands. 'I thought you were in Florence.'

'No, I decided to stay behind this time. Good thing I did, *sì?*'

'*Sì*… thank you.'

But when we arrived at the hospital, I was unceremoniously thrown onto a gurney. Paul held my hand past a few doors and then his lips brushed mine.

'I love you – you'll be OK,' he whispered.

'You betcha,' I whispered back, wondering if I'd ever be able to walk again.

# 15

## I Hear Those Church Bells Ringing

It turned out that August 20th came and went without my becoming Mrs. Foxham. For three whole weeks, I was trapped in bed and I couldn't move a toe, let alone have any hope of walking down the aisle in the near future.

'I'm sorry,' I sobbed to Julian after he brought me home from the hospital. 'It's like fate doesn't want us to get married.'

'Nonsense, sweetheart. We'll reschedule.'

'Again…But what about everybody?'

'They'll understand. You just get better and the minute you're on your feet, we'll do it. OK?'

'K,' I sniffed.

Maddy and Warren spent the afternoons with me on my bed. Every time one of them shifted, I'd stifle a scream.

'Why don't you use my writing desk to draw?' I suggested with what felt like my dying breath, and happily Maddy hopped up, the mattress dipping slightly, but it wasn't as bad as before.

Warren sat by the window, surveying the horizon. It still wasn't a pretty sight, but better than before.

'Are you and Daddy going to get married when you're better?' Maddy wanted to know.

'Of course,' I answered. 'It won't be long now, sweetheart.'

'And I still get to wear my new dress?'

'Absolutely. And… you'll look like a princess.'

She searched my gaze and when she found what she was looking for, gave a satisfied nod.


After three weeks of physiotherapy, I finally managed to get out of bed, ready to reschedule. I wasn't 100% healed, but I could sure as hell walk down that damn aisle, once and for all. I'd have even crawled if Julian had asked me to. But he hadn't.

'Believe it or not, but a couple has cancelled their wedding and now there's an opening with Padre Adolfo next Saturday, September 17th, close enough to our original date. Shall we book?' I asked Julian as I slowly got dressed.

Julian's face fell. 'Sorry, sweetheart. I'm flying to Copenhagen that week.'

Ah. He'd wasted no time.

'But I won't be away longer than two weeks – and then we can reschedule, promise.'

Which meant October 1st. This was ludicrous. How many times would we have to do this? How many times did I have to move the pink square to accommodate all the blue ones that were making no effort to bugger off already? We were practically becoming a joke in town. Not even I believed we were going to go through with this farce of a wedding anymore. And now, without even telling me beforehand, he'd made plans to go away again. Was he trying to tell me something after all, and I was just too thick to get it?

'Did… Sienna already book everything for you?'

Julian chuckled. 'That woman has even my bathroom visits timed. She's a real slave driver.'

'Isn't she,' I replied, and suddenly I saw Julian and me on either end of a church aisle. Like in a psychedelic dream, the aisle stretched and stretched, while I tried to grab his outstretched hands as Julian grew further and further away from me, far, far away, into infinity – until I couldn't see him anymore.

'We hardly ever see you anymore,' I whispered. 'I miss you. The kids miss you. Sometimes I feel that you're more interested in your career than us.'

'I feel the same way about you and the B & B.'

'But you knew I was going to run a B & B…'

'And you knew I was going to write.'

'And run the farm,' I reminded him. 'I know you're busy, but can't you find one day to get married? I don't even care about a honeymoon anymore…'

He sighed. 'You're right. I've been selfish. This whole career thing has overwhelmed me. I wasn't prepared for it to be a rollercoaster all over again. Perhaps it's all turning out to be too much. The writing, the promoting, the farm. I can't be in three places at once. And the farm itself is not just one task. There's the horses, the crops, the orchards. I'm simply stretched too thin, Erica…'

'I know. But you forgot to factor in time for us.'

'Come on, Erica. Can you truly say you've been on the

ball with me and the kids as well? Are you not obsessed with your business?'

'Yes,' I admitted. 'But only because I have to be. If I'm not, it all goes to pot.'

'What does?'

'My financial independence…'

'But that's the thing, Erica. We're a family. My finances are yours. They're ours.'

'I understand that and really appreciate it. But I've worked all my life. I can't not contribute. I have to do this for my own pride.'

'And I have to write. For my own happiness.'

'I understand that. I'm happy you're doing what you love.'

'Thank you, love.'

'You're welcome,' I conceded. 'I'll tell you what. We'll hire even more help. Hell, you make enough to afford it, right?'

'We make enough,' he corrected me.

'OK, then. We. So you continue doing your thing, and I continue doing mine. And the farm, we'll play it by ear. Deal?'

'Deal,' he said. 'Kiss and make up now?'

I looked up into his eyes. My Julian. My rock. 'Kiss and make up…'

And the next day he flew to Sienna's side. I spent most of my time doing some light cleaning and cooking. And some very heavy fuming, scrubbing furiously until I was spent. This wedding wasn't going to happen anywhere in the near future, I had to face it.

So when Alberto called to ask me what kind of desserts I wanted to offer our guests after the cake, I almost answered, *Forget the cake. It's too much trouble. Let's have… cupcakes. Break-up cupcakes.*

Break-ups were to relationships what cupcakes were to cakes. The easier way out. They didn't take as long to make, were pretty and easier to deal with. They represented lack of commitment. With a sigh, I decided to drive down there and give Alberto the news of the indefinite postponing of the wedding. Once and for all.

'Hey, welcome back to the living,' he said, embracing me and giving me the two customary kisses. 'Did you get my cookies?'

'I did, thank you. I'm so sorry about all your hard work for nothing, Alberto.'

'No problem, Erica. Things happen. When have you rescheduled for?'

*Oyoy.* 'Uhm… we have to postpone the wedding again, I'm afraid.'

He threw me a glance as he sliced a bit of pecorino cheese onto a plate. 'Why?'

I sighed. 'I don't know, Alberto. Julian's work keeps getting in the way. He's probably not in a hurry to marry me, after all, who knows?'

'Ridiculous. Who wouldn't want a woman like you?'

'Aww, that's really very sweet.'

He grinned and reached for a pot of honey. 'You want sweet – taste this combination…'

Food? I could see Mr. Clean's face, his eyebrows knitting as he shook his finger at me, and I backed away while I still could. 'Oh, no, I couldn't possibly—'

'*Assaggia,*' he coaxed as usual.

It looked and smelled delicious. Oh, hell – what was one little bite? So I surrendered and tasted the honey-cheese mixture, looking up into his eyes as the flavor-fest enveloped me instantly.

'Oh my God, Alberto, you're a genius,' I murmured.

He smiled. 'You have such beautiful eyes, Erica,' he said softly.

'Oh, stop,' I said, dismissing his compliment with a smile.

I never thought I'd stick around while another man womanized me, but here I was, eating his food, drinking his wine, sucking in all the compliments and even believing some of them. He was right – I did have nice eyes. I was a good mother and I was nobody's fool. Except maybe for Julian.

Yes, I must certainly be a fool, standing around waiting while Julian went on with his own life, treating our home like a hotel and me as (and I would know) the hotel manager.

As I munched away, my cell beeped. Julian, maybe… A sign that he was thinking of me, even if we were miles apart, as usual? As *if* – it was another message from Julian's credit card company. I was getting sick and tired of them. Every time he bought something, I got a message. I could technically (now that was a thought) track him across the globe. Many a surprise had been ruined because I'd already known what was under the wrapping paper. There was no fun in it at all. Tomorrow, I'd phone the company and get the alerts transferred to Julian's number.

I pulled my phone out and stared at the screen. A payment had been made to Hotel Villa Etrusca. Hotel? What the heck did Julian need a hotel for only two hours from home? How tired would he have to be not to make it home for the night? Unless… he didn't intend to?

The only reason I could think of not wanting to make it home was that he had other plans. With someone else. As much as I hated even to think of the possibility, I hadn't exactly shown him my best side lately. So say that he was sick and tired of living with me and say that he'd found someone else without kids who had no demands on his time… Say also that he didn't know how to tell me and was stalling until he found the courage to do so…

And then I wondered. Was he seeing Sienna? Was he cheating on me with her? Had I had my head so deep in my business that I couldn't see what was happening under my nose? Would this be the second time in my life that a cellphone revealed to me that my man had a lover?

And while I was fuming and considering permutations, my cellphone beeped again. *Tattinger*. As in… champagne? Julian was with Sienna. Drinking champagne. What more proof did I need? How much longer was I going to stay in the dark while my man slept with someone else? Never again!

'I have to go,' I blurted and scooped up my bag before Alberto could look up. 'The wedding's off!'

'Erica, why? What's wrong?' he called after me, but I was already in first gear.

Of course, Julian being 'out of town', there was no way I could confront him. I wanted to tell Renata or Paul – *someone* – because the weight of it was killing me. After only two years in Italy and three in a relationship with Julian, we were over. He'd cheated on me. How many times had it happened before – once, twice, a million times? No wonder he always found excuses to put off the wedding. Did everyone on earth but me know?

For a very brief moment, I was tempted to get into my car, go over there and catch him in the act. Just so there would be no more doubts. But I chickened out. If it was true, what would I do? What would I say? The first time it happened to me, I was married to Ira, and perhaps back then it made sense. We had had nothing in common except for the kids. It had seemed to me only natural for it to end that way.

But Julian and I? We were made for each other. And I wasn't so sure I was ready to face something so monumental. I couldn't bear losing him. So I stayed put and worried in silence, something I was getting amazingly proficient in.

That evening, Paul called and he wasn't happy with me.

'You're not serious about calling off the wedding again, are you? Because I had to find out from Alberto that my best friend isn't getting married any time soon.'

'I know, I'm sorry. I was going to tell you when you got in tonight.'

'That would have been nice, seeing as I'm your *wedding planner* and all!'

'I said I was sorry.'

'Is it like the last time? Is it only postponed? Because in that case, some of the foods Alberto chose will soon be out of season. Not to say your dress out of fashion.'

'Ha. Ha.'

'You laugh. Have you checked your calendar lately?'

Was he joking? I lived by those colored squares. Pink, you'll remember, for my ever-fading wedding day, so distant it was now paling towards an off-white. Blue for the days Julian was away. Green for the kids' activities. Orange for appointments. Red for business deadlines. Between that and my colored Post-it notes, from the outside, my life looked like a rainbow. But in reality, it was more like a game of Twister, as I had to hit as many different colors as possible and literally bend over backwards. Not a way to live in rural Tuscany.

I squeezed the bridge of my nose. 'I have to take Maddy to ballet. I'll call you later, OK?'

'I'm looking like a fool, Erica. This is the umpteenth time we've had to reschedule.'

'I'm perfectly aware, thank you.'

'There goes my chance of ever working with him again – or getting into his pants, thank you very much.'

'Paul, what do you want from me?'

'Just choose a damn date already.'

Anything to get him off my back. 'Right. As soon as Julian gets back, I will.' I could also have mentioned Julian's little tryst, but if I mentioned it, then it became real. First, the bloody locusts. Then my back, and now a knife in the back? This was all too much, even for me.

'God, I swear we'll all be old and gray by the time you guys get a move on.'

'Thank you very much. I really needed that.'

'Just trying to motivate you, that's all.'

'Bye,' I snapped and hung up.

A second later, my phone beeped. It was a message from Alberto:

The menu can still be saved, and so can you.

Ha. As if. With Julian booking hotels and buying Tattinger, my dreadful prophecy had fulfilled itself. After barely three years, Julian's famous Superman syndrome had inevitably reached its end.

# 16

## The Kiss of Betrayal

A few days later I drove to Alberto's restaurant in response to his invitation to check on some stuff. 'Hey, Chef, I got your message. What's up?'

He turned at the sound of my voice and grinned as he reached out to wipe his hands on a dish towel. Did this man never leave the kitchen?

'Is that how long it takes you to return your calls? Two weeks?'

'I'm sorry, Alberto. It's been crazy.'

'I know you have your own cake business and that it's doing very well, but a bride should not make her own cake. So I wanted to show you what I can do,' he said, whipping a lid off a cake stand.

I gasped. Was he trying to kill me? It was halfway between a cupcake and a cake, obviously delicious and white, like real love should be. That it looked virginal in its whiteness was beside the point. It was too good for me.

And the guilt for not having gone back (yet) to the gym

was gnawing at me. Mr. Clean must have thought I was a flake, all mouth and no action. But right now, that was the least of my problems.

'Don't be fooled by its apparent innocence,' he said, taking my elbow. 'Inside it's a tiramisu with the wickedest darkest chocolate – a mini version just for you.'

And *of* me, as well, apparently. Layers and layers of sinful thinking. Yep, that was me.

'And you made this just for… me?'

'*Sì*… to give you a taste of what is to come.'

'Thank you so much, Alberto, but I already told you I'm not getting married—'

'I'm sorry for you.'

'Thank you.'

'Here,' he said. 'Just a taste – a small one. You'll love it. I made it to cheer you up. You shouldn't be sad. Ever. Not with those eyes.'

Little did he know his kind gesture had been for naught. This wedding wasn't going to be. Ever.

He took a step closer, waving the cake under my nose. The fragrance of coffee and chocolate caressed my nostrils, which twitched like a rabbit's. My very own wedding cake. Just mine. Mine the wedding cake, mine the wedding plans, mine (and mine only) the dreams of a life together. Because Julian had drifted out of my reach. How long before he packed his bags for good and gave me 'The Speech'? Or would he go on behind my back as long as possible as Ira had?

Was he in love with her, or was she one of the many? And then the Tattinger came to mind again. They'd go to the hotel, pour themselves a glass, clink and drink to themselves. And then he'd take her glass, put it on the nightstand and push her long red hair off her neck and… I burst into tears.

'*Ehi, ehi, che succede?* What's wrong?' he asked as I buried my face in the collar of my jacket, not wanting him to see me like this and most of all, wanting to disappear into thin air.

'The wedding is off!' I blurted. 'This time for good.'

'What? Why?'

'Because he's cheating on me!'

'*Impossibile*,' he sentenced.

At that, I dug in my pocket for the offending credit card message on my cellphone and shoved it under his nose. He read silently, his eyes hardening, shaking his head.

'*Idiota*,' he muttered. '*Che idiota*. If I had a woman like you, I'd treat you like a princess,' he seethed.

The sensation of déjà vu was too painful to relive. Not too long ago, Julian had said the same about Ira. He'd promised to cherish me and love me forever, and yet here I was again. Damn men.

'You all say that in the beginning. Then you get fed up and crave fresh meat. You're all the same.'

'No, that's not true, Erica,' he murmured, way too close for comfort.

I could smell his skin, feel his muscles move under his shirt. Damn cheating Julian. Years dedicated to building a life together. Years of my kids calling him dad and he'd splurged on the best champagne and a deluxe hotel suite for his lover?

'We're not all like that. Here, have some Chianti – it'll warm you.'

I took a sip and instantly felt better. Wine always did it for me.

'What the heck! You might as well taste the other things I made you,' he said.

I stared at him through a rainfall of tears. 'You... made me something else?'

'Of course.' He sauntered over to the stove and lifted a lid. 'Here, try this... ravioli stuffed with poached sole in asparagus and basil sauce.'

'Mmm,' I swooned and smiled despite myself. Was there nothing this guy couldn't cook?

The wine was making me feel better, warm and fuzzy all over. I wasn't feeling any pain at all. Above us, copper pots gleamed, like a galaxy of suns, reflecting the light from the log fire. It was warm and comfy and easy. I could stay here forever and not have to worry about all the pressure closing in on me from a million different directions. The failing B & B that was still empty, my dead relationship with my stepmother, Julian – who seemed more and more distant with each passing day – and even Paul turning on me.

'What man wouldn't already consider himself lucky with you waiting for him when he gets home?' he murmured.

Of course that all depended on what time he got home and if he actually came home every night, as opposed to my man, who returned, if I was lucky, twice a month. And now I knew why.

'Ah, you'd be surprised, Alberto.'

He looked at me, his eyelids heavy with alcohol. He was so kind, so sweet, so protective. Like Julian used to be.

I closed my eyes and sighed sadly, longing for Julian to love me the way he used to, remembering his warm body against mine, his breath on my face as he leaned in… cupping my chin and delicately tasting my mouth…

But when I opened my eyes, I only saw Alberto. Alberto was kissing me, like really kissing me, with his eyes closed, his hands in my hair, really going for it.

I broke off the kiss and gently but firmly pushed him away so that it was very clear – *Valdinievole* white wine clear – that it wasn't happening. Not now, not ever.

What the hell had happened to me? Had I literally lost touch with reality for a moment while daydreaming about Julian? And that was how long it took to let Alberto, or any man, *kiss* me? I jumped to my feet as if the floor had caught fire.

I'd kissed another man! Well, OK, technically, he'd kissed me, but I'd let him. And all this time, hadn't I gone along with the flirting, albeit thinking it was extremely harmless? And that it had been a long time since a good-looking guy had paid me that one-of-a-kind type of attention. If Julian found out, he'd be devastated. Not to mention Paul. I'd just committed a double betrayal.

'I have to go,' I whispered, looking for my bag, which I finally found on top of the counter where I'd let him feed me some gorgeous non-diet food.

I'd actually cheated not twice, but several times over – Julian, Paul, the kids who depended on me, and finally, my diet. 'Kiss the cook' had just taken on a whole new meaning.

'Are you OK?' Alberto whispered back, rising to touch my arm, but I moved away, even if it was too late.

Way too late. I'd kissed another man. Someone who wasn't my Julian. On the other hand, Julian was booking a suite with someone else. And he'd said he'd cherish me until his dying day.

'Erica?' said Alberto, his shirt hanging out of his jeans, his hands still outstretched in a request to have me there. 'Are you OK?'

This was surreal. A lifetime of male drought and suddenly, it was raining men from every direction, when all I wanted was one man. My man. Who wasn't here. I hugged myself, suddenly cold with the knowledge of what I'd done, and tried to take deep, long breaths.

'No, um, I'm OK. I'm sorry, Alberto, but you... I have to go.'

His head dropped as if I'd sliced his neck open. 'The wine, the fire... it was just—'

'I know,' I said hastily, already halfway across the kitchen.

'I never meant to—'

'I know. It's OK.'

'It's just that... you're so beautiful, so intelligent and passionate.'

The same things Julian used to say to me, once upon a time. But not anymore. Now, he was probably saying those words to *her*, Sienna crappy Thornton-Jones.

'And in love with someone else,' I added softly, making to exit, but he'd caught up with me. I looked up into his face.

'I can give you what you need, Erica. All of it. Love, affection. Wild sex.'

That last one, I didn't doubt.

'You don't have to be a white widow anymore.'

I frowned. 'A white widow?'

'When a husband is alive but always away.'

My mouth, formed a round 'O' of surprise. And then

I recovered. 'I'm not a widow of any color, Alberto. My family is just adjusting to a new career, that's all. These are… minor hiccups.' There. I'd set the record straight. So why couldn't I act like I believed it?

'Who are you trying to kid?' he said coyly, trying to sound suave. 'The super-*mamma* attitude. You're a woman – you can't do it all.'

I felt my face tighten. Jesus, not only did he not know me (which was difficult even for Julian at the best of times), but worse, Alberto's years and years spent womanizing had taught him absolutely nothing about women, *period*. The way we always sacrifice ourselves for our loved ones, be they toddlers, teenagers or grown men. Just because we didn't wear crowns with red stars on the front, fly around in transparent airplanes or toss golden lassos to get the truth out of people didn't mean we weren't bloody Wonder Women.

And all these sacrifices we made? Men like Alberto would never understand. We normal women not only *could* do everything, but we also did it *every* day.

# 17

## Here Comes the Bride, There Goes the Groom…

A heavy metal version of 'Jingle Bells' or the theme tune from *The Hunchback of Notre Dame* – I couldn't decide which – was playing inside my head the next morning as I lay sprawled, fully clothed, on my bed. My mouth tasted like I'd chewed on some dead carcass and my tongue felt like someone had Velcroed it to the roof of my mouth.

Did I mention the racket going on inside my head, threatening to spill out of my skull and onto the floor?

I tried to move, but someone had stuck a giant thumbtack into my forehead, nailing me to the mattress. My man was sleeping with someone else in Hotel Villa Etrusca.

So, like I always did when I was desperate (or happy, or sad, or frustrated or overjoyed…), I ate. And ate, like nothing could fill me up. I ate bread and anything I could get my hands on. My zia Maria's sun-dried tomatoes and Parmesan cheese – one heavenly combination; bread and Nutella; bread and my homemade strawberry jam…

Then I started on leftovers from the night before – lasagne, fried chicken... whatever lurked in the refrigerator. And don't forget the cold roast potatoes with onion and carrot that I didn't even bother nuking, so overwhelming was my hunger. And then I had to stop. Not because I was full, but because my stomach was killing me and we'd entered the hug-the-toilet-bowl zone.

The last time I'd eaten like this had been two years ago, when I thought Julian had walked out on me back in Boston. In a perverse sense of self-destruction, I'd eaten a whole chocolate cake. Chocolate and tears – now there's a familiar combination, and one which I *still* don't recommend.

And then, to get over that sense of guilt, I'd slam myself in the gym for days on end. I lifted barbells, did bench-presses and even did half an hour of spinning. And when I still wasn't wiped out, I went back to the main gym room and joined in the damn haka, stomping away so angrily I thought the floor would give way under my feet, ignoring Mr. Clean's repeated gestures to *tone it down*. Tone it down? I'd pound the guilt out of me if it killed me, that's what I'd do. And one day, as the music died, I collapsed onto the floor.

'Erica!' Mr. Clean called, kneeling by my side, immediately lifting my legs in the air.

My head spinning, I raised a hand that readily flopped onto the mat next to me as if it belonged to someone else. 'I'm all right,' I breathed, but saw his face grim.

'Get me some juice,' he barked, and someone scurried off.

'I'm OK,' I repeated, trying to get up, and he gently pushed me back.

'Lie still,' he commanded.

And then I must have passed out again or fallen asleep.

'You're absolutely nuts, do you know that?' Paul barked as Mr. Clean passed me on to him like a baton in a relay race an hour later.

'I'm sorry,' I said meekly to Mr. Clean. 'I didn't mean to scare anyone.'

'Yeah, well, you scared the crap out of me, missy!' Paul scolded. 'Thanks, Gabriele,' he said as he helped put me into the car.

Who the hell was Gabriele?

'Call me to let me know how she's doing,' my coach said, and Paul nodded as he turned on the ignition.

I gave him a two thumbs up and winked. I must have still been a little woozy.

'What the hell are you trying to do? Kill yourself?' Paul cried as he drove me home.

I wanted to tell him how I felt, how everything was a mess. But instead I gulped, trying to swallow back the tears that I'd been holding in for days now.


The next day I was feeling a little better. That is, until my cellphone rang with Alberto's name in bright lights on my screen. I debated, then finally picked up.

'May I offer you an olive branch?' he said.

'Grilled or baked?'

A chuckle. 'I apologize for being a *stronzo, a jerk*, about the woman thing. It's just that... from the day I met you—'

Oh God, please no. 'I can't talk right now,' I cringed, just wanting to rewind the clock to about a minute before he kissed me to prevent it.

'OK… will you call me back when you have a moment?'

'Sure,' I lied and hung up before he could say anything else.

At that point, I should have given Paul the heads-up on Alberto's sexual preferences. But he was angry enough at me as it was about the wedding plans. There was no way I was telling him Alberto had kissed me. It was my first secret from him. *Ever*. And my very first secret from Julian.

'We need to talk,' Julian said a few days later when he returned from Amsterdam.

His face was unshaven, his eyes were wild and red-rimmed, and he'd even lost weight. How he'd changed in the space of a few weeks. That was what shameless all-night cavorting did to you. And now he wanted to have 'the talk'. Meaning that after he'd spent all that time with Sienna, he realized what he was missing out on as long as he was staying with me. And he wanted out.

*How dare you!* I cried on the inside. *How dare you break my heart and do this to us after all this time together!*

A sharp pang, mainly fear, shot through my system. Here it came, The Final Blow. He was going to leave me. My knees began to shake and my stomach went all funny and I wanted to throw up again. No, I told myself. I wasn't going to go all weak and stuff.

I had no choice but to look him in the face, and I stood my ground under his scrutinizing gaze, biting on the insides of my cheeks to stop from crying, at the same time wondering how either of us would pull this off. I couldn't even imagine what his opening gambit would be like, but at this point, nothing would surprise me. I knew where this was going.

'Erica, you and I need to sit down and have a good talk.'

No, no, no! Not yet. He couldn't be the one to leave me. Not again, not now – not like this! I wouldn't be able to stand it. If anything, I should be leaving *him*.

At that, my cheeks morphed into a painful smile. 'Can't now. I'm on my way out.'

'Can't it wait?' he said, surprised.

'I've got a lunch date, actually.' Shit. Me and my big mouth. Now what? He knew everyone in town and would know I was lying.

'A lunch date?'

I did my usual teapot stance with my hands on my hips. 'Do you find that so hard to believe?'

His eyes narrowed. 'Of course not. Who's this lunch date with?'

And then I had a brainstorm, like people do when they're desperate. 'With Paul's chef. The chef from our wedding, ironically.'

'Erica...' he whispered. 'I know you're frustrated, but please hang in there. I promise you we're getting married as soon as I can come up for air.'

'Don't bother,' I answered, yanking my wrist from his gentle clasp. 'I wasn't holding *my* breath. Now, if you'll excuse me, I have to see a man about the rest of my life.' Jesus, I should have joined the local Greek tragedy group.

And that was when he took me by the shoulders, nailing me to the spot.

'Please hear me out, sweetheart. Don't do anything that would ruin us.'

'Me? You're the one who ruined us!'

And then Julian did something totally out of character. He slammed his hand flat against the dresser. 'Erica, why are you being like this? I love you!'

'No, you love – or *desire* – Sienna. Well, you're welcome to her.'

His mouth fell open. 'What the hell are you talking about? Sienna means absolutely nothing to me outside of business!'

I shook my head. 'I'm sorry. I don't believe you,' I finally sobbed.

Really sobbed, with big shudders that made my shoulders shake. Damn. So much for playing it cool.

I made for the door, but he blocked my exit with his big body.

'You have to, Erica. I'm telling you the truth. Can't you see it? Don't you know I've never lied to you about anything? Why would I start lying now?'

'How the hell am I supposed to know?' I spat.

'Listen,' he whispered, stroking the tears from my cheeks. 'If I wanted out, I'd tell you. But I never will and you know why? Because you're *the one*, Erica. There is and never will be another. OK?'

I stood stiff in his arms. God, this was making no sense.

He took my hand and I thought he was going to sit me down for a lecture, Erica-style, but instead he took my bag off my shoulder and led me out through the side door and onto the terrace under the pergola, my favorite spot in the whole wide world.

'Look around you, sweetie,' he whispered.

From the top of our hill I could see the endless patchwork

quilt of acres and acres of green, yellow and brown land, the fields, the symmetrical lines on the farmland where Julian had run his tractor, the paddock with his horses.

'Isn't this what you've always wanted?' he whispered as he pulled me back against him.

I breathed in the fresh air on my face, his warm chest against my back, and I instantly remembered the hours I'd spent in Boston secretly trawling the internet for a home I could afford, knowing that as long as I remained married to Ira, it would never happen – even if I'd won the lottery or found a bargain. Ira hadn't shared my dreams. Julian had – or so I'd thought.

'Is it also what *you* want?' I asked, closing my eyes, the landscape I knew by heart imprinted in my mind.

'Of course,' he said, after a slight hesitation. Or was I imagining it?

'Really? You're not just saying that?'

'Why would I? You didn't drag me here. I was happy to come.'

I turned in his arms and faced him, once and for all. 'And are you still happy now?'

Julian grinned, and I could see the slightest wrinkles at the edge of his eyes, just above his cheekbones. He put his nose against mine, the way he always did, and we were eyes against eyes. I could see the gold flecks inside his dark irises.

'Pack an overnight bag,' he said. 'I'm taking you to the beach. Just you and me. Renata's coming to pick up the kids.'

I debated. I didn't want to lose him. But I didn't want to be lied to. Not again, after all those years with my first husband, Ira. I just couldn't relive any of that ever again.

But instinct – and love – told me to give him the chance to prove himself, that I was too suspicious. I wanted to believe him. So I did as he told me and packed a bag full of dreams and hopes.

As we drove down to the coast in absolute silence, I recognized the hotel in the brochure – Hotel Villa Etrusca – perched high on a cliff facing the sea.

'This is where you and I will be spending some quality time alone, my love,' he murmured, wrapping an arm around me and leaning in for a kiss. 'Surprised?'

Surprised? I was gobsmacked. I was also wrong about the cheating. The room was for me, not Sienna Thornton-Jones!

'Stunned and grateful,' I assured, returning the kiss. Now we were talking!

Hotel Villa Etrusca was a medieval castle that had been well preserved and renovated over the years so that almost everything was original and yet in mint condition. Surrounded by acres and acres of green lawns and parks, five different pools and a botanical garden with a huge ornate glass greenhouse that looked like Palm House at Kew Gardens in London, it was one of the most stunning hotels in the region.

Once inside, it was like being in church. Huge, quiet and cool.

'It's almost intimidating, isn't it?' Julian whispered.

'I feel like I'm going to get down on my knees and start praying,' I whispered back as the polished receptionist welcomed us and a bellboy showed us to our room.

And to think we were both experts in hotels, me for running them and him for staying in them. We thought we'd seen them all. But Hotel Villa Etrusca really took the cake.

Our room was about as big as six Farthington Hotel rooms put together, with polished marble floors covered in antique yet pristine rugs. The headboard of the bed was massive, as was the bathroom.

'You freshen up – I'll see you in a bit,' Julian said as he kissed the tip of my nose.

'If I can ever find my way out of the bathroom,' I quipped, my mood once again restored. This was going to be fantastic!

When I stepped out of the luxurious shower about a lifetime later, a beautiful turquoise gown was waiting for me. A gown my size, and not Sienna's. Proof, if ever I needed any.

Instant shame fell over me, enveloping me with its heavy folds. How could I have ever, *ever* doubted Julian? He was my one true north, my beacon in the night. He was my one constant since I'd met him. And I had let myself be so insecure as to doubt him.

I put on the dress, feeling every ounce a monster. I'd suspected Julian of cheating on me and even kissed another guy out of spite, when all my man had done was organize a romantic getaway. Could I have sunk any lower?

We sat at an elegant table on the balcony, the yachts out at sea like little tadpoles dotting the calm surface, Julian happy and humming as he poured me some wine to go with our amazing cannelloni with game sauce.

But my sense of guilt was catching up with me with a vengeance. Throughout the entire meal I was edgy, trying to smile when all I could see, like in a nightmare, was

Alberto's mouth closing in on me, blotting out everything else. I pushed the horrible memory away so abruptly, I sat up and gasped.

'What's wrong, sweetie?' Julian murmured, taking my hand.

'Nothing,' I lied, wishing I could erase my mistake, wishing it had never happened.

With that kiss I'd fallen to the lowest rungs of a relationship. I was no good at hiding things from Julian, but this would have to be an exception. Things at the moment were rocky and I didn't want to risk pushing him over the edge. It would be my secret. And of course Alberto's. Because he certainly wouldn't be bragging about it. I couldn't confess this to anyone, not even Paul or Renata. I just hoped the chef didn't have a big mouth.

And then I looked back at Julian, who was popping a bottle of...

'Tattinger?' I squeaked.

'I ordered it last week. Two crates, for our happy moments. Only the best for my girl.'

*Ohgodohgodohgod...*

'Erica, I love you so much and I feel awful for what I've put you through,' he said softly, his voice choked, his eyes shining. 'I promise I'll make it up to you. Don't give up on me, sweetie.'

It was all there, in the warmth of his voice, the contours of his face, the tenderness in his hand as he held mine. He truly did love me – and I was a letch.

'Oh, no, no, no...!' I blurted before my hand could stop the words spilling out of my mouth.

Julian's brow creased. 'What's wrong?'

Tears blurred my vision.

'Please tell me that's a happy reaction to Tattinger? I can't bear to see you cry, sweetheart.'

He took my hand and kissed my palm. And I totally lost it.

'I-I have to tell you something...' Now I know I said I wouldn't, but I couldn't start a new life on a lie, now could I? I wiped the seat of my forehead and cleared my throat. 'I-I knew about the champagne... and the hotel...'

Julian's eyebrows lifted.

'The message from your credit card appears on my phone, remember? We never got round to changing that.'

Deflated wasn't exactly the right word. More like devastated, but he kept his cool. 'Oh. Right.'

'But the worst part is... I thought it was for Sienna.'

'Not again...'

'I'm so sorry for doubting you, Julian!' Especially after it turned out that I was the cheater here.

He stared at me sadly. 'Did you really think that I'm capable of having an affair?'

'No. I thought you wanted out.'

'I don't want out,' he groaned. 'I'm not cheating. Now can we stop it with this jealousy bit?'

'Wait, there's much more,' I bawled, my heart a tight ball by now. 'It gets worse.'

'What do you mean?'

'I'm sorry!' I cried. 'I'm sorry I doubted you, but you and Sienna – the two of you were always together... And when you were home, you were always on the phone to her and I was jealous.'

He sighed. 'Cut to the chase, Erica.'

Julian was a rare gem of a man – one in a million. And I couldn't go on keeping it from him. If I was finally going to marry him, I needed to be honest.

'You know Alberto?'

'The chef? What about him?'

Ho, boy… 'When you were in Denver – or Amsterdam or Tokyo – he invited me to his wedding menu sampling…'

'Yeah?'

'Yeah. I told him I couldn't eat because I was on a diet,' I said, my voice cracking.

'Sweetheart, I get it. You broke your diet. It happens. Don't be so harsh on yourself.'

I sniffed. Yeah, if only it were that simple. But no matter how hard, I had to come clean. I cringed as the words spilled out.

'We had wine, too – lots of it – and he… kissed me…'

# 18

## The Beginning of the End

'You kissed another *man*?' he whispered, his eyebrows raised, his eyes wide as if trying to process the information but just couldn't comprehend.

How could he? I lived for him – told him so practically every day. All my actions all day, every day, were centered on him, our family and this life we'd created together here in Tuscany. Another man? It didn't make sense to him.

And then I saw it, as this version of the truth slowly mushroomed inside his brain, growing, growing, pushing everything else – all his certainties – into a tiny corner. It materialized into pain, right there, on his face. I'd cheated on him. I'd cheated on Julian, the love of my life – whom, ironically, I'd always feared losing to another woman.

I needed to dissolve that pain, take it from him and throw it far away where it could never be found again. I stepped forward gingerly, my mouth trembling. And, for the first time, he pushed himself away from me.

'Julian...' I faltered. 'Please – it was just one kiss! I was just trying to be honest with you.'

'There's nothing honest in snogging another bloke.'

Said like that, it sounded even worse. 'No, I didn't snog him. It was just one kiss! And in any case, he kissed me.'

He turned to look at me, his eyebrow going up as it always did when he was disappointed. 'And you let him.'

I did. If even for a second, I did. But that was all it had been. A simple kiss. Nothing more. Alberto knew it and I knew it. But to Julian's eyes, and rightly so, it was the highest form of betrayal. If he'd so much as caressed another woman's cheek, I'd have lost it. And now here I was, begging for his forgiveness. Of course I didn't deserve it. I knew that much. The best man in the whole wide world had chosen me and I hadn't been strong enough to weather the storm with him.

Because at the first sign of difficulty, I'd let a man kiss me. To be totally honest (and I might as well be at this low point), I hadn't expected Alberto to actually come right out and do that. I'd been happy with just the banter and the minor flirting, which at the time had given me a necessary ego boost, as I'd hit rock bottom in the self-love department.

I had thought that Julian was drifting away from me, and what did I do? Rather than asserting myself and making things clear between us, I pushed him away even further. And now he was the one who was hurt. He was the one who had been wronged. And he was leaving.

'Where are you going?' I squeaked as he grabbed his keys and slammed the door behind him, leaving me alone with this demolition ball in my chest, trying to take stock of what I'd done.

In just three days, my life had taken a major flip. Or rather, a major flop. I'd screwed it up all by myself. No one to blame. Moral of the story? I hadn't trusted my husband-to-be and now he didn't trust me. And this was the price I had to pay.

For days, Julian avoided eye contact with me and only spoke to me when we were in front of the kids. Which brought back yet another set of memories. Like with the first man who had ruined my life. And now, apparently, *I* was the Mary Magdalen of the situation, sleeping alone in our huge bed, sobbing like a two-year-old night after night and wishing – no, praying – he'd knock on my door and tell me he forgave me.

If he ever came back to our bed – if he knocked on our door – I'd be happy to let him spend a year in Antarctica with Sienna. Anything he wanted. If only he'd forgive me and come back to me and marry me and be my love again... I swore I'd do anything for him to come back. And I prayed all the prayers I knew.

A few hours – and a great deal of Hail Marys later – my cellphone rang. Had Julian finally seen the light? Was he willing to talk this over and maybe, in time, forgive me? I jumped onto the phone.

'Erica...?'

'Yes?' I prompted.

'It's Alberto.'

Crap. 'I can't talk right now, Alberto...' *Or ever again.* What a stupid thing to have done.

'Please don't be mad at me, Erica.'

I didn't have the strength to be mad. I just wanted to get rid of him.

'I-I hate myself, but I need to talk to you,' he whispered.

'Did you drop the cake?' I quipped, to block a sob that was choking me.

'Worse. I can't stop thinking about you. Can I see you?'

*Oh, God, no, no, no. Please – I have enough problems as it is.* 'I can't, Alberto.'

'Why not?'

I rubbed the space between my eyes, trying not to scream. 'Because I've just ruined the best relationship I've ever had with a man.'

'But you and Julian aren't a good match. He always leaves you on your own.'

'I love Julian. I'm sorry.'

'But don't forget the chemistry between us. You can't deny that.'

I groaned inwardly, the full realization of what I'd done finally hitting me only now that our happiness was in danger. 'That moment happened because I didn't know what I was doing. I was tipsy, but now I'm sober.'

'I don't believe you.'

I shrugged, as if he could see me. 'Look, Alberto, I'm very flattered. But please don't call me again unless it's about the menu.'

Silence. Then: 'So you mean the wedding is still on?'

Very good question. Who knew?

Two weeks had gone by and still I hadn't made any inroads whatsoever into my redemption. We didn't have it out

– Julian didn't yell at me or insult me like I'd have preferred. He just maintained his distance by sleeping in the guest room. And he was polite when I asked him a question in front of Maddy and Warren or anyone else, but that was it. Maybe because he was leaving for Copenhagen, he didn't want to start an argument we wouldn't be able to finish.

On my part, I did my best to be the perfect housewife, the understanding companion who made him all his favorite foods and spoiled him rotten with various gestures of love: Post-it notes, chocolates on his pillow and even digging up the first picture we ever had taken together. But the door had closed on me and I could find no way to get back in. His heart was harder than I'd thought. And it suddenly dawned on me that maybe he wasn't going to forgive me, after all.

And now, maybe he was just biding his time while he prepared to move out of our home. And then, possibly, his lawyer would send me a letter telling me we had to vacate his home. It was half his, after all, and if he wanted to go back to the States or the UK or Timbuktu, I'd have to relinquish my half. And move Maddy and Warren elsewhere, away from our tiny paradise.

Memories of the impossibility of finding somewhere suitable from where I could continue running a B & B surfaced in all their reality. It was, and would be, impossible to find somewhere to live and have guests at the same time. I'd have to go out and find a job, because my own savings alone simply weren't enough to support us. Not with this year's earnings.

A part of me felt guilty for even thinking about money, but it wasn't the money per se. It was Maddy and Warren whom I was worried about, and who, once again, were relying solely on me for their well-being. My poor kids. I wish they had someone better than me to protect them.

And then I remembered... A surge of panic shot through my heart – Julian had adopted them. Would he want to take them from me? He couldn't – he'd never do that.

'Julian, please talk to me. I can't stand it. We've never not talked before,' I finally pleaded when I couldn't take it any longer.

He stopped and eyed me, his eyes expressionless. Jesus, I'd never ever seen him look at me like this It was heart-breaking. Terrifying, actually. Because I couldn't even begin to think of my life without Julian in it, always on my side, always there for me and the kids. I couldn't think of the void that he'd leave. A void I could never fill or want to fill with someone else. If my first marriage had ended for a thousand good reasons, there was no justification for this one ending. I loved Julian and he loved me (I still hoped).

'Julian, you have to forgive me...' I whispered. 'I need to know you can get past this... this *stupid* thing that happened.'

Julian's nostrils flared like an enraged bull and for a moment I thought he'd lapse into a yelling fit.

'Would you want to continue our relationship if I'd kissed Sienna or some other woman?' he asked quietly, and I could feel the hurt in his voice. 'Imagine me doing the same thing you did.'

That wasn't difficult, as I'd been doing nothing else for the past few months. I'd visualized all sorts of scenarios where he was cheating on me. How, how, *how* could I ever have thought him capable of anything like that? He wasn't Ira and he never would be. He was a proper, decent man who happened to be good-looking and abundantly courted and admired. That didn't make him a cheater. Now, I understood – and, God, at what cost?

'Imagine us kissing,' he continued. 'Imagine—'

'Alright, alright, I get it,' I pleaded. 'Please stop now. I understand you don't trust me. But remember – I didn't kiss him. He kissed me.'

'Same difference. You allowed him to get that close. Ask yourself why.'

My mouth fell open. 'Do you think that I wanted him to kiss me?'

'You tell me.'

'Oh my God, Julian, really? It's not my fault. He caught me off guard. And I pushed him away.'

'How noble of you.'

I huffed. 'Look, I promise you it won't happen again. Ever. Can't we just... go back to how we were before?' I whispered.

He looked at me, eyes not softening in the least, dammit.

'Julian, please,' I sobbed. 'You have to forgive me.'

All I'd ever wanted in my life was about to slip away right through my fingers and there was nothing I could do to stop it. All I could do was sob and nod as he quietly proceeded to read me the riot act, of how crazy I'd been behaving, putting my fears regarding A Taste of Tuscany before him and the kids.

He was right. I had acted crazy, convinced I was owed a living. But it didn't work that way. Life was never in debt with you. Just because you'd had a sad childhood didn't mean you were assured happiness after that. Karma didn't work that way. Not good karma, anyway.

Then, as I wiped my eyes and nose, a slight crack appeared in the ice of Julian's face.

'I want to believe that nothing's changed. But *you*'ve changed, Erica.'

I shook my head, tears streaming down my face. 'But I haven't, Julian. I still love you.'

'You have a funny way of showing it. All you care about is waging a war against your so-called rivals and it's exasperating. I've seen a side of you that I didn't know. Or like, for that matter.'

But he was no angel, either, was he, spending all his time with Sienna Thornton-Jones and all?

'What about you?' I replied. 'Before we moved here, you promised you'd wake up with me every morning for the rest of your life. I can't remember the last time you and I went to bed together, let alone...' I swallowed and turned away for a moment to gather my nerves. 'You promised to share my dreams. Only yesterday you'd have referred to my rivals as *our* rivals and now...' I wiped my eyes. 'I was angry and afraid of losing you. And drunk. You know what happens when I drink on an empty stomach.'

'I thought you said you went to sample the menu.'

'The food came later. We started exchanging our tales of woe over the kitchen counter and I told him how sad I felt because...' My voice cracked, but I needed to tell him. 'Because you're always finding excuses to not marry me and instead fly off for your career. So don't say I'm the only one obsessed with work. All you seem to do is come and go, and the time you spend here – with me and the children who *you* wanted to adopt – is minimal. I'm so lonely, Julian.'

At that, his eyes softened. 'I have been remiss. I know.'

I looked up, swiping at a tear. 'It meant nothing to me – or to him.' A half-lie was better than a whole lie. 'I was upset, so I went to call off the venue. We had some wine and then he kissed me. Not vice-versa. But I wanted to be honest before we got married – if you still want to marry me.'

Julian sat down on the bed with his back to me and hung his head, letting out a long sigh. 'I can't – I just hate this. And I never thought you of all people would do this to me. Damn it, Erica, I trusted you with my life...'

'You *can* trust me with your life, Julian. I know this hurts you,' I barely managed to whisper through my swollen throat. 'But I had nothing to do with it. He kissed me. I don't even know the guy well enough to like him.'

'What about your *date* with him?' It was more an accusation than a question.

'What?' And then I remembered. 'I used that word just to piss you off. It wasn't true. There was no date. Please believe me.'

But he huffed, shaking his head. 'I can't. Not yet. I need time.'

'Time?'

He looked up, but not at me. 'To make sure I'm not simply pretending to forgive you for happiness' sake.'

I nodded. It made sense in Julian's wholesome morals, if not for my twisted, complicated mind. 'OK. How much time do you need?'

When he glowered at me, I lifted my hands in a sign of retreat. 'Forget I said that. You'll let me know.'

Now how was that for turning the other cheek?

*

Half-way through September, Julian was in Munich. Or was it Monaco? It might as well have been on the moon, seeing as he wasn't speaking to me, and that in any case, when he was away, life simply went on in his absence. The kids were fully immersed in their school routines, returning by two o'clock, starved and full of stories to tell about their new teachers, the new rules and the promise of a bigger workload. While Maddy couldn't wait to sink her teeth into her studies, Warren was less enthusiastic.

Me, I was still wondering where the summer had gone. And when Julian would be back. And all our dreams. The funny (or sad) thing was that he regularly called the house phone to talk to the kids, but whenever they offered to come and fetch me, he said he had to go.

And so, with my entire future, and that of my children, on the line and with a headful of worries and a heart full of regret, I had nothing else to do, and a whole lot of adrenaline pent up inside me. So I hit the gym – this time I would ease into it, so I wouldn't need a tractor to take me to the hospital again. I have stopped trying to compete with everyone else (I told you I was going to try to change my ways, didn't I?) and avoided the haka-like classes entirely. Instead, I followed Mr. Clean – *Gabriele* – through quiet, cool Pilates, forcing my mind to concentrate on the slow, balanced movements that even I could manage. All the while, I steered clear of thoughts of Alberto, Julian, my thwarted wedding plans, and all the work that Paul, Renata and my aunts had put in for me. And everything that ailed me.

*Forget about it all. I am now going to relax, because I am light, distant and free, like a hot-air balloon (don't I know it) reaching for the highest altitude, up, up and away from it all…*

But just as I was surrendering and letting go of total control, I freaked and slammed back down to earth with a crash.

Forget all this crap about feeling light and distant from my own life. If I didn't care, who would? And just how frickin' long was Julian going to punish me for? Would he ever forgive me? What else could I possibly do to win back his trust besides repenting the hell out of myself? For how much longer did I have to grovel?

'And stretch, stretch as far as you can,' Gabriele whispered.

I'd been honest and told him all about the kiss, when he'd had no idea what I'd done. (Let that be a lesson to you.) I'd confessed mea culpa when I could have just shut up about it. I'd tried to atone. I'd cooked all his favorite meals for days on end, concentrating solely on him while he was home, and had he budged an inch? Not even half... This was going nowhere and every day that went by I felt him slipping further away.

'And now loosen your limbs. Let them go back to their original position...'

And ironically, he was home for quite a while. A phone call would have been enough to get the wedding preparations back on track, at the drop of a hat, seeing that the ceremony would have been officiated in our own home. But as the days dragged by, he was nowhere near forgiving me. It was a lot if he spoke to me at all away from the children. Talk about having our wedding cake and eating it. Or, rather, skating on thin icing.

'And now hang your head and loosen your neck...'

At the table, he'd have lengthy conversations with the kids about everything from Madame Mila, Maddy's ballet teacher, to Warren's soccer kit. They talked about school, their friends, their hobbies, while he told them about the places he'd been.

'Will you take us one day, Daddy?' Maddy had asked.

Julian's eyes had softened as he touched her cheek. 'Of course, sweetie. Daddy will take you anywhere you want. Always.'

Had that been a threat, reminding me that he was legally their father, and that he could do as he pleased, at least half the time? Or was I blowing everything out of proportion? Julian wouldn't do what Ira had done to me, would he? I should be ashamed of even thinking that. And yet, here he is, not talking to me, just like Ira used to. When he wasn't demeaning me, that is.

'Remember that you are free, light and happy…' Gabriele reminded us.

As if. I was anything *but* that.

Let's face it, I'd nailed my own coffin down tight and there was no way out of it unless I managed to convince Julian that it would never happen again. But how? Chain myself to the kitchen sink? I'd already promised never to have anything to do with Alberto again. What else could I do to win Julian's trust back?

I drove back home after the Pilates class, gripping the wheel and wiping the tears from my face. Only in my car was I alone and free to let all my anguish out as a million permutations zapped around my already frazzled brain. Paul was still mad at me. What was I going to do?

When I got home, I slunk into the kitchen and began peeling onions for tonight's shepherd's pie, Julian's favorite, and I remembered how, when married to Ira, I'd be peeling onions all the time to mask my tears. I'd accumulated bag-loads of them in my freezer. No – I couldn't go back to that... ever again. I plunked myself down at the table, holding my head.

'Hi, Erica! What's wrong?' Renata asked as she sauntered in, and I rubbed my face so she wouldn't see the tears.

'Dunno. Just a bit queasy. Something I ate. Long time no see – how are things?'

She ignored my question. 'That's funny. You've always been able to digest mountains.'

'Sorry – need to run,' I said, dashing upstairs to my en-suite bathroom, where no one would notice me, where I *threw up* mountains.

It just didn't stop. If I hadn't known better, I would have said I was pregnant, but Julian hadn't touched me in months and by the looks of it, wouldn't be anytime soon. A loud groan escaped me as I heaved my whole soul into the toilet bowl and Julian appeared.

'Are you OK?' he asked.

A-ha. So he did still care, even if a little.

'No, I want to die,' I said, sticking my head further down the toilet bowl.

He stood there for a moment, unsure.

'Please go away.' The last thing I wanted was for him to see me like this.

Without another word, he turned and left, and I plastered myself to the bathroom floor, totally depleted of any energy. See? In the past, he would have stayed to hold my hair out of my face. Now, it was the furthest thing from his mind.

I don't know how long I lay there, but I was too weak and besides, my back was very happy in that position. And I didn't have to go anywhere. And I hadn't worried about the B & B or Alberto or even Julian since I'd been sick earlier. It was like a short reprieve from reality. I could actually lie here and not think about anything for a while – possibly until next summer. Hopefully, Julian would be able to look me in the eye by then. If only he'd come back to me. How long did he expect me to grovel? Even I had my limits.

As if in answer to my prayers, the door to the bathroom opened again and Julian stood over me, his face a deep, fuming red.

'What? What is it?' I whispered, rolling onto my side to get up.

'You tell me,' he bit off, his voice so faint it seemed to have nothing in common with the killer expression on his face. He looked like two completely different people. 'Tell me to my face. If you have the *gall*…'

I stared at him blankly. 'What…?'

'When were you going to tell me, Erica?' he suddenly exploded. 'How long has this been going on?'

I scratched my head. Oh my God, had he finally found out about Paul's miracle video that I'd shamelessly swapped at the last minute? I'd managed to keep that one under wraps only because Julian wasn't in the area at the time it was released and also because I'd made sure I'd thrown out every single copy of *La Nazione* in the house. I'd promised I wouldn't do anything like that again, but I had and he'd found out. I hung my head in shame.

'Don't deny it.'

Damn rat. 'I'm sorry. It was… just a strong urge. I couldn't control it.'

'And just what the hell am I supposed to do with this information? To think I'd forgiven you!'

'Could have fooled me,' I cried. 'You were going to forgive me and all the same you put me through weeks of this hell?'

His eyes were blazing, shooting flames. 'And this is how you fix things? By getting pregnant?'

I shrank back. 'What the hell are you talking about? I'm not pregnant...'

'Well, not by me, you're bloody not!'

I watched him, dumbstruck, trying to make sense of what he'd said. Did he think...?

'I didn't sleep with the guy, Julian!'

His eyes pierced mine. Relentlessly. 'How do I know? Renata said you thought you might be pregnant.'

And that was when I realized that he really didn't trust me anymore. In his eyes, I'd completely transformed into The Wicked Witch of the West, because nothing in my life would be the same anymore after my mistake, judging by the look on his face.

'Jesus, Julian – you have to trust me!'

Julian stopped and slammed a powerful fist against his thigh, which must have hurt like hell. 'I *did* trust you, and look where it got me – you're expecting another bloke's baby!'

I stared at him in pure horror at the thought. Which, admittedly, could have been mistaken for the horror of being caught out. Was this a comedy of errors, or what? What was wrong with him?

'Julian, listen to me,' I cried. 'I'm not pregnant and I didn't sleep with Alberto!'

But he turned with a snort. 'And there was me, still trying to get over that *kiss*, thinking I'd try to forgive you for that, while you – *you* went the whole nine yards. What an idiot I am.'

'Julian, stop. You're completely off—'

'Yeah?' he demanded, grabbing my cellphone off the sink as if brandishing hard evidence.

He was certain he'd find a palimpsest of wild love texts in there. He really didn't trust me, or know me at all, then.

'Go on – I have no secrets from you,' I challenged him.

'We'll see about that,' he snapped, thumbing through my photos as if he knew exactly what he was looking for, and slammed it back onto the counter with a loud 'There!' before turning his back on me and striding out the door.

What the hell was he talking about? Had he gone off his rocker all of a sudden? I peered at the tiny screen and backed off in horror. There, in vivid colors, was Alberto's smiling face, his arm wrapped around my neck under a sign that read *Via dell'Amore*.

After a few minutes, I heard Julian's steps on the gravel, followed by the roar of his jeep as he took off. Forever, this time.

'What the hell just happened?' Renata poked her head in.

Just the person I wanted to kill.

'You tell me. Why the *hell* did you tell Julian I was pregnant?'

'I was only trying to help. He didn't look very happy with you lately. I thought that maybe if he thought you were expecting his baby—'

'There is no baby!' I boomed. 'We haven't slept together for forever and now he thinks I'm having some other guy's kid!'

Her mouth fell open. 'Oh, shit,' she whispered. 'Oh, I'm so sorry...'

She ventured a couple of steps further into my bedroom – the battlefield of my relationship. 'What's going on with you two, Erica?' She waited. 'Erica?'

I groaned. 'Things... haven't been going too well lately.'

'That I can see. Why?'

I looked up and moved into the bedroom, where she patted the bed and sat me down. Could I actually come out and tell her about the mess that my life was lately, knowing that everyone back home thought I had it made?

'Alberto – the chef in charge of my wedding dinner – kissed me. And I told Julian.'

'No!'

'Yeah, I know, but I had to. Julian and I promised never to have secrets.'

'Never mind Julian,' she dismissed with a wave of her petite hand. 'Did you tell your very best friend, Paul, that you and Alberto kissed? Because I wouldn't. He'd be devastated. He's head over heels in love with him.'

'Alberto kissed *me*,' I corrected her. Just as Paul sauntered into the bedroom like it was Florence Central Station or something.

'What did you just say?' he whispered, his face paling. 'You...? Alberto?'

Oh, God. Was this a nightmare I'd never wake up from? I stood up. 'Paul—'

'I can't believe you'd *do* such a thing to me,' he whispered. 'You *knew* I loved him.'

'Paul, no – you've got it all wrong.'

'This is the worst thing you could ever do to me, Erica! Ever!'

I was shaking my head. 'No, Paul, you've got to listen to me. There is absolutely nothing between us.' Are you having a sense of déjà vu, as well?

'Did he kiss you or not?' he demanded.

I swallowed. 'He did. But only because I was sad.' That didn't convince even me.

He snorted. 'Oh, you poor, sad, unlucky Erica! With the perfect life, the perfect kids and the perfect husband. Oh, I feel so sorry for you.'

'Stop it,' I pleaded. 'I haven't done anything wrong. It's not my fault if Alberto isn't gay. And in any case, I'm not interested. I have my own problems. Julian's left me for good.'

And with that, I got to my feet again and left both Renata and Paul in my room.

Just when I needed them most and they were both on my case. But at least Paul should have believed me. How could he even think that I could want anyone besides Julian? Come to think of it, how could Julian himself believe I'd want anyone else? Didn't he love me enough to doubt that he may have got it wrong for once? Why were he and Paul so ready to believe the worst about me?

Where had I gone wrong? I'd been their rock for years – Paul's especially. Every time they'd needed me, I was there – through thick and thin: hospitalizations, bouts of insecurity and depression. You name it, I was always the first number on their mental Rolodex and Contact Number One on speed dial. I'd always drop everything to be there for them both – to cheer them on, whether with a tiramisu or some good solid advice, when they thought they were kaput. And now they didn't believe me?

This whole bucolic Italy thing was beginning to weigh too heavily on my heart. Nothing – absolutely *niente* – was going as I'd hoped.

If I hadn't left Boston with Julian, maybe none of this would have happened. I certainly wouldn't have had the money to buy a farmhouse – and, consequently, not even the *drive* nor the strength to move to Tuscany, open a B & B and try to live the genuine good life. Maybe he'd still be there working as a principal, catering to some other troubled mother while sporting a pristine suit and a crisp white shirt, not the tatty old jeans that stayed clean for two minutes flat out here in the fields.

*The good life.* Where had it gone? I'd wanted to improve my family's life, but instead I'd only managed to pull us all into a pit of despair. The kids missed me. And they were right. I'd let my A Taste of Tuscany take over my mind. As if financial success was the only way of proving myself worthy of Julian's love and trust. Well, I'd blown it completely. Now, nothing was left of my relationship with Julian. What else mattered? My big fat Italian life was over. Now, it was the beginning of my big fat Italian break-up.

And now, I gulped down my cappuccino and reached for my third homemade cupcake. Who cared if I gained 15 kilos now? I'd lost the love of my life and my best friend, what else did I have to lose? Julian didn't love me anymore and there was no way in hell I'd be looking for anyone else to take his place. So it wouldn't matter if I gained 30 or even *100* kilos. I'd eat my way into oblivion until I was so fat I couldn't fit through the door. And then I'd be stuck in the house – in this kitchen, actually – right next to the refrigerator, where I belonged. They'd have to come and knock the wall down to get me to the hospital for an emergency heart op. Because my heart was breaking for good.

But if you knew me at all, I was never one to dwell and feel sorry for myself (well, once I'd eaten all the chocolate cake) for too long. After the drama spell, I'd always bring the drapes down and pick myself up.

Paul had packed his bags in a huff and left without saying goodbye. He was probably going to be staying with one of his many friends in Florence. He needed to fester for a bit, if I knew him at all. Insisting he stayed wouldn't have done any good. But with two of the three most important men in my life gone, I was completely lost.

'Erica, where's Julian?'

I jumped and turned to see Sienna sticking a leg out of a taxi as it pulled up on our drive.

'I've been calling him, but he's not answering.'

I looked up. God, she came and went, came and went, I'd lost complete track of her. Complete track of everything, actually. My life was spiraling out of control, spinning out into the infinite universe, never to be found again…

I rubbed my face in exhaustion. 'I'm not sure at the moment. He went for a drive.' Probably to Tokyo.

I wanted to take it out on her, tell her this was her fault too, but who was I kidding? This was all my own doing – my insecurity had caused this. If I'd been self-confident, I would have understood that Julian's business trips were to compensate for our lack of income and that he was doing it not only for his personal success as a writer, but also for us as a family. And I wouldn't have vented to Alberto. Any pea-brained woman would have understood, but me? No sirree.

She huffed, running a slim hand through her glorious mane. 'Bloody hell. I just got here and I have to fly back home for an emergency. Can I bum a shower off you?'

'Of course. Come on in. Are you hungry? I've got some roast pork with some rosemary baked potatoes and a nice niçoise salad.'

She swung her other leg out and hefted her wheelie suitcase. 'You're an absolute doll, Erica, thank you! I always said Julian was the damned luckiest sod on earth for having you.'

Huh. Lucky sod indeed.

Wait a minute. He was gone, and she was going. There were no TV appearances or interviews scheduled, as far as I knew. Had I been wrong all along? Were they really…? And was he only pretending to be angry so he could dump me? No – stop it, I argued with myself like a schizophrenic. This is what got you into trouble in the first place, not trusting Julian.

But I still couldn't help but wonder – had Alberto's kiss been providential for Julian?

I don't know how long I had been mulling over this, because Sienna had gone for a shower and now returned, and I was still at it.

'Julian pushing you too hard?' I bit off despite myself as I set the table and joined her for some nosh.

Sienna laughed. 'Nah, I can take him. It's my partner who's worrying me.'

*Yeah, yeah, your partner.*

'She's pregnant and climbing the walls, so I need to be near her now.'

My head whipped up. *She? Her? Pregnant?*

Sienna laughed. 'I get lots of surprised faces – oh, but yours, Erica! You should see yourself! You didn't know because hardly anyone does. I try to protect Nina from the limelight.'

'Nina? You mean your *assistant*?'

'Yeah, I know, I treat her like dirt, but only on the job. At home I'm as cuddly as a teddy bear. We see eye to eye at home, thank God.' Sienna leaned back against the counter. 'You know, Erica, I've been meaning to tell you…'

'Tell me what?'

'You two are my idea of happiness. You put up with so much from him, but I guess most guys are like that, huh?'

I looked up at her. Was all this real?

'You're always there for him, through thick and thin. And your kids – I wish my own mom had done for me what you do for your family,' Sienna murmured, her voice cracking slightly.

My mouth dropped open as she stepped forward and hugged me briskly, then skimmed a *cupcake* off the dessert tray.

'And… she never once baked us anything. See you soon, Erica. Thank you for taking such good care of me.' And with a generous bite, she left, mouth full, eyes shining.

Huh. Imagine that. Sienna Thornton-Jones, woman extraordinaire and completely indifferent to Julian's charms. Me and my paranoia. Was there no limit to how I'd fallen, hook, line and sinker, into the stereotypical trap of some gorgeous career woman being a threat to normal moms like me? Was my brain that lazy that it preferred to settle for the easiest, most immediate interpretation available – that she was a glamorous bimbo whose eyes were set on my man, rather than even remotely considering entertaining another possibility? Did I have no imagination at all?

'Mom, where's Dad?' Warren said as he and Maddy came back and helped themselves to the pork and potatoes. 'I just saw Sienna driving off. He wouldn't have left without saying goodbye, would he?'

Ha. You find your way out of that one if you can. 'Of course not, sweetheart. Daddy's very, very busy with his new book and he needs to promote it so you can both be proud of him.' Now, where's my Oscar, thank you very much?

'I am very proud of Daddy,' Maddy reassured as she popped a forkful of potato into her mouth. 'He's the best daddy I've ever had.'

Warren turned to look at me and I nodded. 'And he loves you both very much. More than anything in the world.'

'More than he loves you?' she asked in awe.

That was an easy one, especially now. 'Of course! You're his little princess and Warren is his best mate... uh, pal.'

It was only then that I noticed how Julian's British expressions had permeated our own Americanisms throughout the years. Julian *had* changed us, in so many ways. He'd had a positive and constructive influence on the kids. With his and my help, they'd flourished from being the children of a single-parent, slightly wary family to confident, thriving children. I know I'd done my part as a loving mother, but Julian? He'd been essential to their well-being and I'd always be grateful to him for that. I'd also love him until the day I died.

'Don't cry, Mummy,' Maddy said, sliding off her chair

to come and put her arms around my neck and planting a huge kiss on my cheek. 'Daddy doesn't love me more than you. It was just a joke.'

'I'm not sad, sweetheart,' I assured her. 'I'm just so happy to be your mother.'

Warren continued to shovel pork and potatoes into his mouth but eyed me furtively. He was no idiot and would soon be asking questions.


As I was thrashing about in bed that evening and missing Julian like crazy, my phone rang. Julian...?

But it wasn't my husband-to-be. Only Marcy, slurring her words. She must be drunk again, I thought to myself. Good for her. If only I could bury myself in some sort of artificial solace and be oblivious to the world, I'd be home free. Home. Free. Right now, I felt like I was neither.

She was stifling her sobs.

I sat up. 'Marcy...? What's wrong?'

'I was young. He didn't even have a name,' she whispered, and I closed my eyes.

The last thing I wanted to hear was another doomed love story she'd had to go through in her difficult life of suitors. But I had no choice.

'And I gave him up. I gave him up so I could marry your father...'

She heaved a soft sigh and I could hear the shakiness in her voice.

'I was young,' she said again. 'If I was to have any chance of making your father love me, I had to appear to be the virgin he thought I was. So I let him go. Forever.'

'Who?'

'My son. He was conceived in England, during my study vacation. And I... I *abandoned* him, like the worst mother in the world. I abandoned him for Edoardo...' And with that, she really sobbed – a soft but gut-wrenching sob that came from somewhere deep inside her fragile birdlike frame.

Dumbstruck at the revelation, I could do nothing but listen.

She'd abandoned a baby? Where had this come from? And she'd managed to keep this from us all these years? Why? And why tell me now?

'It's alright,' I lied. 'It's alright, Marcy.'

'Oh, Erica, the lies I've told!' she bawled. 'And with every lie, it got more and more difficult to remember them.'

'Marcy, calm down, it's OK,' I said as she abandoned herself to a long spell of tears. I didn't know what to say or what to ask, so I simply sat, making shushing, comforting noises.

A baby boy. Who was a man now. A brother to Judy and Vince. And me. Surreal. But I couldn't tell them. I couldn't betray her confidence. She'd be the one to have to tell them. Maybe not tomorrow, or the day after that. But the sooner she unloaded the burden from her heart, the better.

'Why didn't you tell your parents you were pregnant?' I asked, surprising even myself. 'Why didn't you tell Nonna about your baby?' I had to know.

When she spoke, her voice seemed to come from the bottom of the ocean. Or maybe my senses were simply dulled.

'Your grandmother was going through way too much. It would have killed her. Plus, I've never been the bravest girl in the world.'

As if we didn't know.

Marcy cleared her throat. 'Losing her husband and deciding to move to America were enough tragedy in Nonna's life. I didn't want to shame her, as well.'

I listened, eager to know more, suddenly devoid of any of my typical sarcasm. This was Marcy, my stepmother, finally *communicating* with me.

'I gave birth to him in England. A… a n-nun took him for adoption. I've never wanted to go back since. And when you went there so many years ago, all I could think of was what I'd done. And if the same thing happened to you, I wanted to know so I could help you and you wouldn't be like… me…'

'Oh, Marcy,' I whispered.

'I made a terrible mistake, I know, and it's been eating away at me all these years, conditioning my life, not letting me love those around me.'

That was true, but who was I to judge?

'And now, somewhere there's a man who knows his mother abandoned him. How can I continue living with this? I can't – not another day.'

'But you have to stop being afraid, Marcy. Life won't kill you. You should have voiced your fears. You should have told Nonna Silvia about your baby. She would have forgiven you and helped you.'

When the hell had I become so wise? Or was it that I could clearly see solutions to other people's problems, but not my own?

At that, she sniffed. 'I threw away a child so I could have the love of my life. I know I was young, but it was *wrong*. I abandoned my baby.'

I understood now why she'd resented me all these years. In order to be with my dad, the love of her life, she'd abandoned her own flesh and blood to take me on as her daughter. And all those years I'd asked myself what poison was running through her veins, what deep, dark secret could be possibly afflicting her to the point that she couldn't even take care of her family.

Now, it all made sense. All her years of deep depression that had permeated my childhood – days when she couldn't face even getting out of bed, let alone going to work or walking us to school. It had simply been beyond her, the sheer pain of it sapping her very strength. Now, I was able to empathize and not judge.

Now, I knew what it felt like to love and lose love. To understand that all you've ever cherished could disappear from your life with one word of truth, one word said in the wrong moment.

And Marcy's sense of guilt had been her punishment – a punishment for all these years. Too cruel a fate even for someone like her. She wasn't evil, I finally understood, but simply unable to face life's difficulties. And attacking, alternated with indifference, had been her only defense. My shrink in Boston would have been proud of my analysis, if not of my behavior.

But now, I considered, it was time to heal. It was time for her to stop drinking as an emotional crutch.

She was silent now, as if waiting for me to deliver a magic formula that would instantly wipe away her woes. I didn't have one, of course. I only had a simple suggestion. But it could do us all a world of good if we listened to it.

'We need to be more forgiving, Marcy,' I whispered.

'We've all made mistakes – big ones. Everyone has. So let's all stop recriminating and pointing fingers and put the past in the past. Let's all just…' I swallowed as I pronounced my greatest wish. 'Forgive one another. And ourselves. What else is important on this stupid planet besides love? Because if you don't forgive yourself, no one ever will.'

'You always were the wisest little girl, Erica,' she whispered, and there was nothing more to be said between us.

Even if I was living proof of her sense of inferiority to her own twin, I somehow felt we'd be OK.

'I'm going to get my man back, Erica. I'm going to get your father back. And hope he'll forgive me.'

'Of course he will. Dad loves you. Let me know how it goes,' I said softly, and in my voice I heard a kindness and patience that was new to both of us. Because I had to do my part in atoning and being a better person as well as her.

New beginnings, for all of us. That was what we needed.

'Thank you, Erica…'

'What are daughters for?'

I wondered, if Marcy and I could atone, why couldn't Julian, the man who loved me, understand me and believe me? Why couldn't we atone?


A few days later, while trying like hell to keep up appearances with the kids and trying to figure out an excuse for Daddy's leaving without saying goodbye to them – an alarming first in the Foxham family – I noticed Julian had left behind one of his notebooks in his nightstand.

Hmm. I nudged the corner until it was almost facing me and scanned the page.

I look at my wife-to-be as she bends over to hang the laundry. She's done the whites and takes great pride in them. She should. Everything she does, the way she takes care of us, is full of love. She patiently matches the socks on the line, shakes out the creases in my old T-shirts even if she's going to iron them. I always tell her not to – they're only work clothes – but she says she can't have her man looking like nobody loves him.

And I know she loves me. I can feel it in every gesture, see it in the crinkle of her eyes when she smiles, which has been more these past two years in Tuscany than when I first met her, bravely facing adversities of all kinds.

Sometimes I wonder how her first husband hadn't seen how marvelous she is. He didn't deserve her and sometimes I don't think I deserve her, either. How many times have I disappointed her lately with my career choice? But she hangs in there, ever supportive, ever loving.

Now she's stretching, and in the early morning sun I can see the shape of her body through her sundress. It's a good, strong, healthy body, with all those enticing curves that I love so much. Erica is like her body – strong, feminine and sometimes a bit stubborn.

She turns and catches me staring at her, and she smiles. She's loved, like no man could ever love a woman. I'd never felt anything like this before in my life for anyone else and every fiber of my body screams to me that I never will. Erica is and always will be my soulmate.

I sat back, aghast. Julian had written this about me? I wiped at a tear. Wow. I knew he'd loved me, but I didn't know he'd felt like that. I didn't know he had all those feelings inside him. It never occurred to me that as I was performing such mundane chores, he'd actually been thinking something so... profound. He really was a writer.

Men usually, in my meager experience, keep all their feelings bottled inside, leaving us to expose (and injure) our hearts. In my life, I'd always been the weaker one. The one who loved more. Now, I wasn't so sure.

I'd found someone who loved me as much as I loved him. I couldn't lose him now. The only man who I could ever sleep with, be with, love. Never in my mind could I ever replace him with any other man for a simple afternoon stroll down our country roads, or sit across from anyone else at a *locanda* (inn) for dinner, or look to for approval and feel flooded in warmth when that approval came. It had taken me three years to get to this level of intimacy, of knowing that there simply could be no one else for me. I couldn't lose all that. I couldn't lose him. Not without one last fight.

So I brainstormed a plan all by myself. A crazy one, to be honest, but insanity was all I had left. At that point, if I decided to proceed, there would be no turning back. The die would have been thrown. But I owed it to myself and my children to at least try.

Once my plan was in place, not without a few iffy bits, I called a family meeting with the kids for their input. For Maddy's sake, we had a lengthy PG 10 talk about what was happening and why Julian had left without saying goodbye. Like in a board meeting, I itemized the risks of my plan and the possible benefits, and they listened carefully.

Warren looked at me at length and finally said, 'Mom, do everything you have to do to make things like the way they were.'

'You're sure? And you, Maddy?'

At that, my daughter clapped her hands and exclaimed, 'Go for it, Mommy!'

So with their blessing, I picked up the phone, my heart in my mouth. For this to work, I needed every piece in place.

'Sienna? It's Erica.'

'Oh, hi,' she chirped, interrupted by a female murmuring in the background.

'How's... Nina?' I asked, and could almost see her roll her eyes as she laughed.

'Driving me nuts as usual. Can't wait until this baby is born, so someone else will be the center of her attention. What's up?'

Ironically, I needed her help to save my marriage. So I bit the bullet. 'Sienna, I need a favor.'

'Sure. Shoot.'

Oh, but it hurt so much to admit it. 'Julian's left me.'

Silence, then: 'He *what*? I don't believe it! Why?'

And so, with my heart on my sleeve, I told her. All of it. Well, except for me being jealous of her (one can only eat so much humble pie).

She loyally sucked air in between her teeth and tsk-tsked. 'And he doesn't believe you, the stupid bugger. How can I help?'

Ah. 'Glad you asked.' And so I told her all about my plan. It was an absolutely batshit crazy, 'never gonna get away with it' plan. But I was willing to risk it all for Julian.

Silence, then a hearty laugh. 'I love it!'

'You… think it'll work?' I asked.

'I know it will! You just leave it to me.'

'Thanks so much, Sienna. God, I hope you're right.'

'I'm always right. I may be a lesbian, but I know men, Erica. And I know Julian. I'll get to work on it pronto.'

'Where are you now?'

'We're in London.'

'Is Julian there?'

'No, he's at his parents' home.'

His parents. The people he used to turn to when he was in crisis. I'd been right not to underestimate the situation. This thing was getting more and more serious by the minute.

'OK,' I said, closing my eyes and sending out a little prayer. Actually, it was a huge 'I'll sacrifice everything to You' prayer.

I knew what I needed to do, but besides Sienna, I also needed to run it by my best friend, Paul. He'd know what to do. But five days had gone by and still no news from him. I wanted to leave him his space, but his silence was killing me. We'd never fallen out before – not like this.

He was my blood, my family, my confidante – much more than my own siblings could ever be. His happiness was important to me. I'd never meant to come between him and Alberto and needed to tell him that. And he'd have to listen. If only I had the same confidence regarding Julian. I rummaged through my bag for my phone just as it began to ring. It was Paul.

'Paul – I was just about to call you…' I said breathlessly.

'I'm sorry, sunshine. I should have understood.'

I swallowed, tears pricking. 'It's fine. Did you… talk to Alberto?'

'No. I'm not interested in what he might say. He can kiss whomever he wants.'

'Paul, I swear to you – there's nothing between us.'

'I know. I know you'd never cheat on Julian. I was just angry. Damn it, Erica, I really thought he was interested in me, you know? I actually thought we had a connection.'

'You still do. He admires your work. But I don't think he's interested in men. Otherwise there'd be no escaping your charms, Paulie.'

I said it because I meant it. Paul was the most beautiful gay man ever, inside and out. And I could kill anyone who tried to hurt him.

He sighed. 'Yeah, maybe you're right. Maybe I was just jazzed by the fact that we could be a working team.'

'Well, there is someone else whom I've been trying to parlay into your life, but it always seemed to fall on deaf ears.'

'Who, Gabriele?'

'You knew?'

'Of course I knew. He's been badgering me for weeks, so please don't ask me to go back there with you again.'

'OK, I promise.'

'Attagirl.'

'Paul? Come back home. I need you. More than ever now.'

'What's up?'

So I told him – and I told him my plan to win Julian back. I didn't have much time left now. The clock was ticking.

'That's the wildest thing you've ever done,' he said. 'Are you actually up for it?'

'Absolutely.'

'All of it? Because it could actually backfire on you, you do know that?'

'Yes,' I assured.

A long silence.

'Paul?'

'I'm thinking, sunshine. Are the kids OK with it?'

'Yes, but I'm honestly hoping it won't come to that.'

'And if it does?'

'I'll do everything it takes, Paul.'

'Boy, you are one crazy chick.'

I grinned into the phone despite myself. 'I know.'

'OK, then. Let me just jump into my car and I'll be there in a jiffy.'

As good as his word, he was on my doorstep. And in a couple of hours, he and the kids were huddled with me in a taxi as he bellowed orders into the cellphone stuck to his ear.

'Did you do what I asked?' I breathed when he hung up.

He raised his eyebrow at me as if to say, *get real, will you?*

'Sorry, Paulie. I'm just nervous.'

'Of course you are. You're risking everything you worked for all your life. God knows it's necessary.'

'Thanks. That sure makes me feel confident.'

Paul wrapped his arm around a sleepy Maddy in the back seat and kissed her cheek with a tenderness equaled only by Julian himself. My poor, poor kids. Crazy, crazy Mommy. Crazy to think it would work. Even Paul seemed doubtful. What the heck was I doing? Had I completely lost it?

We were in Boston ten hours later, where Julian was scheduled to have a book signing – precisely, thanks to

Sienna, at The Farthington, my former kingdom from my hotel management days.

According to Paul, it had been my name and not Sienna's that had thrown the doors open. I still had a solid reputation here after three years. I only hoped I wouldn't kill it in the space of an embarrassing three minutes.

I took a deep breath and glanced around. It looked the same. The Chippendale furniture, the walls, the paintings. Even Mr. Farthington was still going strong, his shock of white hair as stark as ever. Lesley and Lindsay's peroxide manes hadn't changed, either, and Jackie was now sitting behind the very desk that used to be mine.

Just wandering around the offices and the hallowed halls of my former domain brought everything back – the sense of power that my job had given me – a feeling I was trying to revive ever since we'd opened A Taste of Tuscany. Memories of flooded hotel rooms, broken boilers, rats, a dying prostitute and even a cat fight flashed through my mind.

And I remembered my daily fights at home with Ira. I'd been so miserable in that marriage and it had almost ruined everything else – my children's happiness, my finances and my health. I couldn't go through that again. This time, I'd do everything it took. My family and my marriage were my priority.

Let A Taste of Tuscany fall apart – who cared? Let the whole damn building crumble into the valley. But not my loved ones. They needed me and not my personal business success. I was ready. Or as ready as I'd ever be. With nothing left to do but pray, I swallowed back the terror threatening to choke me and took a deep breath. And, sending up a silent prayer, I pushed through the double doors.

Julian was in the next room, buried by piles of copies of his book, handsome and completely unaware that I'd been standing on the other side of the wall, the threshold between our present and future. Only ten hours ago I was in my own home, crying my eyes out, hopeless and desperate. Now, I was standing here with my heart on my sleeve, in my mouth, in Julian's hands. Well, at least that was the plan.

But what if it didn't work? What if he still didn't believe me (which was very probable at this point)? What if he really didn't want me anymore? He was right – I had changed from the Erica he'd proposed to. All these months I'd acted crazily. First, with my obsession with the B & B, working all hours and forgoing all things family-related, as if the only thing that mattered was my personal success. And then with my lack of support for his career.

Never once had I cheered him on like I should have, always doubting Sienna's good faith. And his. I'd doubted Julian just because I'd lacked self-confidence. And I'd believed he could only love me if I continued being the businesswoman he'd met, the one who was afraid of nothing and no one.

And, worst of all, when his interest in the farmhouse had become second to his career, I'd started to resent him. I'd made the very mistake that Ira had made and that had led, among other things, to our divorce. When would I learn? Was it too late?

My heart was about to explode. I could still see him through the open door, could hear every inflection of his voice as he spoke to Sienna, and I could almost *feel* his muscles flexing under his shirt as he forced a laugh at something she said. I'd made him miserable.

'Thanks for fitting this in, Julian,' Sienna said as she began to pull copies of his latest book off a nearby table and pile them onto the corners of his signing table.

He shrugged. 'Yeah, no biggie.'

'Terry's off sick and has asked me to deal with your American book signing,' she said, as per our plan.

'What are all these flowers for?' I heard him ask, lips tight again.

'Right... About that... Sorry – there's a wedding here later,' she explained.

His face fell. 'Oh.'

'What is it, Julian?' Sienna said. 'You look like absolute shit.'

Julian shrugged, his hands stuffed in his pockets.

'You can tell me. Am I not your super-duper agent who has your well-being at heart?'

Julian made another attempt to smile, but I could tell it wasn't working. What had I done to the poor guy?

'This,' he said softly, 'is where Erica used to work.'

'And? Something you want to tell me?'

'We... h-have a few problems... Erica and I,' he said evasively.

'Who doesn't?' she said. But when he didn't answer, she said, 'Is it serious?'

Silence, then: 'Pretty much. We're... over.'

*No, no, no!* I cried inside.

'I even left without saying goodbye to the kids. But I sent them a letter.'

'Jesus, Jules – a letter?'

'I don't want to be like their biological father who just walked out on them. I don't want them to relive that.'

'Looks like they already are. How could you do that to them?'

'I had no choice.'

'Nonsense. Talk to her. Call her.'

*Exactly*, I wanted to scream at the top of my lungs. *Why don't you just call me? Talk to me? I'll be there in a jiffy. In half a second, actually.* I bit on my knuckle, willing him to say he'd do just that, willing him to reach into his pocket and pull out the cellphone that was always practically glued to the palm of his hand.

But he just sighed and shook his head, and my heart splintered into a gazillion shards so violently, I was sure he could hear them pinging against the glass window across the room.

'It's not that simple, Sienna. I don't know what's happened to us. I wanted to be with her for the rest of my life, you know? Of all the people I've met in my life, I knew that she was the one for me. She really was.'

My heart stopped. *Was*, definitely past tense… And now?

'And?' she prompted.

He shook his head sadly. 'It didn't work out.'

*No, no, no… This can't really be happening to us, not after all we've been through!*

Sienna shrugged. 'Well, I know for a fact that she loves you deeply and it's obvious you love her.'

He sighed heavily. 'It's not that easy, Sienna. And the kids – I love them so much, you know?'

*And me?* I wanted to ask. *Is there absolutely no hope for me? Not even when you see what I've come up with to win you back? Is there no hope at all?*

'Jesus, Julian, when is love ever easy?' Sienna countered.

'Look at me and Nina. I had to fight my family tooth and nail and look at us now – we're having a baby.' She took his hands and kissed his cheek. 'Love is always worth the pain, Julian. So get over whatever issues the two of you have and marry the woman, already.'

When after all that, Julian was still silent, Sienna groaned.

'God, I'm *so* glad I'm not with a man. Right, I'm letting your fans in. Got your pen ready?'

I saw him hesitate, then take a deep breath – and by reflection, I inhaled deeply, as well. He nodded.

'Good man. And remember – good love is always worth a good cry.' And then she turned and left him, giving me the thumbs up as she left me the stage.

Swallowing my terror, I wiped my forehead, careful not to mess my make-up. I hadn't actually planned what I'd say. I always thought that spontaneity was the best form of communication. So before I could stop myself and think of what I was doing, I burst through the door and into the center of the hall.

He was standing on the far side now, facing the window, his familiar lean silhouette black against the crimson sky.

Forget Mr. Darcy in *Pride and Prejudice*. Forget Heathcliff in *Wuthering Heights*. Julian was the romantic lover of all the books ever written, all rolled into one. His was the face I wanted to wake up to every morning, his was the laughter I wanted to be the cause of. The voice I wanted to hear say *I love you*.

And now I only hoped he wouldn't freak out and send me packing. If only I could say something romantic, something soulful, to attract his attention and win him back. But no words came out. Not even a mousy, terrified squeak.

Then, as if sensing my presence, he turned and saw me, his eyes flashing as he took in my wedding dress.

'What the f…!' he cried under his breath, and for the life of me I couldn't tell what he was thinking.

Was it good? Bad? Confusing? I could still work with confusing.

'What the hell are you doing here?'

With a desperate but silent prayer, I closed the distance between us and stood directly under his shocked gaze. Well, shock was better than hatred, right? I swallowed hard and took a deep breath as raw emotion burned up my throat, seeping through to my face and into my ears.

This was it. My whole life, the kids' well-being, our future – *everything* – depended on how he reacted now. Assuming I'd make it to the end of this alive, because let me tell you, the way my heart was jackhammering its way through my rib cage, I thought it would pop out of my dress and straight into Julian's hands any second.

'Julian!' I babbled. 'I'm so sorry for the pain I've caused you. I love you and I want to make it up to you!'

He stared at me, his eyes narrowing. It wasn't looking too good from where I was standing (shaking), but I soldiered on. It was do or die. I licked my lips.

'To show you how much I love you, Maddy and Warren and I are ready to move back to Boston – or London or Liverpool or Budapest or the North Pole, wherever you want – to be closer to you.'

Silence.

'Because you, dear Julian… are all that matters to us. Forget… forget Tuscany, the B & B – *everything*.' For emphasis, I sliced my hand like a karate champion in a definitive gesture, barely aware of the bouquet of calla lilies flying out of my hand.

But Julian's eyes registered it before they swung back to my face, trying to understand what I was babbling on about and probably how on earth I'd come up with something so stupidly crazy. I dared a step closer, both my (sweaty) hands on my heart.

'All I want is to be with you, Julian. And for you to believe me. I'm not pregnant and I didn't cheat on you. I love you with all my heart. That's all I can say. And having said it, will you please marry me? Here? Now?'

But he just stood there as if I'd hit him over the head.

'I-I got a dress, see? It's not Italian, but it'll do. As a matter of fact, we don't have to have anything to remind us of Italy, or the past...' I swiped at my face, aware of the foundation coming off in chunks under my tears, but I couldn't care less. 'No flowers, no big dinner, nothing. I've wanted to be your wife ever since you killed that spider and tore my clothes off in the ladies' room almost three years ago. I was yours already then and I still am. No one else's, Julian. And that's the truth.'

Julian was silent and my heart contracted into a tiny ball and fell to the pit of my stomach. And then finally, he shook his head, his eyes solemn.

'Please – don't say anything yet,' I begged him before he could say no. 'Think about it. But could you make it snappy? I'm going to have a coronary any minute.'

Still, he was silent. And just like before death, my whole life with him flashed before my eyes: the time I'd walked into his office with my horrible burlap coat and fallen off my chair, the ever-so-slow courting, the time he saved me from Ira's violent wrath, our first kiss, the first time we made love. The time I'd waited for him at his house stark naked on a chaise longue and he'd arrived with his mother. There had been so much love between us. I hadn't known so much love could even exist between two people.

I caressed his face with my fingertips, trying to bring back that love – and the comradeship that had once upon a time made us special.

'Please, Julian,' I whispered. 'I did some crazy things. But I did them because I was afraid of not being good enough for you. All I want is you, Julian.' I swiped at my cheeks as my voice took a fall. And I laughed. 'I've even been offered my old job back.'

But Julian just stared at me standing in my wedding dress. OK. This was getting awkward. I didn't expect *total* silence.

'Erica…'

He sighed unhappily, and I caressed his beloved face once more, possibly for the last time ever, sobbing like a leaking faucet. What was a little groveling compared to a life without his love?

'If there's any bit of love left in you for me, Julian…?'

He sighed and walked away from me to the door. Was he leaving the room or just going to close the door? I had a fifty-fifty chance, so when he reached the door, I held my breath.

If he left, I wouldn't pursue him. If you love somebody, set them free and all that. But if he was only *closing* the door, that meant I had – well, still a 50 per cent chance, but I'd be damned if I didn't make the most of it.

He – yes, thank you, God! – closed the door and turned to me, coming back to stand in the same spot, his eyes disappointed but kinder than in the last few times we'd argued.

'Erica.'

Ho, boy.

'I don't want to leave our life in Italy. And for the record, despite all your shenanigans and schemes, I never stopped loving you. Never…'

'What?' I squeaked. 'You mean…?'

He took a step closer and reached out to cup my face with his beloved hands, his dark eyes liquid. 'Yes, Erica. I'll marry you. Here. Now.'

I slapped my hand over my mouth, tears plopping down my cheeks.

He peered into my eyes. 'If you don't take your hand off your mouth, I can't kiss you…'

My hand dropped to my side and I watched in shock as his face filled my field of vision and his lips caught mine in a long, soul-burning kiss. He'd *forgiven* me. I reached up past his shoulder blades and clutched at his arms and tasted salty tears, a mixture of mine – and his.

'Never ever do that to me again,' he breathed against my mouth, and I kissed him back hard like never before. 'You almost killed me.'

'I won't,' I promised. 'I'm so, so sorry, Julian.'

'How the hell did you manage to organize this so quickly?' he asked when we came up for air.

I shrugged and pulled him back down to me. 'Quickly? It's been years in the making,' I answered before we kissed again.

Whether it was minutes or hours later, I'll never know, but in came the kids, who threw themselves at him, and he pulled them to him, covering them with kisses.

'Daddy is so, so sorry for leaving without saying goodbye,' he wept, and my heart went out to him. 'It'll never happen again.'

Warren hugged him back. 'Dad, it's cool. Sometimes Mom drives me nuts, too!'

'Me too!' Maddy chimed in, and I wiped the last of my mascara from my eyes.

I knew I should have worn waterproof.

With a happy cheer, in came Julian's parents, who were anything but stiff upper lip, and they wrapped us in their warm embrace. And finally, not wanting to be any less, my family burst in, including Marcy and my aunts and siblings, and it was a warm embrace of pastel silks and loving words for us all.

Even Marcy said, 'I couldn't imagine a couple who deserve each other more!'

Which was a monumental milestone, because we all knew how highly she thought of him.

My father pulled me close and kissed my cheeks. 'Your mother would have been so proud of you, Erica.'

I pulled him closer. I didn't think I had anymore tears left, but I was wrong. 'Thanks, Dad.'

'Be happy, my sweetheart. As happy as you can be. Love each other always and don't hang onto the silly things, like whose turn it is to take out the trash.'

Which was meaningful, seeing as he did all the chores in his house.

I laughed. 'I promise.'

Paul, still teary-eyed himself, brought up the rear, lugging a suit bag as he yanked Julian out of the circle.

'Hurry up, Jules. Put this on. The priests are due any minute – one Catholic and one Protestant,' he called. 'You can all cry later!'

Alone in the Groom's Suite, Julian took me in his arms and kissed me like he hadn't in a long, long time.

'You even hired a Protestant priest?' he asked.

'I'm taking no chances this time, Julian.'

His beautiful face suddenly crumpled and more tears flowed. 'I love you, you freaking nutter.'

I laughed, swiping at my cheeks. 'I love you, too!'

'I can't believe you just risked everything for me,' he whispered against my mouth, and I giggled.

'Me neither. Boy, you must really be worth it.'

He grinned, white teeth against his Tuscan tan. 'You know damn well I am.'

I play-slapped his rock-solid pecs. 'I can't believe you made me grovel like that when you knew you were going to take me back!'

He caressed the tip of my nose. 'Let that be a lesson to you. From now on, no one kisses these lips except for me. Got it?'

'Got it!'

He nuzzled my neck, tugging at the shoulder of my wedding dress. 'Now, how about a little pre-conjugal visit before I finally make an honest woman out of you?'

My heart jumped and my body responded immediately. Oh, God. Finally. I was beginning to think I was going rusty down there.

'You promise you'll still respect me afterward?' I quipped.
'Uh-huh...'

'You done in there yet!' Paul called many moments later.
'The priests are here and they're at loggerheads!'

'Go away,' Julian called back lazily.

'You go, girl!' Judy chimed in.

'Erica, don't forget your veil!' Marcy called.

'You comin' or what?' My brother, Vince.

'Oh, you've got that right!' Judy cackled.

Jesus, were they all out there listening against the door?

'Coming!' I called, getting up, but Julian pulled me back
down onto the rug.

'Are you in a hurry, love?' he asked huskily as his eyes
traveled over my naked body.

'What, are you already ready for round two?' I chuckled.

He glanced down at himself and grinned. 'It appears so.'

I crawled up his body and nibbled on his ear. 'Round two
it is, then...'

We had our entire lives ahead of us. So what was the rush
to get out and get married in the next few minutes?

The rest of the story, you can imagine. If you look beyond
the break-up, the flowers, the wedding party, the exchange
of the rings and the usual wedding stuff, you'll see Julian
and me with all our faults and our one extraordinary Italian
love.

# Epilogue

Back home in Castellino, our garden twinkled in the sunset with white fairy lights, the crystalware and white linen tablecloths gleaming as the children's voices rang happily.

Everyone was there for the Italian replica of our wedding dinner – my family, Julian's parents Maggie and Tom, Renata, Marco and their kids, Sienna, Terry, Mr. Clean (I mean Gabriele), our friends and farmhands and even Eva Santos, whom Julian and I had invited as a surprise for Paul. And when she saw what he'd managed to pull off in a couple of *days*, she immediately signed him a check and booked him – and our newly landscaped property – for her own wedding. If he could organize this miracle at the drop of a hat, she marveled, then he was the wedding planner for her.

In the end, it all turned out well. Mom and Dad made up (as they always do). She continued to ignore her sisters (as she always did) and I was beating VIP guests away with a stick.

Yes, my little boutique hotel had been a great idea and a success. But I had learned one important lesson: priorities.

Nothing, absolutely nothing, matters when you have the two most important things: health and family.

As far as I was concerned, success, a healthy body and all those things we crave were legitimate aspirations. But first came love, and self-love. I had finally learned that it was now and forever time to live, love and be happy.

The End

# Apology

Unfortunately, Castellino is a fictitious town. But it sums up everything I love about Tuscany – my home for six years and where some of my very best friends still live today.

# Acknowledgements

This book was inspired by many Italians I know and love, i.e., my university buddies that have become family. I have lived with them for over six years during the most formative part of my life and they are all forever imprinted in my heart: Antonella, Arianna, Rolando, Liz, Simona!

Two more amazing Italian/English talents had my back during this entire process, i.e., my editor Martina Arzu and my agent Lorella Belli. You both rock!

Many thanks to everyone at Aria/Head of Zeus and LBLA for all their hard work in making sure my book got the best of everything.

And finally, to my friends and family who make it all worth while.

But did you think I'd forgotten about you, my Dear Reader? Never! Thank you so much for reading and reviewing this book! I hope you enjoyed it enough to continue Erica's journey!

Much love,
Nancy Barone

# About the Author

Nancy Barone grew up in Canada, but at the age of twelve her family moved to Italy. Catapulted into a world where her only contact with the English language was her old Judy Blume books, Nancy became an avid reader and a die-hard romantic.

Nancy stayed in Italy and, despite being surrounded by handsome Italian men, she married an even more handsome Brit. They now live in Sicily where she teaches English. Nancy is a member of the Romantic Novelists' Association and a keen supporter of the Women's Fiction Festival at Matera where she meets up with writing friends from all over the globe.